PRAISE FOR *THE MAGICIAN'S WIFE*

"*The Magician's Wife* is Brian Moore at his very best. This compelling and expertly wrought tale about a French couple in Algeria is both an amazing historical portrait of the hopeless misunderstanding with which the French entered Algeria, and a meditation on why people insist on believing in each other's illusions."   MATT COHEN

"A page-turner . . . saturated with the political and moral awakening of a fascinating woman."   *The Financial Post*

"With overtones of Thackeray or Balzac, a most remarkable book."   *The Globe and Mail*

"*The Magician's Wife* is a stylish historical adventure . . . gripping entertainment . . . Employing taut prose, Moore puts every cog carefully into place . . . The polished, precise surface of the tale . . . is matched by an irresistable narrative . . . impressive."   *The Toronto Star*

"Moore's forte is suspense and mystery. In his new novel, *The Magician's Wife*, he delivers a hefty dose of both."
The Halifax Chronicle-Herald

"This is a superior performance, rich in historical detail, acute in its psychology, a story that in less skilled hands might have bloated to 500 pages, but in Mr Moore's seems a bulging 229 . . . he transforms a historical fact into a story both true to the time and relevant to the present day . . . Mr Moore has left no seams between reality and fiction."   *New York Times*

". . . the novel's magnificent story grips and delights . . . he weaves an account of class conflict and of the role of religious faith, as well as a portrait of a marriage in crisis, of a young woman isolated and in doubt . . . Moore is a writer of supreme efficiency."   *Washington Post*

The Lonely Passion of Judith Hearne
The Feast of Lupercal
The Luck of Ginger Coffey
An Answer from Limbo
The Emperor of Ice Cream
I am Mary Dunne
Fergus
Catholics
The Great Victorian Collection
The Doctor's Wife
The Mangan Inheritance
The Temptation of Eileen Hughes
Cold Heaven
Black Robe
The Colour of Blood
Lies of Silence
No Other Life
The Statement

BRIAN MOORE

The Magician's Wife

**VINTAGE
CANADA**

A Division of Random House of Canada

VINTAGE CANADA EDITION, 1998

Copyright © 1997 by Brian Moore

All rights reserved under international and
Pan American Copyright Conventions.
Published in Canada by Vintage Canada,
a division of Random House of Canada Limited Toronto,
and simultaneously in the United Kingdom
by Flamingo, an imprint of HarperCollins*Publishers*,
Hammersmith, London, in 1998.
First published in the United Kingdom
in 1997 by Bloomsbury.
Distributed by Random House of Canada Limited.

Canadian in Publication data

Moore, Brian, 1921
The magician's wife

ISBN 0-676-97140-7

I. Title.

PS8526.O62M33 1998 C813'.54 C98-931288-7
PR9199.3.M66M34 1998

Set in Baskerville

Printed and bound in Great Britain by
Clays Ltd, St Ives plc

FOR JEAN
comme d'habitude

Part One

France, 1856

ONE

The Colonel left the house at five o'clock. As his carriage drove out towards the main gates Emmeline put down her *petit point* and went to look through the window of her sitting room. She wondered about this visitor. He must be important. For the last two weeks her husband had refused to see anyone, remaining locked up in his workroom with orders that he not be disturbed. As the Colonel's carriage reached the gates, a painted mechanical gate-keeper wheeled jerkily out of its lodge, legs moving on an electric track as it approached and touched the lock of the gates. The gates swung open, the automaton stiffly raising its right arm in salute. When the carriage had crossed the hidden trip wire which lay at the entrance the gates began to close. As the carriage moved off in a wall of dust down the rutted road which led to Tours, the automaton trundled back into its lodge and an electric bell sounded within the house signalling that the visitor had departed. A moment later she heard a second bell. She looked up at the bell panel installed in her sitting room. That would be for Jules. Soon Jules would come upstairs to tell her that the Master could not leave his work to join her for supper.

Two weeks ago a new mechanical figurine had arrived on time from the workshop where her husband's artisans had constructed it exactly to his specifications. But something was wrong with the mechanism. The automaton's hand, which was supposed to draw silhouettes in ink on a sheet of paper, behaved erratically, producing a series of scribbles. He had at once begun to take it apart painstakingly, obsessively, as always when a marionette developed some flaw. There was

3

no reasoning with him, not that she had tried. He no longer thought of himself as a magician. Now he was an inventor, a scientist. But would a real scientist spend his days making mechanical marionettes?

A bell jangled on the panel above her head. That would be Jules. She went to her escritoire and pressed a button. The door opened electrically.

'I beg pardon, Madame. Monsieur sends his compliments and asks you to meet him in the green salon in ten minutes' time, if that is convenient?'

'Tell him, yes.'

As Jules withdrew, the electric beam automatically closed the door behind him. She went to her dressing table and sat in front of the triptych mirror, beginning to brush her hair. She set great store by this brushing and did it three times daily, tugging at the long thick mane of her hair, counting the strokes. She was not brushing it for him. These days she sometimes wondered if he noticed that she no longer used mascara or rouged her cheeks except on the rare occasions when they went out to dine. And even then, what was the point of dressing up and trying to look pretty? It was always the same: when they entered a room people looked at him, not at her, he, the famous Henri Lambert, and she? May I ask you, Madame Lambert, what it is like to be married to a great magician? It must be exciting to be the wife of a person like that?

At first it *had* been exciting. She was happy to escape Rouen for the pleasures of Paris. They lived in a furnished apartment in the seventh arrondissement which he told her was a gift to him from one of his admirers. He also owned an atelier in Neuilly where he employed three artisans in the manufacture and painting of automata and electric devices, and a small theatre near the Palais Royal where each season he performed his celebrated 'Magical Evenings'. In the first two years of their marriage he took her with him on two foreign tours, once to Berlin and once to Madrid. She had enjoyed seeing these cities and had hoped to see others. But after her first miscarriage Lambert decided that he no

4

longer wished or needed to keep his Paris theatre or go on foreign tours.

'I've long ago made my name as a performer,' he told her. 'Now I must devote more time to my inventions. And so, my darling, I've decided that we shall live in the country with servants and comforts in a home where we can bring up our children and I can work undisturbed.'

At once, in his usual secretive way, he bought and furnished this manor outside Tours without even showing her the premises. And so, when she first entered the Manoir des Chênes knowing it would be her home, she was pleased, disquieted and disappointed. Pleased because the rooms were larger and more grand than those in her parents' home, disquieted by the strange displays, disappointed because the manor was down a rural road that led to Tours, a dull town far from Paris. It was, she felt, less a country house than a theatrical museum. There were magic boxes in almost every room, a large puppet theatre in the front hall, its stage electrically lit, and on the walls portraits of magicians from a bygone age and large framed posters of Lambert's command performances before the Queen of England, the Empress of Russia, King Louis Philippe and Emperor Napoleon III. In addition to the chimes and tickings of forty-two clocks, an electric carillon sounded constantly in different tones, each tone telling the master of the house that a visitor had arrived or departed, that a servant was preparing a certain meal, that the gardeners were working in a specific area of the grounds, that the morning mail had arrived or been sent out, that the electric grottoes and displays had been activated by someone's entering them. In his workroom in the dungeon-like basement, Lambert controlled and watched over each of these activities.

And now, minutes after Jules' visit, clocks throughout the house began to chime the quarter-hour. She hurried out of her sitting room, down the main staircase and into the ground-floor reception room. As she entered she looked at once to the clock over the chimmneypiece, strategically placed to astonish all who had not seen it. Five feet in height, made of transparent glass, it kept perfect time. He kept perfect time. She knew that in less than one minute he would appear in the doorway.

'Emmeline!'

As always, coming into a room he made an entrance, now opening his arms as if to embrace her, palms up to show that he had nothing to hide. Normally, while working at home, he wore an old velvet coat, an open shirt and checked trousers, which he bought in a shop that provided uniforms for chefs and kitchen staff. But today he was dressed as for a performance in a dark frock coat, a white linen waistcoat, a formal shirt with red silk cravat and narrow trousers of dark-grey wool. This was the attire that had made him famous as the first magician to appear, not in ornate oriental robes or other extravagant stage costumes, but dressed soberly, a person no different from his audience and therefore ever more mysterious, ever more the sorcerer. Now, in a conjuring gesture, he slid his slender white hand into an inside pocket of his frock coat and produced a gold-lettered invitation card which he held in front of her.

'We are going to Compiègne, my dear.'

'Compiègne?'

'Yes. We have been invited to a *série* for the last week of October.'

A *série*? The Emperor inviting his guests to a week of hunting, shooting and parties, everyone had heard of those grand affairs, everyone in Paris talked about them, was Henri to perform, that must be it. But why me?

'Henri, if you're going to perform there, why would I be invited? Aristocrats, grand people. They don't want me.'

He handed her the gilded card. 'Read it.' She stared at the ornate lettering:

Maison de l'Empereur,
Palais des Tuileries, 20 October 1856
  Monsieur,
By order of the Emperor I have the honour to inform you that you have been invited, together with Madame Henri Lambert, to

spend seven days at the Palace of Compiègne, from 22 November to 28 November.

Court vehicles will be waiting to bring you to the Palace on the 22nd on arrival of the train which will leave Paris at 2 hours 30.

Accept, sir, the assurance of my distinguished sentiments,
The First Chamberlain,
Vicomte de Laferrière.
Monsieur,
Madame Henri Lambert.

'It's an invitation for both of us. And I am *not* being asked to "perform". I'm told the Emperor wishes to see me on a matter of national importance.'

She stared at him. 'What are you talking about?'

'I can't discuss it, not yet. It's highly confidential.'

'But, Henri, I can't go there. I'd be terrified.'

He turned away and went to the window which looked out on the main drive. It was his habit when irritated to lapse into silence.

'Henri, there must be some mistake. Please?'

'There's no mistake. It's a great honour, don't you understand that? Everyone – society, aristocrats, millionaires, artists, everyone dreams of being invited to Compiègne. You who complain that life is dull here! This is the chance of a lifetime. We are to be the guests of Napoleon III. And of the Empress! We have been invited for a whole week.'

'A week? What are we going to wear? We don't belong in that world.'

'Don't worry. Colonel Deniau has given me a list of the items we will need for our visit. In my case, I'll have to be fitted for court clothes. You'll have to have at least twenty dresses. The style for the ladies is that they should not be seen twice in the same costume. Emmeline, it's going to be wonderful. We'll be entertained, we will mingle with the *gratin*, we'll be in Their Majesties' company each night for dinner.'

'But it's not – I don't want to go! Besides, it will cost a fortune!

My dressmaker here wouldn't be able to make anything suitable. I'd have to go to Paris. I won't have time to do all that. And in Compiègne, what would I do all day among a lot of titled ladies who'll be looking down their noses at me. And you dressed up in court dress, dining among marquesses and counts. Henri, it's not our place. We must apologize, you must invent some excuse.'

'Nonsense! And what do you mean, it's not our place? I've met royalty many times, I've been to the Tuileries, the Emperor knows me – '

'But as a performer, not a guest!'

'Emmeline, I am not being invited as a performer. I am being asked to do something for my country, something of the highest importance. That's why the Emperor wants to see me. They are trying to persuade me.'

'Persuade you to do what?'

'I'll tell you later, *if* I decide to do it. Listen to me. When Colonel Deniau first spoke about this matter, that was two months ago. He came here specially, at the end of August, do you remember?'

'No, I don't. I didn't see him, you didn't introduce him. And today I just saw the back of his head as he was leaving. Who is he, anyway?'

'He's the head of the *Bureau Arabe*, the political office of France in North Africa. At any rate, last August I refused his request. My mind was quite made up. I was too busy here. Now they have come back with this invitation. The Emperor himself wants to persuade me.'

'The Emperor?'

'Yes! I am being wooed by Napoleon III. Think of it! And as far as being made to feel uncomfortable, you'll be treated as the wife of an inventor, which is just as high a calling as a sculptor or writer or any of the other intellectuals who have attended these *séries*.'

She looked at him, standing there by the window, his hand tucked into a fold of his waistcoat, like Bonaparte whom he admired, cocking his head slightly to the side as she had seen him do on stage when he listened to a question from his audience, his smile, his soft tone of voice aiming to distract her, to shift her attention away from her fears. But of course it wasn't a matter of how *he* would be treated, it was a matter of how she could survive a week in Compiègne, a week of blushes, feeling looked down on, not knowing what to say.

'I've read about the *séries* at Compiègne,' she said. 'Everyone knows you bring your own servants. I'd have to have a lady's maid. Can you see Thérèse in the part? She doesn't even have a uniform. And Jules, is he to be your valet? Henri, listen to me. Say that I'm ill. Tell them you'll go alone. If they're so anxious for you to do whatever it is, then it won't matter that you haven't brought me with you. *And* it will be a lot cheaper. Have you any idea what all those dresses will cost if I have them made up by a Paris dressmaker?'

'Don't worry,' he said. 'I'll pay for it. And you can engage a lady's maid for the trip. We'll dress Jules up.'

'But that's only the beginning – '

'Listen to me, Emmeline. This is what we're going to do. I'm going to send you to Paris at once. Madame Cournet will advise you. She knows about these things. I've always consulted her when I'm giving a royal performance. She'll find a dressmaker, a maid, everything you'll need. You'll have to stay in Paris for the fittings.'

'In Paris? That could take weeks.'

'We leave for Compiègne on the 22nd. That's four weeks from now. That will give you time. A month in Paris, it will be a holiday for you. You're always saying how dull it is here.'

'So I won't see you for four weeks?'

'I don't know. I may have to come to Paris for a day or two but in the meantime I must get on with my work. Now what about you, do you think you could leave tomorrow? If so, I'll order the phaeton to be ready to take you to the station. The Paris train leaves at noon.'

'But what if I say I won't go?'

'My dear, I have already accepted for both of us. Tomorrow,

Colonel Deniau will convey my thanks to the First Chamberlain. Emmeline, we must do it. I can't give you a choice.'

She felt tears. She heard him ring for Jules.

'Perhaps, you'd like me to join you for supper this evening,' he said. 'I'm at a delicate stage in my work but if you're leaving tomorrow?'

'No. I'll have supper in my room. If I leave tomorrow, I'll have to pack.'

He came towards her. She held back her tears. She did not turn to him. He bent and kissed the nape of her neck. 'You're a darling,' he said. 'What would I do without you?'

The Emperor. Society. The Second Empire. Everyone talked about this new Paris. The year before last in the Rue de Rivoli at eight o'clock on a September evening Emmeline stood in a crowd of spectators, watching a file of carriages move into the courtyard of the Palais des Tuileries. From these carriages she saw, descending, gentlemen in knee breeches and silk stockings, officers in dress uniforms and decorations, ladies in billowing crinolines, their breasts almost bare, their necks and arms adorned with pearls, rubies and diamonds. A woman beside Emmeline pointed out two famous beauties, the Duchesse de Pourtales and the Marquesa de Contadades, as the guests moved under a marquee into the entrance hall of the Pavillon de l'Horloge. Swiss guards stood to attention there, halberds to hand, plumed helmets on their heads. It was a sight Emmeline would not forget, a sight she had gazed on that night with the pleasure of watching actors in some theatrical extravaganza, a glimpse of a grand world she would never know. And now, suddenly, her husband had entered it.

*   *   *

'My dear child,' Madame Cournet said, smiling. 'If you're worried about how you will be received, remember it's all important that your clothes be designed by Monsieur West. Compiègne is a fashion show. In a West toilette you will be recognized as someone of the first rank. He's not a dressmaker, he's an artist. He dresses the Empress herself.'

'The Empress?' Emmeline said. 'But then it will cost a fortune.'

Madame Cournet smiled and tapped the end of her nose with the silver lorgnette which she deployed much as a schoolteacher uses a pointer. 'Not quite a fortune,' she said. 'Although an original toilette of the sort Monsieur West designs for ladies who attend the *série* will cost your husband a great deal. It is *de rigueur* that you change three times daily. You will need eight day costumes, including a travelling suit, seven ball dresses and five gowns for tea. But it will be worth it. You will be the height of fashion, I assure you.'

'I'll have to speak to my husband,' Emmeline said. A flutter of hope rose within her. Twenty dresses made by the Empress's dressmaker? Perhaps now, Henri would see sense.

'There's no need,' Madame Cournet said. 'I've already received Monsieur Lambert's permission to make the appointment. It's arranged for Thursday at 3 p.m. in Monsieur West's villa at Suresnes. Believe me, it will be one of the most delightful experiences of your life. Such taste, such an artist. You'll be enchanted.'

That Thursday, arriving with Madame Cournet at precisely three o'clock in the afternoon at a Parisian villa in the suburbs of Paris, Emmeline wearing her very best daytime dress, coat and hat was shown by a servant into a reception room crowded with gilt-edged chairs, gold mirrors, embroidered pillows, small tables covered with knick-knacks and silver-framed photographs. She and Madame Cournet were invited to sit on a large red satin sofa. In an adjoining room a fountain of eau-de-Cologne spurted continuously, filling the air with a sweet yet pungent odour. Monsieur West made his entrance ten minutes later, accompanied by three young male assistants.

He was enormously fat and spoke French with an English accent which Emmeline found hard to understand. He wore a loose silk smock, black velvet trousers and a huge velvet beret which fell over his right eye. He described himself as an artist and in the next hour, having inspected Emmeline as though she were a piece of furniture, he made sketches and notes which in subsequent weeks evolved into morning costumes of grey velvet, black velvet and dark-blue poplin adorned with sable tippets. There were also sable and chinchilla hats with coats to match; five afternoon gowns and seven sumptuous evening dresses, each costume, gown and dress made to emphasize that it was unique and indisputably the work of an artist in *haute couture*. Because all of the evening dresses were crinolines, Emmeline had to practise walking in them, so difficult were they to manoeuvre. In addition, under their wide hoops she must wear pantaloons. And as she lacked certain items of jewellery which Monsieur West considered essential, Madame Cournet took her to a discreet boutique where decorated fans, bracelets and bandeaux were rented out to her for a period of a month against a large deposit.

Finally, when the toilette was assembled, Madame Cournet engaged on a temporary basis an old woman named Françoise who been employed for thirty years in the household of the Count de Maine as lady's maid to the Countess. This old woman, servile yet censorious, was yet another reason for Emmeline's feeling of panic when, alone in her bed in the Hôtel Montrose on the night of 21 November, she waited for the arrival of her husband next morning, the day the *série* was about to begin.

'The servants will travel in a separate section of the train,' Madame Cournet had advised. 'But it will be your responsibility to see that they and your baggage are on the station platform one hour ahead of departure time.'

So, on the morning of the 22nd, Emmeline, dressed in Monsieur West's elegant travelling clothes, took the old woman to the Gare du Nord where Jules, uncomfortable in his new uniform, stood at the station entrance guarding four trunks and the six huge wooden boxes that housed the

West crinolines. When porters had been summoned, the two servants followed the luggage into the station, Emmeline remaining outside the entrance not wanting to be the first guest to arrive. At 2 p.m. when at last she went in, she saw at once, on Platform Number One, a smart train, its carriages adorned with the Napoleonic eagle, waiting under a sign, *Extra et Imperial*. Standing near this sign was a gentleman who, when he saw her approach, introduced himself as Vicomte Walsh, an imperial chamberlain. She was obliged to tell him that her husband had not yet arrived.

'But it is early, Madame. Perhaps you would like me to show you to your seat? I will let him know where to find you.'

He ushered her on to the train and installed her in a large salon carriage fitted out with comfortable armchairs and tables strewn with illustrated newspapers. She thanked him and sat uneasily alone until two-fifteen when, suddenly, the seven first-class passenger coaches began to fill with gentlemen in morning clothes and ladies in travelling cloaks and hats, many of whom seemed to know each other, bowing, nodding, exchanging conversation about acquaintances, receptions, balls and other matters of which Emmeline knew nothing. Her unease became panic. Where was Henri?

At two-twenty-five precisely the train engine sounded a piercing signal. At that moment, as though he had planned it, Lambert came strolling down the platform. He stopped to consult the imperial chamberlain and on entering her carriage, came to Emmeline, kissing her formally on both cheeks.

Although he had not seen her for a month, his first words were: 'Where's Jules?'

'He's here, but the servants are in another part of the train.'

'Does he have my portfolio?'

'What portfolio?'

'You know the one. It looks like an artist's portfolio, one to carry drawings in. You've seen it on stage.'

'You mean the one you take things from?'

'Yes, that's it. If it was with my luggage, you couldn't miss it.'

'We have so much luggage, I didn't notice.'

'Well, where are the luggage coaches?'

'Henri, we don't have time. The train's leaving. Look, they're closing the doors.'

Reluctantly, he sat facing her after bowing to the other gentlemen and ladies in the carriage, strangers who formally and distantly bowed back. At 2.33 p.m., with a second piercing shriek and a sudden convulsive jerk, the imperial train left the station.

The portfolio? She sat, twisting her gloves in frustration. He lied to me. He's going to perform. We're not invited as guests but as the magician and his wife.

She leaned forward. 'What's this about your portfolio?' she whispered. 'You said you hadn't been asked to do that.'

He smiled and held his slender hands palms upwards. 'I told you the truth, darling. But Colonel Deniau thought it might be an appropriate gesture if I would, perhaps, take part in one of the evening's entertainments.'

And then as though he sensed that the other people in the carriage were listening to this conversation he turned to them and said, 'I'm sorry, we haven't met, as yet. This is our first visit to Compiègne. But I've been told we guests are expected to entertain each other during the *série*. Is that not so?'

One of the gentlemen, dressed in clothes of English cut, his right eye permanently drooping in a way which gave him a sinister appearance, nodded. 'Yes, indeed. But I warn you, these entertainments are exceedingly dull. Yet you are Lambert, are you not? I've seen you on stage.'

'Henri Lambert. And may I present my wife.'

'My respects, Madame. I must say, with your husband on hand I am confident we shall be splendidly entertained.'

Emmeline felt her face grow hot. Just as she had feared, the others in the carriage were aristocrats whose every glance in her direction seemed to warn that despite Madame Cournet's coaching and Monsieur West's elaborate toilette she would remain for them beyond the pale, a doctor's daughter, half educated in a Rouennais convent, provincial beyond redemption and, despite his fame and pretensions, the wife of a person who performed on stage.

Exactly one-and-a-half hours after leaving the Gare du Nord, the imperial train arrived at Compiègne, fifty-five miles from Paris. As they came out of the station the passengers were met by a large crowd of townspeople and tourists, assembled to see the nobles, diplomats, artists and foreign dignitaries invited by the Emperor to his latest *série*. Emmeline, drawing her new travelling cloak tightly around her because of the November chill, watched as valets and maids scuffled about, supervising the loading of scores of trunks on to luggage carts. At the station entrance ten *chars à bancs* were lined up, their painted dark-green coachwork outlined in red, each drawn by four horses. Mounted on the lead horses were postilions in short red velvet jackets, wearing black velvet caps over their white wigs, their small pigtails tied with a black bow which flapped up and down behind them as, blowing their horns and cracking their whips, they rumbled the *chars à bancs* through the quiet town of Compiègne. Behind the *chars à bancs* came the servants' coaches and in the rear the luggage carts on which a mass of trunks swayed to and fro as the procession left the cobbled streets of the town. Soon they were travelling along the roads and crossroads of a huge royal hunting forest where at every turn red-painted signposts pointed towards the Château of Compiègne. And when at last the procession clattered into the main courtyard of the château, Emmeline stared up at huge eighteenth-century buildings, at wings and turrets and an immensity of windows.

'Beautiful, beautiful,' her husband said, turning to her with a satisfied smile as the postilions reined their horses to an abrupt stop in front of the entrance arches. 'What a wonderful place to spend our week!'

But Emmeline looked uneasily at the great stone staircase where servants waited to help the guests alight, servants whose court uniforms and powdered wigs brought back that evening two years ago when she, anonymous in the crowd outside the Tuileries, had her first sight of this intimidating world. Now she must step down with the other guests, pretending to be like them, as they walked towards the First Chamberlain. After a formal greeting he passed them over to a head usher who conducted them through a series of ornate ground-floor reception rooms into a long hall where a line of valets waited to show them to their apartments. As Emmeline followed their particular valet, she saw Lambert wave to a handsome army colonel with a scarred face, military moustache and sun-darkened skin.

'Who's that?'

'That's Colonel Deniau. I'll introduce you later.'

'He's the one who arranged all this, isn't he?'

'Yes. I've told you already. He's my liaison here.'

She studied the Colonel as the valet ushered them towards a wide marble staircase which led to the upper floors of the château. At the foot of this staircase, a second valet handed each set of arriving guests a numbered card tied with a yellow ribbon. They then followed their particular valet up the staircase. On the first floor some of the guests, including the Colonel, were led off down various corridors. This process was repeated when they reached the second floor. Emmeline noticed that the rooms to which these more privileged guests were led seemed to be suites, many of them overlooking the park. The remaining guests must climb yet another staircase to reach the upper floors of the château. At last, with just one other couple, Emmeline and Lambert ascended a final staircase leading to a floor just under the roof.

At this point, the lady ahead of Emmeline angrily announced to her husband, 'You must complain, Théophile. This is disgraceful.'

'Please, Florence, I know about these things. The allocations are made according to a plan. There's absolutely no way we can change it now.'

Their valet led them to a door. On it was a white card tied with a yellow ribbon, similar to the one which had been handed to them earlier. In its elegant calligraphy, Emmeline saw a number and their names. The valet held open the door, showing them into a cold attic room with a sloping wooden ceiling and a view from its window of turrets and roofs. Adjoining this room was a small, dark bedroom. As Emmeline went into it to remove her hat and cloak her husband called to her from the sitting room.

'I think that room's going to be a little small for both of us. I'll sleep on the couch out here.' As usual, he was being discreet.

There was a knock on the door. Three soldiers of the royal guard entered, bringing in their trunks and the large crinoline boxes which took up most of the space in the living room. Lambert went at once to his portfolio, opening it with an air of relief, then placed it against a wall.

'Your servants will be sent up at once, Monsieur,' the valet said. 'And the First Chamberlain wishes to remind you that dinner is at seven-thirty and that the Emperor and Empress will welcome you in the *grande salle des fêtes* at 7 p.m.'

The door shut. In the room outside she saw Henri bend down and poke the fire.

'It's freezing cold,' she said. 'I think these must be servants' rooms.'

He pretended not to hear. She sat down on the bed. She felt dizzy. It was nerves, she knew, but knowing it did not help. Madame Cournet had told her one must change costumes three times daily. It was now four-thirty. As she must prepare for the imperial reception in the *grande salle des fêtes*, she would not have time to change into afternoon costume but must put on the evening dress of black lace over white tulle with twisted green velvet bows, a décolleté and crinoline. Madame Cournet had recommended it as the proper choice for a first meeting with the Emperor and Empress.

Shortly before seven, having completed her toilette with the aid of Françoise, the old but skilful lady's maid, Emmeline went out into the sitting room. Her husband, following instructions which had been given him earlier, had dressed for this first evening in court dress of white knee breeches with white silk stockings and a dress frock coat. She saw him rub his hands together for warmth as he stared at his image in the pier glass which was placed in a corner of the sitting room. The fire had long gone out.

'Are you ready, Emmeline? We mustn't be late.'

'How will we know where to go?'

'I told you,' he said. 'Everything is planned here. You'll see.'

He was right, she supposed, for as they left their room a valet was waiting for them in the corridor. With a bow, he indicated that they follow him, leading them downstairs and through long corridors to arrive at last at the *grande salle des fêtes*. Here, footmen stood at the doors of an immense salon. Emmeline looked up at the painted frescoed ceiling, the glitter of crystal chandeliers and then, in trepidation, at the guests now coming into the room. At precisely ten minutes past seven a footman announced the arrival of the First Chamberlain, the Vicomte de Laferrière, and the Grande Maîtresse, the Duchesse de Bassano, who moved down the lines of guests murmuring formal words of welcome. Emmeline did not know whether to curtsy or bow and so stood, bobbing her head foolishly as these grand persons passed by. Although she guessed that by now there must be almost a hundred people in this huge salon, it still seemed half deserted. A chamberlain came up to Henri.

'Monsieur, the lady you will escort in to dinner is Madame de Deauville. That is the lady over there, with her husband, Monsieur de Deauville.'

'And who will take *me* in?' Emmeline whispered as the chamberlain moved on.

'I've told you, darling. Everything is arranged. You mustn't worry. The Colonel says it's just like a military operation.'

Ten minutes later, the doors to the *grande salle des fêtes* were closed as though to signal that the last guest had arrived. The First Chamberlain disappeared through a smaller door halfway down the room. At once the guests began to form two long lines. The small door opened and Emmeline saw the Emperor and Empress appear. The Emperor differed from his photographs and paintings, seeming to be shorter, stouter, his waxed moustaches longer, his eyelids drooping languidly as though he had just wakened from sleep. He wore the same court dress as the other men, white knee breeches, silk stockings, low pumps, his sole decoration the ribbon and star of the Légion d'Honneur. But it was the Empress, majestic in white-spangled tulle, with a tiara of diamonds and a necklace of pearls, who fascinated Emmeline. She saw at once that the Empress's gown, while, of course, more splendid than her own, was, no mistake about it, the work of Monsieur West. Suddenly she felt less unsure. Because of Monsieur West she was part of this gathering. They both were. After all, Henri was wearing the same sort of court dress as the Emperor.

Moving slowly down the lines of guests, the Emperor turned towards the men, the Empress towards the ladies. As Their Majesties passed by, the gentlemen bowed and the ladies curtsied with a great dip of crinolines. When the Empress came abreast of her, Emmeline sank down so low that she seemed almost buried in the multiple folds of her gown. The Empress smiled on her as on the others, and murmured, 'Good evening,' before passing on. As Emmeline rose from her curtsy, her face flushed with relief, she saw lackeys draw open the doors as the Emperor went to the Empress, giving her his arm, leading her out in procession towards the banqueting hall. Around her Emmeline saw gentlemen approach ladies and offer their arms. Her panic flooded back. Who would . . .? But coming towards her, his arm extended, was Colonel Deniau. Gratefully, she put her hand on his sleeve, joining the procession as it moved into the long gallery, afraid that her new shoes would slip on the highly waxed floor.

Now, the guests began to pass between two long lines of the Emperor's *cent gardes*, soldiers in a uniform of light-blue jackets, white breeches and silver helmets from which manes of white horsehair flowed down their backs. The *cent gardes* stood rigidly to attention, staring straight ahead, ignoring the passing parade of ladies in glittering jewels, officers in dress uniforms, diplomats in decorations and ribboned orders. As Emmeline walked past these statuesque soldiers and turned her head to glance surreptitiously at her escort, she felt a sudden giddy confidence. Somehow, in her splendid dress, on the arm of this officer, she was part of this great event.

When the procession entered the dining hall the first Chamberlain led the Emperor and Empress halfway down the room, seating them on opposite sides of the long table. As soon as they were settled, chamberlains showed the guests to their places. Colonel Deniau, who did not seem to need a guide, walked Emmeline past the royal personages down to the lower end of the table, seating himself on her right. The table, a field of white linen, was decorated at set intervals by formal arrangements of flowers, white epergnes filled with bonbons, and larger dishes filled with fruits. The service was of white Sèvres porcelain with the letter 'N' in gold, surmounted by the imperial crown. At least fifty lackeys waited to push the guests' chairs into place. In a large circular loggia above the french windows a military band began to play music which was, for Emmeline, a reprieve from speech. She pretended to smile and nod her head in tune to the melody, leaving the Colonel free to pay attention to the lady on his right.

When a new set of lackeys entered, carrying a first course of soup, Colonel Deniau leaned towards her: 'I must warn you, Madame, there will be a great deal of food tonight, but we will be obliged to eat it quickly. The Emperor will not spend more than an hour over dinner. Still, that may be a blessing, don't you agree? These affairs can be tedious.'

'I don't know,' she said. 'I've never been to anything like this before.'

'I'm surprised. You seem to fit in so perfectly. If this is your first invitation to a *série* I'll wager it won't be your last. You are Compiègne's latest adornment.'

'I hope you're wrong,' she said, but felt a rush of pleasure at his words.

'Why do you hope that?'

'Because I don't belong here. It's not my world.'

'Dear Madame,' the Colonel said. He leaned towards her,

his fingers gently touching her bare arm. 'I am not trying to flatter you. You're young, charming and – what can I say? Your husband must have used some of his magic to conjure you away from the attentions of other men. There is no world that is not open to you.'

She avoided his eyes. I mustn't be deceived. Men like him throw compliments like confetti. 'Monsieur, you're too kind. I am a provincial, a very ordinary person. To be honest, I'd be happier at home in my room, eating my supper from a tray.'

He laughed. 'Is that really true? But won't you remember this evening as something special? After all, that man sitting further down the table is the nephew of Bonaparte. And he himself is an extraordinary figure. Think of it. He has come from exile, seized power and crowned himself as Emperor of France. An amazing achievement! And tonight you are part of his court. I might even say that tonight we are making history.'

'So are ordinary people doing their evening shopping in the streets of Rouen.'

'Ah! You are a revolutionary, I see.'

'No, no,' she said, blushing, surprised that she had been so frank with him. 'As I told you, I'm just an ordinary person. That's why I said it.'

'Well, we won't argue. Although now that I've met you I can't believe that you are anything of the sort. But, as it's partly my fault that you *are* here tonight, I hope I'll be able to show you that a week in Compiègne can be very pleasant. There are beautiful walks in the grounds and in the forest. If you wish to go for a drive, or visit the town, there are all sorts of carriages to take you. If you care to ride, there are one hundred and fifty horses waiting in the imperial stables. Do you enjoy card games or charades? The Empress is fond of them. And of course, ladies can attend the shooting parties, or watch the hunt. It's quite a splendid sight.'

'Watching men shoot birds, or hounds chasing a stag and killing it,' Emmeline said. 'No. I am too fond of animals. As for cards I am without skill. And charades with the Empress! I'd be terrified. Now, do you see why I wish I were at home?'

He laughed. 'Indeed I do. I feel ashamed to have imposed this visit on you. Still, I'll try my best to amuse you. If you will let me?'

As he said this he smiled and, as though ending the conversation, turned to speak to the lady on his left. What did he mean? Was he just trying to flatter her, to make her part of whatever it was they wanted Henri to do, or was he the sort of rake who might, here in Compiègne, ignore the fact that she was Henri's wife? He looks at me in that way. Is it this dress that makes me into someone I'm not? And that old woman had a way with my hair tonight, far better than I could manage myself. Imagine if I *were* part of this, dressing every evening in grand clothes, dukes and counts bowing to me, the Colonel leading me in on his arm?

At that, as though he had heard her, the elderly gentleman on her left introduced himself as the Count de Burgos, and at once began to talk about hunting dogs. 'I am particularly looking forward to the hunt, Madame – it's the day after tomorrow, you know. The Emperor has a wonderful pack. English dogs. He has an excellent trainer who treats the dogs with kindness and lets them follow their natural bent. It's a mistake to beat them, you know. They lose their initiative, if you do. I'm told it's quite a sight to see this pack in full cry. A hundred hounds. Imagine. You'll enjoy that, won't you, dear lady? You'll be there, hah?'

She nodded in a way which she hoped could mean either yes or no. And again felt panic. Aristocrats, hunting dogs, things she knew nothing about. How was she going to get through this conversation, this evening, this week? But then she looked again to her right. The Colonel, talking to his neighbour, caught her eye and gave her a complicit smile. Reassured, she picked up the menu. There were six courses, soup, foie gras, fish, roasts, lobsters, desserts. How could they possibly eat all of this in an hour? But as the band continued to play and the dishes were put in front of her it was, at least, a reprieve from having to talk to the Count de Burgos, who, once he saw food, abandoned all attempts at speech. Coffee and liqueurs were served at the table and precisely at eight-thirty the Emperor and Empress rose. At once, lackeys came forward and drew chairs from under the guests, forcing everyone to stand up.

Emmeline, unsure, looked to the Colonel who, offering his arm, escorted her in procession back down the long corridor where the *cent gardes* stood immobile as before and into the *grande salle des fêtes* where he excused himself and went off to another part of the room. Far away, down the enormous salon, a gentleman sat down at an upright piano and began to play a tune.

Emmeline, alone, ignored by those around her, walked aimlessly among the groups of chatting guests. A few people had begun to dance, urged on by the chamberlains who circulated like anxious nursemaids, shepherding them towards the piano music which sounded faint and false in this enormous place. And now she saw the Colonel moving among the crowd, looking for someone. With him was Henri, they must be looking for her. She hurried to them, waving to attract their attention.

'At last!' her husband said when she came up. 'How are you, my darling? Are you enjoying yourself? The Colonel tells me you were his dinner companion.'

'And how fortunate for me,' the Colonel said and again gave her that special smile. 'Well, now that I've reunited you two . . .' He turned to Lambert. 'By the way, I've been told it will definitely not be this evening.'

Bowing to her, he moved off and was at once accosted by two gentlemen with whom he began a conversation. She stood abandoned, with Henri, Henri who had not looked after her, Henri who was so honoured to be here among these people that he did not see the obvious: he and Emmeline were at the lowest rung of this social ladder, ignored, shut off in cold attic quarters under the roof.

'*What* will definitely not be this evening?' she asked. 'What's he talking about?'

'Our audience with the Emperor. I'm not surprised. I imagine it will take place in private. It's too important to discuss in front of other people.'

'If it's so important and you're so important, why are we stuck up in that cold attic?'

'Darling, at dinner tonight Gounod, the composer, said that his room is damp and cold and looks out on the stables and that other people are complaining of the same thing. Apparently it happens all the time at these *séries*. Compiègne is part of French history but that doesn't make it comfortable.'

'And what about Colonel Deniau? I'm sure he's not in some damp room.'

'I don't know. I didn't ask him. Why are you being so disagreeable? I've spent a lot of money to bring you here. You might as well try to enjoy it.'

She did not answer for at that moment a chamberlain approached and asked if they would like to dance. 'If we can get the dancing properly started,' the chamberlain said, 'then the Empress may join in.'

At once, as though he were a servant not a guest, her husband took her arm and led her on to the floor.

'Why are we dancing?' she said. 'You don't like dancing. Why do something we don't want to do?'

'It's just good manners. Besides, I think it's better to dance than to stand around among a crowd of people whom I don't yet know. By this time tomorrow we will have met several interesting men and women and you'll feel more at home.'

'Will I?'

Turning her in a wide waltz step, he looked up at the ceiling and sighed. 'I'll never understand you. Do you know that tonight you look more beautiful than ever? That dress is wonderful, simply wonderful. And your hair and those jewels. I'm so proud of you, my darling.'

What was there to say? Whatever it was he wanted to achieve by coming to Compiègne, he would, as always, be ruthless in pursuit of it. If that meant spending a fortune on dresses for her, then so be it. If it meant a cold damp attic room, then so be it. If it meant that in the next days she would be ignored or snubbed, then so be it. He was not Henri Lambert for nothing, he was the man who had sat alone in a room for hundreds and hundreds of hours, his fingers manipulating cards and coins until he had learned and could perfectly reproduce every form of prestidigitation found in books of magic lore: he was the inventor of mechanical marionettes that made pastries and potions, opened gates and balanced on tightropes, an electrical wizard who used the new secrets of science to instil in his more gullible audiences the belief that he might be in league with the powers of darkness. Yes, he was kind and, yes, she believed that he loved her. But his love was not that of an ordinary man. It was, like everything he had achieved, like everything he sought to do, bound up in some way with his life of illusion.

Shortly after nine the Colonel rejoined them, introducing them to an elderly banker who had seen Lambert perform at St Petersburg before the Empress of Russia. 'An astonishing evening, sir. I remember that the Empress was most impressed. I can't tell you how delighted I am that you're to be with us this week. It's going to be a much more interesting *série* than the last one I attended. I assume we will have the honour of a performance?'

'I am not here to perform,' Lambert said stiffly. 'But if I am asked, I may take part in some entertainment.'

'The old banker smiled. 'Wonderful. I look forward to it, sir.'

'And the *série* you attended last time?' Colonel Deniau asked. 'Who were the guests?'

'Prince Metternich, that crowd. And a few titled foreigners. The Duke of Hamilton came for the shooting and there was a Russian grand duke. That's known as the elegant *série*. Actually, very boring.'

She saw that Henri was not pleased by this. 'So there are several different *séries* then?' he asked.

'Oh, yes. The Emperor gives four different *séries* each season. And people worry about which one they've been asked to attend. Everyone wants to be invited, of course, but to which one? It's a matter of status. There's a story – ' The old banker broke into an alarmingly loud laugh. 'They say one lady asked another, "Are you in the elegant *série*?" "No, indeed," was the reply. "I'm in yours."'

'And which *série* is this?' Lambert asked.

'The political, I'd say. There are some engineers concerned with the Suez canal project, and bankers like myself – because these great works have to be financed, and, of course, Baron Haussmann is here with further plans for the Paris boulevards. And there are quite a few political figures. Like yourself, Colonel. You're part of the Emperor's African adventure, no?'

The Colonel smiled. 'I serve in Africa, yes. But I'm here as a friend of Monsieur Lambert. The Emperor is fascinated by his skills.'

'Well, I hope we shall all have a chance to enjoy them,' the old banker said. 'Ah! They're going in now.'

Emmeline, looking in the direction he indicated, saw the Emperor and Empress enter the small private salon, accompanied by a dozen guests. 'Now, the dancing should pick up,' the old banker said.

'Madame, may I have the honour?' Colonel Deniau asked her. And in a moment he had swept her off to the strain of waltz music echoing faintly from the far end of the enormous room. They danced. He smiled at her but did not speak. She felt the intimate touch of his hand in the small of her back as he guided her through steps and swirls. And when the dance ended she realized that he had manoeuvred her to a part of the room, far away from her husband. 'You dance beautifully,' he said. 'Shall we continue?'

And so, between dances, making innocent conversation, but with far from innocent glances, he managed to monopolize her until the Emperor and his suite emerged from the private salon. Tea and cakes were served and a few minutes later Their Majesties bowed to their guests and walked to the doors, turned on reaching them and with a last sweeping inclination of their heads, disappeared from sight. At once Lambert, as though he had been dismissed, hurried across the room and took hold of Emmeline's arm. 'Let's go up, now, darling. You must be tired.' He turned to Deniau. 'Till tomorrow, then, Colonel.'

The Colonel looked at her. 'Till tomorrow, Madame.'

TWO

She woke – where? Dark wooden ceiling, blear winter light from a window, damp linen sheet against her neck, woke as she had in the night, cold, confused, from a dream of the *cent gardes*, a smiling Empress, *chars à bancs*, a dark handsome face, but this was morning, her husband in his dressing gown in the adjoining room, watching as a bewigged and powdered footman put down a tray with silver jugs of *café au lait*, then withdrew.

'What time is it?' she called.

'Nine o'clock. Everything here runs like clockwork. They've left a timetable of events.'

She watched him pick up a sheet of paper from the coffee tray. He read: 'Programme for the day. Morning coffee, 9 a.m. Lunch, 11 a.m. Shooting party, 2 p.m. Musical concert, 9 p.m.'

He poured a bowl of coffee and brought it to her in the bedroom. 'I'm going to go over some work notes,' he said. 'What will you do? We've got a couple of hours before luncheon.'

'Is it raining?'

'No.'

'Then I'll go for a walk.'

He nodded and went back to the desk in the sitting room. It was no different from home. It was up to her to amuse herself. She looked at the trunks, half-unpacked in the clutter and discomfort of this small dark bedroom. What would she wear? Which, among these morning costumes, was most suitable for a walk in the grounds? Madame Cournet had said that at the end of the morning she must change for lunch. She decided not to call Françoise, the supercilious old lady's maid, not just yet. I'll dress and go out and then when I change for lunch I'll ask her to do my hair.

She chose the plainest of the morning costumes, a brown cloth suit, trimmed with bands of sealskin, with coat, hat and muff to match. Lambert did not even look up when she went, dressed, into the living room.

'How will I know where to walk?'

'There are footmen outside,' he said.

A lackey in green livery led her down through the labyrinth of the château's stairways and corridors to a door which gave on a series of formal gardens. 'It might rain, Madame, so I would advise the trellis walk. You will be sheltered there.'

The trellis walk, one thousand metres long, dark, with the umbrella foliage above her head. She the only walker for the first thirty minutes was joined by a cleric in purple robes who, reading his breviary as in a monastery cloister, acknowledged her presence with a nod as she passed by. In her sealskin-trimmed coat and hat, her hands snug in a sealskin muff, she imagined herself as one of those elegant society ladies she used to see taking their morning stroll under the arcades of the Place des Vosges. Wearing Monsieur West's clothes, invited to Compiègne, curtsying to the Empress, seated at the same table as Louis Napoleon, a handsome colonel smiling at me, a lady's maid to dress me and do my hair, and yet this time next week I'll be back in Tours in the Manoir des Chênes, my husband shut away in his workroom, his mechanical marionette opening our gates to local tradesmen who think us in league with the devil, the carillon warning him of every movement in the house and, day and night, forty-two clocks ticking out the seconds, the hours, the years. Compiègne, the *cent gardes*, the *chars à bancs*, the royal train, the Emperor and Empress, will be something that happened once, long ago. My new wardrobe will fill my dressing room, crinolines packed away for ever, for whom would I wear them – even on a visit to Paris there wouldn't be any occasion. The afternoon dresses I can wear in Tours, but we have no friends there, no one to admire them.

The coats and hats and morning clothes I'll wear, yes, over and over again until they're out of fashion and put away as relics beside my wedding dress and my first-communion frock.

She heard the spatter of rain, but the walk ahead remained dry, protected by the thick foliage above her. Imagine this huge château filled with servants, furniture, paintings, tapestries, yet used only for a few weeks of each year. If Maman were still alive, I could tell her about the dresses, the dancing, the *cent gardes* and my curtsy to the Empress, but Papa won't believe we were invited because the Emperor wants Henri to perform some service. What could that possibly be, he'll say, your husband isn't a soldier or a diplomat, what can they want of him, what use could they make of him and his tricks?

At the end of the trellis walk, she saw hedges, paths, formal gardens, deserted, curtained by rain. What time is it? She looked back. The cleric had gone in. Suddenly worried she ran back down the dark, now interminable trellis walk to the doorway where her lackey sat on a high stool, waiting. He told her the time. Luncheon at eleven, less than thirty minutes to change. He led her back to her rooms and went off to summon the old maid. Frantic, Emmeline sat, her shoulders bare, while the old maid, mouth full of pins, began to put up her hair.

In the adjoining sitting room, Lambert closed his notebook and said crossly, 'Why did you leave it so late? We're late already. It's five minutes to eleven. How can you do this?'

'Go then, if you want to. You can make my apologies.'

'Maybe I will. One of us should be on time.' He shut the book with a snap and went out of the room.

'Perhaps I won't go down,' she said, half to herself, half to the old maid. 'I won't be missed.'

'No, Madame. It would be noticed. Which dress, Madame?'

She chose the dark-blue poplin, trimmed with dark-blue plush, and struggled into it as the old maid fussed to lock the clasp of her bracelet.

'You are ready now, Madame. *Bon appétit.*'

A lackey waited by the door. She followed him down the stairs, through interminable corridors, into the great hall where, a bad sign, the *cent gardes* stood at ease, stiffening to attention as she rushed past. The dining-room doors were shut. A footman hurriedly opened for her, as her lackey led her in.

Luncheon had begun. Head bent, blushing, she followed the lackey down the long table. Where was Henri? Where should she sit? Did the Emperor look up as she hurried past him? The First Chamberlain did.

'There is no formal seating for luncheon,' the lackey whispered. 'Madame might sit here?'

A chair was drawn back and she sat at last. The lady sitting opposite welcomed her with a smile then turned to whisper something to her neighbour, an aristocratic young gentleman who put his hand over his mouth as if to stifle a laugh. What are they saying? Making fun of me? And then at the far end of the table she saw Henri leaning forward to catch her attention, giving her an angry look. She tried to stare him down but he, as if to rebuke her, turned his head and spoke gaily to a lady on his left. Where is the Colonel? But the table was so long, the number of guests almost a hundred, he could be anywhere in this crowd. She turned to the gentleman on her right.

'Good morning,' she said.

'Not the best of mornings, is it, Mademoiselle. It's raining outside. I suspect they'll have to cancel the shooting party this afternoon. Is your escort a gun?'

What did he mean? At a loss, she smiled at him. He called me Mademoiselle. A gun?

'There are some very good guns in this *série*,' the gentleman said. 'Prince von Lowenstein, an Austrian, is here. Last year at Compiègne, he shot one thousand, two hundred birds in one day. Astonishing. As for me, I'm glad that it's raining. I'm afraid I'm a very poor shot.'

'I hope it rains all week.'

The gentleman smiled. 'For my sake, Mademoiselle? How sweet of you.'

'No,' she said, 'I mean, for the sake of the birds.'

He laughed. 'You have a tender heart, I see. But I notice you are about to eat pheasant.'

She looked down at her plate. A lackey stepped forward and filled her wine glass from a crystal decanter.

The gentleman raised his glass to her in toast. 'I'm sorry,' he said. 'That wasn't fair. Forgive me. Let me introduce myself. I am Jean de Courcel. And you, Mademoiselle?'

'Lambert,' she said. 'And it is Madame.'

'Lambert? Are you, by chance, the wife of the magician? I was told that he is here.'

'I am.'

He smiled and looked at her again, now, she sensed, with a certain condescension. 'Ah! So we are in for a treat, are we? You must introduce me to your husband. I've always been fascinated by magicians and magic tricks.'

The rain had stopped. As the guests left the luncheon table, a cold November sunlight shone through long french windows which faced the formal gardens at the rear of the château. Emmeline waited by the door of the dining room until Lambert joined her and then in angry silence walked with him up the long corridor lined by *cent gardes*. At the end of the corridor a group of chamberlains was in conversation with certain guests, one of whom was Colonel Deniau who, at sight of her, came over, bowed and kissed her hand, a true kiss, his lips moist on her skin.

'Good morning, Madame. And Lambert, my dear fellow, I have news for you. Do you shoot?'

She saw Henri look at her, in warning. 'Not regularly,' he said, laughing a false laugh. 'But I can point a gun. However, I don't have guns or a shooting costume.'

'Nor do I,' the Colonel said. 'But we'll be outfitted after a fashion. The Emperor has asked us to join his party this afternoon. Madame also, of course. The carriages will be waiting in the main courtyard at two o'clock.' He turned to her. 'The Empress will be joining us, so you may have a chance to meet her. Don't forget to dress warmly. I look forward to being with you this afternoon.'

With a bow and a smile, he turned and went out into the gardens.

'What's come over you?' she said. 'Why did you say you shoot, you've never gone on shooting parties, you told me you have no interest in that sort of thing. Besides it's cruel, horrible, stupid.'

'I know, I know. But I've got to go, I've *got* to! This is a personal invitation from Louis Napoleon himself. For God's sake, Emmeline! Please, darling. You've been invited as well. It would be an insult to the Empress if you refused. Please? I haven't asked a lot from you, have I?'

'No.' Suddenly, she felt as if she would weep.

'Then, *please?*'

At two o'clock, footmen helped them into *chars à bancs*, tucking them under heavy rugs. The Colonel sat next to Emmeline, his leg touching hers under the rug. Lambert, at the far end of the *char à bancs* engaged his neighbour in sporadic conversation.

In the main courtyard trumpets sounded a fanfare as the Emperor came through the main entrance arch in company with a gentleman, who, the Colonel said, was Prince Metternich, the Austrian Ambassador. The two men climbed into a small dog cart and the Emperor took the reins. Then the Empress came down the great stone staircase, wearing a green shooting costume and an elegant three-cornered hat trimmed with gold braid. With her was Princess von Lowenstein, the wife of the famous gun. These ladies were seated in a victoria. With a flick of his whip, the Emperor started up his dog cart, leading the cavalcade of vehicles out of the courtyard on to the network of private roads which criss-crossed the vastness of the royal forest. Emmeline, snug in her travelling cloak, her sealskin-lined boots tucked under a heavy bearskin rug, was aware that Colonel

Deniau and she were being jostled together and that this both amused and pleased him.

'Are you warm enough?' he asked. 'I'm afraid it will be chilly at the shoot.'

'I'm quite comfortable,' she said. 'In fact, I wish I could stay in this carriage and not have to watch.'

'But you've been to *chasses à tir* before, haven't you? I suspect that your husband is quite a good shot.'

'Did he tell you that?'

He laughed. 'No, but he seems to know a lot about guns.'

'I've never seen him shoot,' she said. 'He takes birds and rabbits out of a hat.'

Again, he laughed and looked at her with a delighted, complicit smile.

Why did I say that? Anger against Henri, yes, but it's something more. I want us both to make fun of him.

Ahead, they could now see a large open space surrounded by thick forest. Assembled there, a crowd waited for their arrival. As they descended from their carriages it seemed to Emmeline as if the entire population of Compiègne had turned out as beaters and spectators. Now, guided by chamberlains, the sportsmen took their places in a long line, the Emperor in the middle, with Prince Metternich on his right and Prince von Lowenstein on his left. She saw that her husband and the Colonel were placed near the end of the line.

Once the sportsmen were in position the ladies were asked to stand behind them, much too close, Emmeline thought, for directly behind the ladies were gamekeepers, darting forward to load and hand fresh guns to their masters. Suddenly, Louis Napoleon raised his hand and in an enormous hubbub the lines of beaters moved through the forest, forcing birds to fly up above the trees and rabbits and hares to come scuttling into the open. Hundreds of animals had been frightened and hoarded into an area from which they could not escape and now were being driven to their deaths.

Emmeline stood, deafened by the roar of guns, shutting her eyes to the rain of dead animals falling from the sky, aware that all around her beaters were rushing about, picking up the dead and dying animals and putting them into numbered sacks, thus making a tally of each sportsman's kills. Henri? And the Colonel? She turned and looked down the line. Lambert raising his gun, firing, exchanging the empty gun with his loader, skilful yet theatrical in this movement as he was in everything, the butchery of sport forgotten in his eagerness to be seen as one of these rich and idle aristocrats. She looked past him, to Colonel Deniau. His scarred face impassive, he stood like a soldier firing implacably at some unseen enemy in the sky, ignoring the pitiable dead and dying creatures that fell at his feet.

Ill, turning this way and that to avoid the gun loaders, the men picking up the dead birds, the jolting echoes of firing, the smell of gunpowder, the stench of death, Emmeline suddenly knew that she would vomit and so, holding up her long skirt, ran back towards the carriages. As she did she saw, ahead, the Empress and a lady-in-waiting hurrying towards the victoria as a postilion readied a wooden step to help them to mount into the carriage. The Empress, turning back, saw Emmeline, her pale face, her panic.

'Are you all right, my dear?'

Unable to speak, Emmeline nodded, choking back the bile in her throat.

'It's too cold,' the Empress said. 'It's this November damp. We are going back now. I advise you to do the same if you're not feeling well.'

With that, the Empress and her-lady-in-waiting were helped up into their seats. Emmeline turned away so that they would not see. She retched.

A chamberlain came running across the grass. 'Madame is ill. Would you like to go back, Madame?'

Miserable, she nodded her head, fumbling in her muff for a handkerchief to wipe her mouth. She heard the chamberlain call, 'Georges!'

A coachman came up, touching his fingers to his cap in salute. 'If Madame will follow me?'

He led her to a phaeton, helping her up and tucking her in

under a heavy robe. Some of the watching villagers turned to look at her as the little carriage trundled off down a royal road. In the distance the angry staccato of guns sounded strangely like the cawing of crows. And then she was alone, quiet, away from the noise of carnage, hearing only the clop of the horse's hoofs, the coachman on his bench in front of her, head nodding as the phaeton jolted towards the château of Compiègne.

The sky went dark. Spits of rain increased to a drizzle. The coachman raised an umbrella, handed it back to her, then whipped his horse into a gallop. Emmeline sat, eyes shut, head bent, the umbrella stick clutched in her hands like a processional cross, nausea again rising within her. If this rain continues the shooting will end and they'll come back to the château looking for some new diversion. Killing birds, hunting stags, tea parties, banquets, charades, concerts, dancing, anything and everything to get them through the boredom, snobbery and indifference of their lives. Why did I pretend the Colonel wasn't one of them, he's the one who brought us here, how could he ever be attracted to someone like me, whatever it is he wants from Henri, it suits him and amuses him to flirt with me, I'd be a fool to think it's anything else. If only this carriage were taking me to Rouen. Papa would give me medicine to stop this retching, Marie would undress me, make me a tisane, and put hot-water bottles in my bed. I'll tell Henri I'm sick, I'll say I have a fever, I'll say I can't be sick here, I'll ask him to send me back to Tours with that old servant, she'll take care of me, he doesn't have to come, he can stay on for the rest of the week, showing off, talking to the Emperor about whatever it is they want him to do, anyway he's angry with me, he was furious this morning when I was late for lunch and when I didn't want to go to the *chasse à tir.* No one will miss me. I'll go to bed now. Tomorrow morning, I'll leave.

The phaeton rumbled through the great arches, leading to the central courtyard. As it crossed the courtyard, a major-domo who was standing in the main doorway signalled that a carriage was approaching. Two lackeys came running out to help Emmeline descend.

'Madame was taken ill,' the coachman called down. At once, the major-domo looked at a list and called out the number of the Lamberts' apartment. The lackeys like solicitous nurses led her up the long flights of staircase and into her room. A third servant brought in firewood and laid a fire in the sitting-room grate.

'Will we summon your maid, Madame?'

'No, thank you.'

She went into the dark bedroom, shut the door, took off her dress and stays and got into bed. The nausea came back in a wave, then passed. Within minutes, exhausted, she fell asleep.

'Madame? If you please? Could you drink this?'

She woke to a darkened room lit only by two flickering candles. Standing over her was the old maidservant, offering tisane in an elegant porcelain cup, her hands' slight tremor causing the cup to jiggle on its saucer.

'What time is it?'

'It is eight o'clock, Madame.'

Eight o'clock. They will be finishing dinner.

'I didn't wake you earlier,' the old maid said. 'The doctor advised that you be allowed to rest.'

'Was the doctor here?'

'Yes, with your husband, Madame. They looked in some time ago. Monsieur is dining now. He said he will come to see you before the concert this evening. How is Madame? Are you feeling better?'

'I don't know,' she said. But she did know. The nausea had passed. She no longer felt cold. The sickening sights of that afternoon were now a memory. *I'm well, but if I'm to be allowed to go home, I mustn't say so.*

'Thank you for the tisane, Françoise.'

'Rest now, Madame.'

*　　*　　*

When next she woke it was to find her husband kneeling by her bedside, stroking her hand. And at once, looking at his worried face, she saw that side of him she could not ignore: despite his self-absorption, his inability to understand her loneliness, her boredom, despite his inordinate ambition, he loved her.

'How are you, darling?'

How can I lie to him?

'Better,' she said.

'I can't forgive myself. I didn't know what had happened until I came back here after the shooting party. I looked for you at the game tally and when they said you'd already gone back I admit I thought you'd done it to spite me. Oh, darling, I'm sorry. I should have taken better care of you.'

'It's all right,' she said. 'I just couldn't watch those animals being killed.'

'Well, at least, now, we know what to do,' he said. 'They will be having a stag hunt on Saturday and afterwards there's some sort of hunting ceremony. I'll speak to Deniau. We will make your excuses.' He got up from his kneeling position. 'And I have good news, darling. You and I and Deniau are to be received in private audience by the Emperor on Friday. So we can relax and have a pleasant holiday until then. I hear we're to have a theatrical evening tomorrow. The Théâtre Français, no less. Let's hope you're well enough to enjoy it.' He bent over her and kissed her cheek. 'Sleep now. Good night.'

THREE

The court theatre, large as any in Paris, was lit by thousands of wax candles, creating a brilliant, romantic glow, which set off the jewels and gowns of the ladies in the audience. The Imperial Loge, designed in the shape of a shell, reached from the first tier of boxes to the last seats of the parquet. Their Majesties' seats were in the centre of the Loge with lady guests and the most important gentlemen of rank placed beside and behind them. Other gentlemen sat in the parterre and circulated throughout the theatre between the acts. In addition to the Emperor's guests a large house party from a neighbouring château had been invited to fill out the audience.

Now, in a sudden hush of conversation, the Empress appeared in the Imperial Loge, followed by the Emperor, smiling, his fingers touching the long ends of his waxed moustache. At sight of Their Majesties everyone rose, ladies curtsying, gentlemen bowing. Their Majesties bowed in response. The Master of Ceremonies gave the signal and at once the curtain rose. The scenery had been brought in from Paris. The principal actors were the great Coquelin, Madeleine Brohan, and Madame Favard, all members of the Théâtre Français.

Emmeline, wearing the most beautiful of her West gowns, sat in the second tier of boxes. Looking around her, she was enchanted by the setting, the jewels, the gowns, the sense that, despite her feelings of hostility, this evening would be one of the great occasions of her life. Almost from the moment the play began, she was caught up in the story enacted on stage. Coquelin and Madeleine Brohan became for her the living incarnation of the characters they played. The play itself was moving: she wept, her lace handkerchief wet, as she watched the story unfold. At the *entracte*, her husband and Colonel Deniau joined her in the box. They too seemed transformed by the evening. Even Lambert, to whom a theatrical performance had always been something he judged as a professional, was tonight enthusiastic and delighted as a boy who has just seen his first play.

At half-past ten the performance ended, after which the entire audience followed the Emperor and Empress into the *grande salle des fêtes*. The Emperor then sent for the actors, who, having changed out of their costumes, appeared to a round of applause. Emmeline watched Coquelin talk to the Emperor and saw that he was able to put the Emperor at ease, laughing and chatting with him in a casual way which none of the distinguished guests seemed to have managed in the preceding days. For some reason this comforted her and made her feel more secure than at any time since her arrival in Compiègne. The Emperor was a man, he was human, he wanted to enjoy himself; he who was at the top of the social ladder did not look down on Coquelin who, like her husband, was a person who performed on stage.

At eleven o'clock refreshments were brought in, the carriages were announced and making a 'reverence' to Their Majesties the artists took their leave. The Emperor and Empress then withdrew. The guests from the neighbouring château departed in their carriages leaving the guests free to go to their rooms.

On the following morning her changed mood still held. She felt light-headed, free, no longer intimidated by the grandeurs around her. After *déjeuner* when the Master of Ceremonies approached, as usual, to ask what they would like to do and Lambert, as usual, said that he would like to sit and read, she, to her surprise, asked if she could visit some sights in the region.

'An excellent idea,' the Master of Ceremonies said. 'There is a wonderful castle nearby, the Château de Pierrefonds, a former ruin which the Emperor is renovating. It's one of his great projects. Well worth a visit.'

At that moment, Emmeline saw that Colonel Deniau had come up and was standing directly behind Henri. 'The Château de Pierrefonds, did you say? I very much want to see it. Would you allow me to join you, Madame?'

'Wonderful,' Henri said, turning to the Colonel. 'If you go with her it will make me feel less guilty.'

She noticed at once that the Colonel in his usual complicit way managed to ignore her husband's remark and, instead, kept looking at her, waiting for her answer.

'I must put on my travelling clothes,' she told him. 'But I can be ready in, say, half an hour?'

'A landau and a picnic hamper will be waiting in the main courtyard, whenever you come down,' the Master of Ceremonies told her.

She smiled at the Colonel. 'Will that suit you?'

'Indeed, Madame. À *bientôt*.'

The forest of Pierrefonds adjoined the royal forest of Compiègne. Sitting side by side in the landau wrapped in furs and rugs, they set out in November mists, down twisting forest roads, dead and dry leaves rustling under the horses' feet. At first they sat in silence looking around them at vistas of trees and lake, then as the drive continued Deniau made polite conversation about last night's play and the actors. Suddenly, he said, 'You seem happier today. I don't mean because you're no longer ill. You no longer hate being here. Am I right?'

'Yes.'

'I'm glad. Bringing you to Compiègne was my idea, you know.'

'No, I didn't know,' she said. 'But tell me. Why would you want me here?'

'Because you are part of my plan. I realize it sounds confusing, but when we meet the Emperor on Friday I think it will all become clear. You are very important in this affair. Yes, yes

– I made a mistake. I thought you'd be delighted to visit Compiègne. When I saw that wasn't true, I was alarmed. But now – was it the play last night that made you change your mind? I hope so.'

What did he mean? 'Why am I part of your plan?' she said. 'Tell me.'

'Not now. But I promise you, I will.'

Their drive through cold November mists ended at an abrupt turn of the road when, suddenly, they saw the enormous fortress-château of Pierrefonds, rising above the little town of that name. Following the road which led up to the château they came to a gateway, then through a second gateway into a court until, finally, their carriage clattered over a drawbridge to pull up at the main entrance.

The Colonel helped her down, saying, 'Let's not have a guide, shall we? They talk too much. Let me be your guide. I know a few things about this place. Don't you think it will be more fun to explore on our own?'

And so, waving aside the servant who waited to conduct them, they passed through a dark vaulted chapel, climbing more than a hundred stone steps to reach a platform which overlooked a view of the little town and the surrounding forest. A cold wind blew through the ramparts as they stood, side by side, looking down. She shivered and turned away. Seeing this, he took off his fur-lined cape and draped it about her shoulders. It was a gesture any gentleman might have made but when he did it he did not release the cape, instead holding it against her body for a long moment.

'I can see that you were made for warmer climes,' he said. 'You need the sun, you need space, you need the desert. The desert has a beauty one can't imagine until one sees it. You must visit Africa.'

At that, he released his hold on the cape. She pulled it tight about her. 'Africa? Why would I go to Africa? I don't understand.'

'You will.' He took her arm. 'Let's go down and look around. The Count de Vogué visited this castle the other day and he tells me it's not really interesting. A hundred years ago someone managed to buy it for only eight thousand francs. Imagine! Now, as you know, the Emperor is restoring it. Vogué said there's one astonishing thing, a huge chimmneypiece in the *salle des gardes*. Let's find it for our picnic, shall we?'

Their coachman, summoned by a castle servant, brought the picnic hamper up to the *salle des gardes*, a huge deserted hall, furnished only with ancient stone benches and dominated by the fireplace, its hearth large as a stable, its chimney forty feet in height, ornamented with carvings of hundreds of squirrels which peered down on them with stony curiosity. The coachman spreading a carriage rug on the hearth unpacked cold meats, fruit, cakes, wine. The castle servant, aware that they were visitors from the Emperor's *série*, brought in logs and kindling, lighting a small fire under the great vault of chimney. Servant and coachman then withdrew leaving them alone in the echoing vastness of the hall.

Through the high narrow windows a late afternoon sun, veiled by cold November mists, filled the shadows about them with a cloudy golden light. Emmeline drew back the hood of her cloak, baring her neck, letting the heavy coil of her hair fall down against her cheek. The fire crackled and blazed, smoke rising in swirls up the blackened chimney walls. She leaned towards it, the golden misty light falling on her shoulders and hair.

'You look like a medieval angel,' Deniau said. He reached for the wine bottle and sat close to her, handing her a glass. 'Do you know that German toast, the *Brüderschaft*? No? Let me show you. Hold up your glass.' He leaned forward, entwining his own glass of wine through her arm in a gesture which brought them almost face to face. 'Now let's drink,' he said. 'It's a toast to friendship.'

Embarrassed, for there was something dangerously intimate in this linkage, their bodies touching, his dark, handsome face so close to hers, she drank down the full glass of wine without realizing what she had done. As she withdrew her arm from his he looked at her strangely.

'Friends? Are we?'

'Of course.' She bent her head, avoiding his eyes.

'Madame,' he said. 'You are a mystery.'

'Why?'

He laughed, and shook his head. 'I don't know why. But you are. Your smile is enigmatic as the smile of La Gioconde. Tell me. How did you come to be the wife of a magician?'

It was her turn to laugh. 'Because he called me up on to the stage during one of his performances.'

'Cast a spell over you, is that it?'

She smiled. 'More or less.'

'And are you still spellbound?'

She looked up at the small cold circle of sky at the top of the great chimney above her. *What do I say to that? Yes? When it is no.*

'I'm sorry,' he said. 'I was being facetious. I know that Lambert is spellbound by *you*. You have enchanted the magician. You should hear how he talks of you.'

He refilled her wine glass and held it out to her. She looked into those dark eyes which sought to make her his accomplice. She did not accept the glass.

'Thank you, but I must go back now. The rule is that ladies must be in their rooms by four o'clock. That's when the Empress will send for me if she invites me to tea.'

He smiled. 'Tell me. Will you be invited, do you think?'

'No. But I want to go back. Please?'

He rose at once. 'Of course, Madame.'

At four-twenty, in her room in Compiègne, having changed from her travelling dress into an afternoon gown of blue faille, she heard a knock on the door. The old maid went to answer and there in the corridor was a lackey and a small boy.

'Monsieur Lambert?' the lackey asked.

'Monsieur Lambert is in the theatre,' the old maid said. 'He left word that you are to bring the boy there.'

When the door closed, Emmeline, weak with relief, asked, 'Françoise, do you think it's still possible that she will invite me?'

'At this hour, I doubt it,' the old maid said. 'Invitations are usually issued at a few minutes after four. And as I recall, Madame, as a rule, they are given only to ladies of the Empress's acquaintance.'

'So Monsieur Lambert is down in the theatre,' Emmeline said.

'Yes, Madame. He is there with his man Jules. Jules tells me they are preparing for a performance.'

'A performance? When?'

'This evening, I believe, Madame.'

At eight o'clock she was escorted in to dinner, not by Colonel Deniau but by a gentleman whose name she did not catch, a stout dyspeptic person who talked constantly throughout the meal. 'Are you cold?' was his first question and then without waiting for an answer he complained that his room was in a part of the château filled with draughts and a fireplace that smoked. 'If you're not a prince or a baron or some *grande horizontale* who the Emperor is trying to entice into his bed you will always be freezing in this place. And the entertainment! I was here two years ago and on four different evenings we were forced to take part in boring charades. They have rooms full of theatrical costumes and you are asked to choose some ridiculous getup to illustrate an idiotic sentence. Luckily, this isn't one of the aristocratic *séries*. Aristocrats love charades. I don't know about you, Madame, but I find the aristocracy incredibly stupid. *Dieu merci*, this is what they call a third-tier *série* where the great majority of our guests, are, as you may have noticed, not the *gratin* but rich bourgeois, bankers or moneyed foreigners, people the Emperor wants to use in some way. Is your husband here?'

'Yes, he is.'

'I'm sorry. I hope I didn't put my foot in it. He's not a banker, is he?'

'No.'

'Good. By the way, having said that about the entertainment, I thought the theatrical performance the other evening was not bad. What did you think, Madame?'

'I thought it was wonderful.'

'If only they would have something like that every evening, we wouldn't die of boredom. That's what we need. Professional entertainers. I wonder what they have in mind for tonight?'

Emmeline looked down the long table to where Lambert was as usual in animated conversation with his fellow diners. Not a first-tier *série*, this man says. Foreigners, bankers, people the Emperor wants to use in some way. What can he want from Henri?

A footman removed her dessert plate and served coffee. In less than an hour Henri will stand in front of all of these people, not as a guest but as a magician, here to amuse and divert the company. And my charade will have ended. I will be the magician's wife.

At nine o'clock when Their Majesties acknowledging the curtsies and bowings of the audience had seated themselves in the Imperial Loge, the Master of Ceremonies announced that two of the invited guests would entertain the company before the evening's dancing began. At that, the curtain went up. Standing at a podium, a tall gentleman began to read a poem. Emmeline's neighbour whispered, 'Who is he?' and someone answered, 'That's Théophile Gautier.'

At least, Emmeline thought, Henri's in good company. Even she had heard of Gautier: her father had once informed her that Gautier was a writer of genius. But during the reading, when she looked up at the Imperial Loge, she saw that the Emperor was slumped in his seat, his eyes closed as though asleep. After half an hour when the writer finished his reading and bowed to his listeners, the Emperor still seemed to be asleep. The Empress led the applause. Emmeline then saw the Emperor open his eyes, clap feebly, and turn to talk to his guests. The curtain descended.

After a short interval the Master of Ceremonies, strolling among the gentlemen in the parterre, looked up to the Imperial Loge trying to catch the Emperor's eye. When the Emperor waved assent the Master of Ceremonies rapped his staff three times on the floorboards. The curtain rose on a stage, completely empty except for a small deal table at the rear, and at centre stage a plain wooden trestle of the sort used by artists for stacking their drawings. On this trestle stood a long green leather portfolio emblazoned in gold letters with the legend:

Henri Lambert
Carton du Dessins

The audience waited. After thirty seconds of silence, Lambert appeared from the wings, dressed in the frock coat he had worn at dinner and carrying a small ebony baton with olive-shaped ivory tips at each end. He smiled, bowed to the audience and walked all around the portfolio, using the baton to show that there was nothing concealed under the wooden trestle. He then put the baton down on the table at the rear, walked back to the trestle, opening and closing the long narrow portfolio to show that it was empty. He turned to face the audience, bowed, then reopened the portfolio, taking from it a sheaf of engravings. The audience applauded. He again opened the portfolio, taking from it four turtle doves which he released into the air. The applause increased as he closed the portfolio, smiled, then reopened it, this time taking out three large copper casseroles. He opened one to show that it contained green beans, the second to show that it contained a burning flame, and the third to show that it was filled with boiling water. Having displayed the contents of the casseroles to his audience he returned to the trestle and the portfolio, this time taking out a large cage filled with tiny birds which flew from perch to perch inside it. The applause was now generous and Emmeline looking up at the Imperial Loge saw the Emperor smiling and clapping, his sleepy lizard eyes lit with approval.

Lambert bowed to the Imperial Loge, then turned again to the empty portfolio, flipping it open with his index finger. At once, the head of a small boy appeared, smiling at the audience. Lambert reached in and lifted the boy out of the portfolio, setting him down on the stage. The boy was the same boy Emmeline had seen outside her room earlier that afternoon. Silencing the applause with a raised hand, Lambert gestured to the wings. At this point Jules, his servant, appeared, carrying a low wooden bench to centre stage. He then brought out three small stools which he placed on top of the bench, together with three long canes. Lambert, facing the audience, with the little boy at his side, took from his pocket a small flask.

'Your Majesties, ladies and gentlemen, I have discovered in ether a new and marvellous property. When this substance is at its highest degree of concentration, if one allows a human being to breathe it in, his body will become as light as a balloon.'

All of this he spoke in what Emmeline thought of as his professorial voice, a diction he had carefully studied to make him sound like a scientist, not a performer. He now made the little boy climb on to the middle footstool and extend his arms. He placed a long cane under each of the boy's arms to hold them in a cruciform position, then uncorked his flask and held it under the child's nose. A smell of ether pervaded the theatre. The child at once fell asleep under the anaesthetic. Lambert, bending down, slid the footstool from under the child's feet, leaving the child apparently suspended in mid-air, his only support the long canes which held up his arms in the cruciform position. The audience watched in a mixture of fascination and unease as Lambert removed, first, one of the long canes from under the child's right arm, his only support the long cane under his left elbow. Lambert then placed his index finger under the child's waist, and tilted the body sideways, raising the child to a horizontal position, leaving him apparently weightless, his only link to earth the slender cane under his elbow which rested on the small footstool, which, in turn, rested on the low wooden bench. Lambert bowed to the Imperial Loge. Applause and cries of 'Bravo!' filled the theatre as Lambert, turning to the child, again with his index figure, moved the weightless body back to a vertical position. Touching the child's face with his hand, he wakened him, catching him as he began to tumble, then placing him securely on the stage. He took the child's hand and again bowed to the Imperial Loge.

The curtain fell.

That evening, the music in the *salle des fêtes* was a new marvel, a mechanical piano, its handle turned dutifully by one of the chamberlains. But few people were dancing. All around her Emmeline heard talk of her husband's mysterious and magical performance.

'Lambert? This is the first time I've seen him perform, but of course he's famous.'

'I remember a few years ago he had his own theatre in Paris. At that time his "magical" evenings were all the rage.'

'*I* thought he'd retired.'

'Hortense, do you remember, *we* saw a performance while I was stationed in Madrid. It was at the court. The King was present.'

'Yes, of course. I know it gave me a peculiar feeling, almost as if I were witnessing something supernatural. And I had the same thought tonight.'

'No, it's just trickery. But damnably clever.'

'Well, I must say he's a cut above any magician *I've* ever seen. The levitation of that child was uncanny.'

These and similar comments came to her as she moved through the groups of guests, searching for Henri and Colonel Deniau. But her husband was nowhere in sight and it was only after twice wandering up and down the entire length of the great room that she saw Colonel Deniau who at once broke off a conversation with an elderly lady and hurried to join her.

'Ah, Madame! Emmeline! I have been looking for you everywhere. In a few minutes we'll be going into the *petit salon.* Your husband is surrounded by admirers but I'll prise him away in time. If you will just stay here, I'll bring him to you and then we can all go in together.'

Alone again in this crowd of strangers, Emmeline looked nervously at the entrance to the *petit salon* where at ten o'clock each evening the Emperor and Empress withdrew for a private hour of conversation with certain privileged guests. It was now ten-thirty. Turning to the mirrored walls she hastily inspected her hair. I will be presented to them. I will have to speak. No, let Henri do the talking. I'll just bow or curtsy. Which? I must be calm. I don't even have time to re-comb my hair. Why didn't I think of it sooner?

But at that moment in the vortex of her confusion, Deniau and Lambert came to join her. Lambert was smiling, not in the least nervous about the coming audience. 'Ah, there you are, darling. It went well, didn't it? Everyone has been most enthusiastic. As a matter of fact, I haven't had a minute to myself.' He turned to Deniau. 'Charles, you were right. It was a very good idea to arrange for me to entertain them tonight. Not too much, not a real performance, but enough to give the Emperor a *soupçon* of what I can really do.'

'I know that His Majesty is delighted,' Deniau said. 'I watched him while you were on stage. You're the star of the evening.' He smiled at Emmeline. 'Are we ready then?'

He took her arm. The chamberlains on guard at the doors of the *petit salon* bowed to Deniau and stepped aside. Suddenly, Emmeline found herself in a drawing room ornately furnished and dominated at its furthest end by a huge white marble statue of the Emperor's uncle, Napoleon I, in a familiar pose, hand inserted in his vest. There were about twenty people in the room, most of them members of Their Majesties' intimate circle, who at dinnertime were always seated in places favourably close to the imperial couple. Emmeline saw the Empress, surrounded by admirers, talking to Gautier, the writer who had performed earlier that evening. The chamberlain now beckoned them to follow him, leading them through the clusters of people directly to the far end of the room where, under the statue of his ancestor, the Emperor sat like a king on his throne listening to a stout gentleman who stood humbly before him like a petitioner. When this man had bowed and backed away from the throne-like chair their chamberlain approached the Emperor and whispered something into his ear. The Emperor looked up, his sleepy eyes picking out Emmeline and not her husband. His glance, to her astonishment, was the appraisal of a lecher, an impression heightened by the fact that his face, adorned with long thin waxed moustaches and goat-like pointed beard, made him resemble a satyr in a Rubens painting.

The Emperor, turning his glance to Deniau, said, smilingly. 'Ah, Colonel, there you are.'

'Your Majesty, may I present Monsieur and Madame Lambert?'

Emmeline, sure that she would trip on her crinoline, made a hasty and awkward curtsy. Her husband bowed in almost oriental fashion.

'That was indeed wonderful tonight,' the Emperor told Lambert. 'You, sir, are a necromancer. I believe I saw you perform a few years ago. Was it at Fontainebleau?'

'Yes, Your Majesty. I had that honour.'

'And this delightful lady is your wife? Oh, how I would like to sit now and talk to you, my dear. But the trouble with these evening *conversaziones* is that there is no real conversation. Too many people. Colonel, I believe we are to discuss our project tomorrow afternoon?'

'That is correct, Your Majesty.'

'In that case I must beg Madame Lambert to honour us with her presence. It will make the meeting something that I specially look forward to.'

As the Emperor said this Emmeline saw that the Empress and Princess Metternich had come up and that the Empress had heard what was said. She saw the Empress give her a cool appraising glance and then turn to her husband: '*Mon ami*, I think it is time for us to rejoin the company.'

The Emperor rose at once, bowed to Emmeline and took the Empress's arm. They moved towards the doors which led to the *grande salle des fêtes*. At once, the chamberlains indicated that all of the guests in the *petit salon* should follow.

Later, when the imperial couple had retired and the guests were going upstairs to bed, Lambert, pausing at a landing, turned to her, put his hands on her shoulders and looked at her intently. 'This was your evening,' he said. 'Not mine.'

'What do you mean?'

'Don't you know? The Emperor has an eye for you. And Deniau took you off this afternoon to Pierrefonds. *Picnic à deux.* Should I be jealous?'

She smiled and shook her head.

FOUR

'Madame? Madame Lambert?'

Emmeline, walking in winter sunlight among banks of fuchsia in the château's formal gardens, saw the old lady's maid hurrying up the path.

'What is it, Françoise?'

The old woman, out of breath, stammered, 'Madame, the Marquis de Caux has sent word that you are to sit beside His Majesty at *déjeuner*. You must be ready at the doors of the *grande salle* as soon as Their Majesties enter the dining room. I think you should dress now, Madame.'

'And my husband?'

'The invitation is for you alone.'

At five minutes to eleven, Emmeline, waiting with the other guests outside the *grande salle*, saw the doors open to allow the imperial couple to enter the dining room. At that moment a gentleman who introduced himself as the Marquis de Caux came up to her, gave her his arm and led her down the long room to that part of the dining table where the Emperor and his party had just taken their seats. On His Majesty's right was an empty chair. The Emperor did not rise, but smiled at her as she slipped into her place. Across the table the Empress nodded to Emmeline in a queenly manner. The Emperor then gestured to the *maître d'hôtel* and at once the first dishes were brought into the dining room. Behind the Emperor's chair his personal *chasseur* took the dish from the hands of the *maître d'hôtel* and presented it to His Majesty who then helped himself, whereupon the *chasseur* handed the dish back to the *maître d'hôtel* as a signal that guests could now be served.

53

'Do you know the game of croquet, my dear?' the Emperor said, turning to Emmeline.

'No, Your Majesty.'

'I'm told it's now the rage in London and I want to know what the fuss is about. As a matter of fact I've ordered a set from Paris. If they arrive before we leave Compiègne, you and I must learn this game together. Would that amuse you, my dear?'

'Is it a card game, Your Majesty? I'm afraid I'm very stupid at cards.'

The Emperor laughed. 'No, it's an outdoor game. Hitting a ball with a mallet. Anyway, we'll see. Tell me. Will you go to Africa with your husband? That is, if I can persuade him to help us. I want you on my side this afternoon. On my side and by my side.'

He smiled and put his hand on her arm. She felt herself flush as she looked at the Emperor's hand, hairy, its long buffed fingernails gently tickling her bare flesh. This man, the son of Hortense de Beauharnais, the nephew of Bonaparte, his lecher's eyes appraising her, his covetous, faintly mocking smile. And Africa? What *was* this about Africa?

'And let us not forget the *chasse à courre.*' His fingers tightened on her forearm. He leaned forward, his long waxed moustaches only inches from her face. 'You will be my guest at the *curée* on Sunday evening.'

Curée? She smiled at him vaguely. 'What is that, Your Majesty?'

'The finale of the stag hunt. Did you not know about it? Well, why should you? You are so young. How pretty you are. Indeed you are. So pretty.'

Having said this he pushed aside his plate which was promptly removed by his *chasseur.* A second dish was served at once and as the Emperor sampled it and turned to the lady on his left, an old gentleman on Emmeline's right began to talk to her about a dance called the lancers. 'I dread it,' he said. 'I am too old for it, but it is mandatory that if one is asked to take part one cannot refuse. Do you enjoy it, Madame? I may tell you that the Emperor is very fond of the lancers.'

It was at this point that Emmeline sensed the rule of conversation in high society. She did not have to understand what was being said to her, she had only to answer with the vaguest of assents, smiles and nods. It was conversation without purpose, a brief break in the quick and ruthless service of food, necessary to the fulfilment of the Emperor's demand that lunch or dinner must never take more than an hour at table.

And so when, fifty minutes later, the Emperor stood up, his *chasseur* drawing the chair away from the table, lackeys at once stepped forward and put their hands on the back of the guests' chairs, as a signal that all must rise. The chairs were drawn out and the procession followed the Emperor and Empress out to the *grande salle*. Emmeline, escorted by the Marquis de Caux, was suddenly accosted by her husband who bowed to the Marquis then took her arm and led her out on to the loggia.

'What did he say to you?'

'Who?'

'The Emperor. I saw him talking to you. Did he say why he invited you?'

'He wants me to go to Africa. With you. Henri, what's this about? Why won't you tell me?'

'Because it's confidential. You'll know soon enough. What else did he say?'

'He wants me to be on his side this afternoon, whatever that means.' She saw that this pleased him.

'So they really want me.' He smiled. 'What did he say about me?'

'Nothing.'

'By the way, I was watching him all through luncheon. He was laughing and smiling at you. I saw him put his hand on your arm. You know, of course, that he has the reputation of being a terrible roué. Did he . . .?'

'Did he what?'

'When he had his hand on your arm. What was he talking about?'

'Croquet.'

'Croquet?'

'Yes. It's a game. He wants us to learn it together.'

'You and me?'

'No. Louis Napoleon and me.' She began to laugh. He looked at her as though she had slapped him.

'Deniau will meet us at the foot of the main staircase at two o'clock sharp,' he said. 'Don't be late.'

And walked away.

When Colonel Deniau came down the central staircase of the château that afternoon, Emmeline did not at first recognize this imposing figure in dress uniform with long cape and gold-leafed kepi. Previously the Colonel had worn civilian clothes like most of the other gentlemen attending the *série*. But now, in uniform, his dark good looks and military bearing were heightened to a point that seeing him approach she suddenly felt a quick, guilty excitement. Instinctively, she hurried towards him and as he bent to kiss her hand it seemed as if he, too, were caught up in her mood.

'Where is your husband?'

'He will arrive exactly three minutes before the time of our meeting,' she said. 'It is always like that.'

'Just like the Emperor,' Deniau said. 'As you may have noticed, *he* divides his time into neat compartments. Of course, who can blame him? He has a great deal on his mind, these days.'

She did not know what could be on the Emperor's mind. Croquet, perhaps? But she held her tongue.

Lambert appeared exactly as she had predicted and they all three went down a long corridor and through a door which led to an antechamber where two chamberlains waited. Precisely as a clock chimed the half-hour, three gentlemen emerged from the inner chamber, deep in whispered conversation. As these gentlemen went out, one of the chamberlains beckoned to Deniau, who turned to Emmeline. 'After you, dear Madame.'

And so it was Emmeline who led the way into the Emperor's study. The Emperor came to greet her, taking her hands in his and leading her solicitously to a chair on the right of his desk. He sat her down on this chair, then sat at his desk, close to her, waving absent-mindedly to Deniau and Lambert to seat themselves opposite. It was then that Emmeline saw that the Emperor seemed ill: he grimaced with pain as he bent forward to pick up a folder on his desk; his eyes were circled by dark shadows, his face was puffy and she realized, with shock, that his cheeks were rouged. Nevertheless, when he began to speak his voice was forceful and filled with conviction.

'Gentlemen, we know why we are here today but perhaps Monsieur Lambert does not know how badly I need his help. I believe that some months ago Colonel Deniau asked you to assist us and that, for good reason, no doubt, you refused.'

'If Your Majesty will excuse me,' Lambert said. 'I did not realize that the request had come from Your Majesty.'

'But you were right, my dear fellow. The request did *not* come from me. I was unaware of the proposal at that time. Now let me explain why I see this as an important project. As all of France knows, our armies have given us a great victory in the Crimea. Generals MacMahon and Pelissier will be honoured by me in a special ceremony on my return to Paris next week. Our soldiers will also be decorated and rewarded. The Army has fought hard and well and because of that' – he looked at Colonel Deniau – 'I have informed our Governor-General in Algeria that I do not want us engaged in what I hope will be the final struggle for the conquest of that country until our troops have enjoyed a period of rest at home. Accordingly, I told him he must wait until spring before we commit our armies to this task. However, I can understand why Governor-General Randon is worried about this delay. He fears that a certain powerful and dangerous marabout could launch a holy war before then. You are the Arab expert, Colonel. What do you think?'

'There *is* that risk, Your Majesty,' Deniau said. 'And if the final campaign is to be delayed until spring, all the more reason for us to try the gambit I have proposed.'

The Emperor turned to Emmeline. 'This must be confusing for you, my dear. I don't know how much you have been told.'

Emmeline, having learned her lesson at luncheon, smiled and nodded vaguely, whereupon the Emperor lit a long cigar and blew the match out with a whistling sound. 'Never mind,' he said. 'It will become clear soon enough. Now' – he turned to Lambert – 'I know that what you showed us the other evening is but a fraction of your talents. What we need to convince the Arabs is something even more spectacular, something which will both frighten and amaze them. Colonel Deniau tells me that you are our man. He says he has seen you demonstrate illusions so astonishing that even we might be tempted to believe you have supernatural powers.' The Emperor laughed, puffed on his cigar and turning to Emmeline, winked at her like a wicked uncle. Then, leaning back in his chair, he said to Lambert, 'Let me explain what I have in mind. I have great plans for Algeria. I see it as the meeting ground between East and West and the key to our empire's economic expansion. Next year, in the spring, I will bring our armies to Africa, subdue the Kabylia region and complete our conquest of the entire country.'

The Emperor looked at Deniau. 'Now, Colonel – tell us about the marabout.'

'The marabout, Your Majesty? First let me explain that Muslim countries are very different from ours. There, marabouts or saints have a political and spiritual influence which is greater than the power of any ruler.'

The Emperor blew smoke. 'An unfortunate situation for the sheikhs.'

'Indeed. And because of that, only the marabout can proclaim a jihad or holy war against us. At the moment, Your Majesty, all of Algeria is in thrall to a certain Bou-Aziz, a charismatic marabout who has risen up in the South and is said to possess miraculous powers. Because of his influence, should he call for a holy war, the Arabs will believe that God is on their side and that, if they fight, they will defeat us. It was my suggestion, and Governor-General Randon agrees, that if we can bring Monsieur

Lambert to Algeria to put on a series of performances for native audiences, we may convince them that Islam is not alone in possessing miraculous powers. In other words we will present him as a greater marabout than Bou-Aziz and convince them that God is not on their side but on ours.'

'I think it's a capital notion,' the Emperor said. 'It's a gamble of course and may well come to nothing. But if we win it? If you succeed, Monsieur Lambert, you will be saving thousands of our soldiers' lives.'

At once Lambert made a small bow in the Emperor's direction. 'Your Majesty, I am honoured by your confidence and, of course, I will do my utmost to be worthy of it.'

'Good.' The Emperor turned to Emmeline. 'Madame, your husband will be in Algeria for several weeks. He may have to travel to different venues. Colonel Deniau has suggested that it might make his stay more pleasant were you to accompany him. It's up to you, of course, but Algeria is, I am told, a very interesting country and it will be part of our plan to send your husband there with all the ceremony we would afford our highest ambassador. You will be fêted and dined by both the sheikhs and the French community. You will be housed in Algiers as the guests of the Governor-General.'

Emmeline looked at Lambert who, with an almost imperceptible nod of his head, was urging her to accept. 'I will be glad to go, Your Majesty,' she said. 'As you say, it will be very interesting.'

At once, the Emperor leaned towards her and again put his hand on her arm, his fingers moving from her elbow to her shoulder in a long lascivious caress. 'Good, good. What a lucky man you are, Lambert, to be married to this charming girl. Don't forget, you will both be my special guests at the *curée* tomorrow night.'

He rose and, lifting her hand in his, put his moustachioed lips to her skin. 'Till then, dear Madame.'

A few minutes later, walking down the long draughty corridor between her husband and Deniau, she was filled with a sudden rush of excitement. 'But *when* will we go?'

she asked Deniau. 'And what sort of clothes will I need in Africa?'

'There is a ship sailing from Marseille to Algiers on the 27th,' Deniau said. 'And a second one sails three weeks later. It depends on whether your husband can assemble what he needs in time to make either sailing. What do you think, Henri?'

'I have already decided on what I will need,' Lambert said. 'I can be ready for the sailing on the 27th. What about you, my dear?' He turned to her as if in question but she knew it was rhetorical. 'Yes, we can be ready,' he said to Deniau.

'As for clothing, at that time of year it will be like a dry summer's day in France,' Deniau said, smiling at her. 'Don't worry, we will go over all the necessary arrangements. You know, I'm delighted that you'll be with us on this adventure.'

'The Emperor is an extraordinary man, isn't he?' Lambert said. 'I've met many kings and queens and rulers, as you know, but no one like him. Obviously, a man of great vision.'

Emmeline, listening, knew now that her husband had not needed to be persuaded to accept this mission. In the five years of their marriage she had never seen him so happy as at this moment. Now he was more than a magician. Now, he was France's emissary on an important mission. But at the same time she sensed that Deniau was aware of this conceit and amused by it. For, turning to her with his usual intimate smile, he asked, 'What did *you* think of him, Madame? He has an eye for the ladies, no?'

'But we ladies have eyes too,' she said, laughing. 'The Emperor uses rouge.'

'That could be,' Deniau agreed. He turned to Lambert. 'But you're right, of course. He *is* a man of vision. Think of it. Nine years ago he was a simple member of the National Assembly. Then, four years later, he staged his *coup d'état* and now he's Emperor Napoleon and the victor of Crimea. And by this time next year I hope he'll be the conqueror of Algeria. With your help, of course.'

'My help?' Lambert laughed. 'He doesn't need me.'

'He does, my dear fellow. We all do.'

But when he said this, Deniau turned to her and winked.

And at that moment she sensed that in a strange exotic country she would face a new dilemma. For, in that momentary covert closing of an eye, was proposed the ultimate betrayal.

Next morning the valet who brought to their rooms, as usual, coffee and the programme for the day handed Emmeline an envelope containing a note from Vicomte Walsh, one of the Emperor's chamberlains. It informed her that today's programme, the last of the *série*, would include the stag hunt and, in the evening, the *curée* or celebration of the day's sport. The Vicomte's note added that a place had been reserved for her in the carriage of Madame de Fernan Nunez so that she could have a good view of the chase. No mention was made of her husband. She passed the letter over to Lambert.

'I don't to want to go,' she said. 'And why didn't they ask you?'

'It's a carriage for the ladies,' he said. 'Don't worry about me. I'll be looked after.'

'I still don't want to go. Remember, I was ill after the shooting party. You promised you'd make my excuses.'

'But don't you see, when they've made these special arrangements for you it will seem very rude if you refuse. Besides, darling, it won't be as bad as the shooting party. I very much doubt that you'll be close enough to see the kill. And they say it's a truly wonderful spectacle – the hunters' costumes, the hounds, the pageantry. And remember, this evening we'll be the guests of the Emperor. If they sent you that note, it must mean that he's behind this invitation. You know that he's fond of your company. Please, Emmeline. This is our last day here. Let's not spoil things.'

And of course he was right. The Emperor must have spoken to Vicomte Walsh. She could not refuse. And so, a few hours later, a chamberlain presented her to Madame de Fernan Nunez, the wife of a Spanish banker, and soon she was seated beside Madame Nunez and two other ladies in a stately Berlin carriage, *en route* to the Carrefour l'Étoile, the rendezvous point in the royal forest where other carriages were drawn up at the side of the road awaiting the arrival of the Emperor's retinue. Already, the imperial *équipage de chasse* and the gentlemen of the hunt were assembled at the crossroads and Madame Nunez who, Emmeline realized, had been chosen as her chaperone because she was expert in hunting matters, began to point out the various members of the Emperor's *équipe*. There were ten in the team, huntsmen, whippers-in and valets on horseback, managing the pack of one hundred English hounds. The sight of the gentlemen riders in red coats and top boots, reining in their prancing horses as they waited for the Emperor's arrival, reminded Emmeline of a scene in a painting. Unlike the guns and the brutal preparations for the shooting party, this was a pageant, and now the Emperor's special group rode up to the crossroads, an astonishing sight in green velvet frock coats trimmed in crimson and gold braid, white kid breeches and tricorne hats. The waiting hunters fell in behind this official cortège, the pack of English hounds mingling among the riders in a great tail-wagging cluster, their movements kept in check by the professional huntsmen of the *équipe*. And then, to a sudden mournful peal of hunting horns, horses, men and hounds galloped off into the forest in a cloud of dust and flying leaves, the ground shaking under the drumming of hooves.

In a confusion of cracking whips and shouting coachmen the guests' carriages set off down the broad *allée* in an effort to follow the progress of the hunt. At last, at a crossroads, they came upon a lone rider who told them that the stag, far ahead, had just taken to water, swimming desperately, pursued by the pack of hounds. Madame Nunez, upbraiding her coachman, tried to move ahead of the other carriages to witness the kill but to Emmeline's relief this was impossible and within minutes someone called out that the stag had been cornered, whereupon Madame Nunez reluctantly decided that, as their way was blocked, they might as well return to the château.

*   *   *

Two hours later Emmeline sat in an iron tub, warm and relaxed as old Françoise sluiced jugs of hot water down her naked back. Tonight she would dress for this last evening in an elegant Worth crinoline, her hair arranged as she could not do it herself, wearing the bracelets and earrings which must be returned next week to the Paris jeweller from whom she had rented them. After the pre-dinner reception in the *grande salle des fêtes* she would walk for the last time down the great corridor past the silver helmets of the *cent gardes*, to take part in a final gala dinner after which she and Henri would join the Emperor and Empress on the balcony of the central courtyard to witness a final torchlit ritual. Tomorrow, after Sunday Mass and an early luncheon, the imperial train would bring them back to Paris. By Monday evening she would be home in Tours, where she lived amid chiming clocks and ringing bells, her companions four servants, dozens of mechanical marionettes and a husband hidden away like a monk in his workroom. This week in Compiègne, with its embarrassments, its luxuries, its seductions and snubs, would it be a once-in-a-lifetime memory, the grand gowns packed unused in tissue paper, the daily programmes yellowing in her escritoire? Or was it possible that this was the beginning of a new life in which Henri on his arrival in Algeria would be treated as an ambassador, where, if he succeeded in what he was being asked to do, he and she might, on their return to France, be invited by the Emperor to attend yet another of these imperial *séries?*

As her maid sluiced a last jug of warm water over her breasts, Emmeline stood up in the tub, wet and glistening. In the long pier mirror opposite she saw her naked body, young and slender; no one could guess that twice I have carried a dead child in my womb. I look like a virgin. It's Henri who is old, not I. And in these clothes, in this world – Compiègne has changed me.

*   *   *

Monsieur de l'Aigle, an elderly gentleman whose patent leather evening shoes made a scuffling sound on the waxed floorboards of the long corridor, escorted Emmeline from that evening's pre-dinner reception to the dining room for the final banquet. At once she saw that the table decorations and service were even more elaborate than usual. When she admired them Monsieur de l'Aigle informed her that this was the *biscuit de Sèvres service de chasse*, traditional on the night of the *curée*. 'This is a very special evening, Madame.'

And indeed she noticed that the guests' conversation was more animated than usual, the lackeys especially anxious to refill the gentlemen's glasses, the long table loud with laughter and anecdotes about the incidents of the day's hunt. Even the Emperor seemed roused from his usual sleepy watchfulness and in a departure from custom ordered that coffee and liqueurs be served not at the dinner table, but later, at the post-prandial reception, a reception at which chamberlains circulated among the ladies warning that as the night was cold they would be well advised to provide themselves with shawls and wraps for the *curée*.

At nine o'clock precisely Vicomte de Laferrière, the First Chamberlain, approached His Majesty to announce that all was ready. Amid a hubbub of anticipation, the Emperor and Empress led the way into the long gallery which over-looked the *cour d'honneur*, the vast central courtyard of the château. The Empress, accepting a sable cloak from her lady-in-waiting, followed the Emperor on to the balcony as chamberlains, circulating among the guests, discreetly advised certain favoured ladies, including Emmeline, to follow the imperial couple out into the night. Most of the remaining guests positioned themselves at the twenty windows of the long gallery, while some of the gentlemen, including Lambert, sat on an exterior flight of steps which led down to the *cour d'honneur*.

Emmeline, bracing herself against the night chill, pulled her shawl tight around her shoulders as she walked outside. The Emperor, catching sight of her, beckoned her to join himself and the Empress at the front of the balcony. Beneath, in the courtyard, the château's lackeys, valets, grooms and maids stood in a wide circle, keeping back the crowd of Compiègne townsfolk who had come to watch the *curée*. A rank smell of tar came from a ring of flaming torches, held aloft by liveried footmen, giving off a light which cast a raw, savage redness on the scene. At the far end of the courtyard, positioned directly opposite Their Majesties, the chief huntsman held up the head and antlers of the stag slain that afternoon. Attached to it was the skin of the animal, folded into a sack which contained bones and entrails. Directly beneath the imperial balcony, under the steps on which some of the gentlemen guests were seated, eight hunt servants held back a pack of yelping, struggling hounds. As Emmeline watched in horror, the chief huntsman bowed to His Majesty then waved the skin aloft and with a sudden blaring fanfare of hunting horns, the dogs were released to rush towards their meal. But within seconds the chief huntsman cracked his whip and, obedient, the pack of hounds stopped short of their prey as if fearing to be flayed. Again, a fanfare of trumpets released them and again, within feet of the sack of entrails and bones, they were stopped by a crackling whip command. Now, the lackeys lifted their torches high in the air as the hounds cowered down in silence. In the darkness of the outer circle, the local populace loosed a great cheer. Emmeline felt herself tremble. At that moment a hand touched her back, pushing askew the hoop of her crinoline and sliding down to fondle her buttocks. She turned to face the Emperor's sly concern. 'Are you cold, Madame? Do you need another wrap?'

Emmeline shook her head and was about to speak when, with a blast of hunting horns, the hounds were released to devour their reward. Emmeline, staring ahead, saw the hounds tear apart the sack of skin, heard yelps and growls and the horrid noise of crunching bones as the pack fought over the bloody entrails. Unable to watch she turned to her companions, seeing the ladies' faces, masked in tight smiles, the gentlemen openly laughing. The Emperor's hand no longer caressed her. Instead, he stepped forward magisterially to the railing of the balcony and raised his arms in a gesture of triumph. The hunting horns sounded in a new and deafening fanfare, the whips cracked, the hounds, having devoured all but the head and antlers, were quickly brought to heel and leashed. The Emperor turned to her, smiling. 'We can go in now,' he said. 'I hope you did not catch cold?'

She shook her head. Her trembling had nothing to do with the cold. At any moment she felt she would vomit. She tried to smile, for at that moment the Empress came up and nodded to her, whereupon the Emperor gallantly claimed his wife's arm.

'At least it was short,' he said to Emmeline. 'Would that *our* banquets took so little time.'

Next morning in the shuttered darkness of their bedroom, she woke to a sound of knocking. She heard her husband get up from his couch in the living room and go to answer. It was not as she expected the valet with their coffee, but Françoise, her maid, coming into the bedroom, drawing the shutters and laying a black lace veil on her bed.

'I am sorry to disturb you, Madame, but Madame must wear this to Mass this morning. It is *de rigueur*. Ladies must wear mantillas in the Spanish style as Her Majesty is Spanish and prefers it this way. And if Madame will permit me, I must begin to pack Madame's toilette.'

And so, that last Sunday morning began with Emmeline wearing a black veil as if in mourning and Lambert sending Jules to borrow missals for they had forgotten to include prayer books in their luggage. Then, after their morning coffee, they followed a lackey through endless corridors to arrive at the château's private chapel where Mass was to be said. There, as Emmeline's maid had predicted, the ladies attending the *série* appeared in headdresses of black lace, draped in the Spanish fashion. The Empress, who wore her mantilla with the ease of long custom, entered and knelt alone above the other worshippers in a private alcove overlooking the altar. The Emperor was not present. As soon as the Empress entered the alcove a priest and two acolytes appeared on the altar. The Mass began.

Emmeline knelt at her pew and put her head down as if in prayer. But she did not pray. After a few moments she looked at the congregation and saw that, as so often at Mass, she was not alone in this absence of prayer. The ladies in their lace veils were covertly studying their neighbours. The gentlemen perused their missals like inattentive students and everyone from time to time looked up at the alcove where the Empress knelt, her hands entwined in a rosary, her eyes fixed on the altar. Emmeline glanced sideways at her husband and saw that, as always in church, he read his missal carefully, from time to time studying the movements of the priest on the altar as though by paying close attention he might one day solve the mystery of changing bread and wine into the body and blood of Christ. What *did* he think of miracles; did he, who had said that all such things were illusions, include in his condemnation the mystery and miracle of the Mass? She had never thought to ask him but this morning, her mind filled with the brutal tableaux of last night's *curée* and her memory of the Emperor's hand on her thigh, she felt herself now, more than ever, her father's daughter for it was often rumoured that Dr Mercier was a freemason. Of course no one knew if this was true, for it was certain that if he proclaimed these beliefs his medical practice would suffer. Freemasons, like Jews, were frequently cited as the enemies of religion and although Napoleon III was known to be more liberal than his predecessors the Church had lost none of its power to punish transgressors.

And yet in her early years Emmeline had emulated her mother's piety. She was a child who did not fidget at Mass but often lost herself in a dream of one day becoming a nun, young and pure in a white veil, kneeling before an altar filled with candles, flowers and incense, a nun who tended to the sick, following in her doctor father's footsteps, but, unlike him, toiling only for the greater glory of God, a nun who might one day be beatified like the nun-martyr-saints the Sisters spoke of at school, a nun who, when she died, would go straight to heaven to sit at the side of God the Father, no longer Emmeline Mercier, but Blessed Sister Anne Marie, of the Order of the Sacred Heart.

All of that was long ago. In her last year at school she had begun to see nuns as jailers, reproving distant figures, not women as her mother and aunts were women, but childless, shut away from life, obedient handmaidens in a male church. One could heal the sick as a nurse, or teach poor children how to read and write without submitting to the harsh rule of a religious order. And, of course, one could marry.

'What *do* you want to do?' her father had asked. 'You said once that you would like to work in my clinic. Do you still want to do that?'

This made her mother angry. 'Working in a clinic will not prepare her to be a wife. There are certain things a young lady must learn. She should stay with the nuns for a year or two more. By then, she will be of an age to decide what course her life might take.'

In the end, Emmeline defied her mother. For two years before her marriage she had worked three mornings a week as a nurse in Dr Mercier's clinic. And in that time her father's view prevailed. She was Catholic but no longer devout. She no longer said her nightly prayers, she attended Mass and took communion regularly but without thought: she rarely remembered her old dream of sainthood or her adolescent fears of damnation. Religious observance became an obligation, not an act of worship. In large measure, she had lost her faith.

This morning the Mass was not, as might have been expected in these surroundings, a High Mass, sung, with a choir. Instead it was a Low Mass as it might be celebrated in any provincial chapel, the priest seeming to hurry through it, as though, as with most events in the *série*, Their Majesties would permit no dawdling. And so, within fifteen minutes, the moment came for the elevation of the Host. The little Sanctus bell tinkled in the silence, warning the congregation to look up in devotion as the priest raised aloft the wafer of unleavened bread and the chalice of wine transubstantiated into the body and blood of Christ. But in that moment, Emmeline, raising her head as she had been taught to do since childhood, saw the chalice and thought, not of the blood of Christ, but of the bloody spectacle of last night, the red, tarry torches flaming in the darkness, the growling hounds, their jaws flecked with blood, the crunch of bones. Above her, the Empress knelt in a tableau of devotion, hands joined in prayer, her eyes on the upraised chalice, the same Empress who last night had smiled in pleasure as she presided over the satanic celebration of the kill. The Sanctus bell rang again, signalling the end of the elevation. The congregation shuffled and coughed, relaxing as the Mass moved towards its end. Soon they would all file out of the chapel, this ceremony completed, a ceremony which, to Emmeline this morning, seemed only that: a ritual of society, a service which, in the court of Napoleon III, had no more meaning than a military parade.

When she and Henri handed their prayer books to a valet at the chapel's exit and moved into the salon where the guests were assembling for a final procession down the great corridor past the statue-like rows of *cent gardes* to attend the last luncheon of the *série*, she saw the Emperor in the centre of the room, acknowledging the bows and greetings of guests who clustered around him. As she stood watching this scene, the Emperor turned towards her, came over, took her hand and kissed it, smiling his sleepy smile.

'This is always a sad time, is it not, my dear? Parting. Yes, I find that on these occasions, when I make some charming new acquaintance like yourself – and your husband – then, almost before we have time to get to know each other, the train leaves for Paris and we must part.'

What should she say? When she hesitated, her husband rushed in. 'It has been a pleasure and a great honour for both of us, your Majesty. I'm sure we'll never forget your hospitality and kindness to us in this past week.'

But the Emperor did not even look at Lambert. Reluctantly,

he released Emmeline's hand, saying. 'However, when you come back from Africa, I shall invite you to Fontainebleau. Fontainebleau, dear Madame, has some pretty sights which I would take pleasure in showing you. We have canoes, punts, all sorts of boats which we float on a very pretty lake. We have even a Venetian gondola. I can see you in a gondola, my dear. Well, perhaps I *will* see you in a gondola. I hope so.'

When the Emperor said this he bowed to her and signalled to the Grand Chamberlain who hovered in the background. 'Now, we must go into luncheon. À *bientôt*, dear Madame.'

À *bientôt*? But, at the final luncheon, and afterwards, on the drive to the Compiègne station and during the train journey to Paris, they had no further chance to speak to Their Majesties, who, surrounded by sycophantic guests, seemed hurried and distraught as though, the *série* ended, they must rush on to yet another engagement. And so it was that at five o'clock that same afternoon on their arrival at the Gare du Nord they watched Colonel Deniau, his luggage carried by two soldiers, striding down the platform as though he also was in a hurry. He saw them and came over, saying to Lambert, 'We shall be in touch next week. I'll make all the necessary arrangements. And thank you again, my dear fellow.' Then, turning to Emmeline, he kissed her hand and oddly enough, said goodbye with the same phrase as the Emperor. 'À *bientôt*, dear Madame.'

Amid the bustle of guests, the swarm of porters, the piles of luggage, his military figure was quickly lost to her view. A sadness came upon her. She turned to Lambert.

'Will we see him again before we go?'

'Possibly not. He is leaving for Algiers next week.'

And then it was time for Lambert to pay off Françoise, the old lady's maid, who, when she had received her money, curtsied perfunctorily to Emmeline and set off down the platform, dragging her little trunk behind her. Lambert sent Jules to hire two fiacres to bring them with their luggage to the Hôtel Montrose where they would spend the night before returning, next morning, to Tours.

It was raining. The street lamps burned bright in the symmetrical boulevards of this new Paris, created for the Emperor by Baron Haussmann, a city of thoroughfares fifty metres wide, of great squares, of green parks, of huge monuments, many moved brick by brick from their old sites to fit the dreams of the man who, that very morning, had kissed Emmeline's hand.

But soon her fiacre turned off the broad, brightlit boulevards into the crumbling ruins behind these grand façades, back into the city she had known all her life, that Paris of ill-lit alleys, of narrow pavements, loud with the noise of pedlars, jugglers, plumbers, knife grinders and other relics of the old medieval city which had grown like a carapace, over the centuries, that Paris of *quartiers* where provincials clustered close to provincials from their own region, that warm, dark, dirty world which the Emperor's grand plans would now destroy.

Lambert, as was his habit, retired early. In their bedroom at the Hôtel Montrose he lay, his face to the wall, asleep or feigning sleep. She walked towards the mirror in the small entrance hall, her mind filled with thoughts and memories of the week just past. On the dressing table was her jewellery box. She opened it and fingered the bracelets, the necklaces, the earrings, the brooches which she must return tomorrow before leaving Paris. And then at the bottom of the box she saw a small velvet sack and drew it out. From it she took the ring her husband had given her when their engagement was announced, a blue sapphire, set in tiny pearls. She remembered that when he gave it to her he pretended to take the little sack from between her breasts. For a moment she had wondered whether the ring was false and this was some trick. But when she took it to Froment-Meurice on the Rue Saint Honoré to have it fitted, the jeweller said, 'Mademoiselle, this is an exceptional stone in a beautiful setting.'

Now, she put the sapphire on her finger and raised her hand, looking into the mirror, staring uncertainly at the Emmeline who stared back at her, remembering the time five years ago when Lambert had wooed her with this ring. The other day in Pierrefonds I made a joke when Deniau asked how I came to be Henri Lambert's wife. I said he had called me up on stage. We laughed and Deniau asked if Henri had cast a spell on me. I made a joke of it, but was it a joke? Is everything in my life an accident, a coincidence, or was it fate that sent me to the theatre that evening to see a performance I'd never have seen if one of Papa's patients hadn't given him two tickets for a special engagement by the world-famous Henri Lambert who would be in Rouen for three nights only. And if my cousin hadn't wanted to go with me, I'd never have gone alone. And if Henri had looked like a magician in some theatrical costume, I wouldn't be in this room with him tonight. But, no, he looked like a gentleman and when he came down to the footlights early in the performance and pointed to me, asking if I had a scarf he could borrow, I remember I took my silk scarf from my neck as if I *were* under his spell and went up on stage, half blinded by the flickering footlights, to stand by his side, looking out into the darkness. And this strange man, the magician, took my scarf, pressed it into a ball, let it shake out, turned it in every direction to show there was nothing concealed in it, then, holding it at its apex, shook it out again and to everyone's astonishment a long feather plume fell on to the floor. He turned the scarf around to show its other side and at once a second plume fell out, then a third and a fourth and suddenly at a drum roll from the orchestra pit a rain of plumes fell from it, covering the stage at my feet. I remember that he turned away from me and went downstage, showing my scarf from every side to prove it concealed nothing. Then he tied a knot at each of its four corners and suddenly, waving his hand over the knotted scarf, shook it out, the knots untying to reveal a bouquet of real flowers which he presented to me amid the sound of applause. And then the moment I will not forget. As he handed me down from the stage he leaned towards me and said in a quiet voice, 'Mademoiselle, something special has happened to me tonight.

I must see you again.' And as if by magic a notepad and pencil appeared in his hands. 'Do me the honour of writing down your address. I will send a messenger tomorrow. This is important for both of us.'

All of this while the audience still applauded and I, like someone under a spell, wrote down my address. And then he went back up on stage and for the rest of the evening's performance, in every marvellous magical thing he did, he made me aware that he was performing for me, and me alone. Of course I didn't tell anyone what I'd done. Papa would have been furious if he'd known that I'd given my address to a total stranger. But I remember I was excited and when I came home next day after teaching my class at Sainte Sulpice there was that envelope waiting, delivered by messenger, together with a bouquet of roses. Would it be possible for us to meet that night after his performance? Would it be possible for us to have supper together? And what was it that made me say yes? It was the last two sentences in the invitation. 'Believe me, dear Mademoiselle, this is the first time in my life that I have asked such a favour of any member of my audience. For you, and I know it in my heart and in my intuition, are the woman I am destined to join in life.'

Looking back now, I believe that on some occasions he does have a sort of magical power, or at least a summoning of his will so strong that he can make people do things they would never dream of doing. And certainly I, my parents' obedient daughter, would not have gone in secret to meet him in the Hôtel Impérial where, over champagne and supper, he told me he would come back from Paris very soon to speak to my parents, because he knew, from the moment he looked out into the audience and found me, that this was the most important meeting of his life. 'Dear Mademoiselle, I am not like other men, I have the gift of foreseeing my future and I know, from this evening on, that my most important aim in life must be to win your affection.'

I was twenty-two years old, I was bored with Rouen, I didn't fall in love with him, but I was flattered, I was excited, he offered to take me to Paris, London, St Petersburg, the Riviera, all of those places were like home to him, and he did come back to Rouen three days later to speak to my parents and ask permission to go on seeing me, and yes, he didn't allow Papa's contempt to wound him, he knew instinctively that if he pleased *me*, he had won the wager. And because of his will, because he's a man who will always persevere in what he seeks to do, seven months later we were married.

The Emmeline in the mirror smiled at her, but the smile was false. She turned her back on her mirror face and taking up a novel by Victor Hugo slipped into bed beside her sleeping husband. After a few desultory pages, she put aside the book and snuffed the candle. Her father had told her that Hugo was the greatest of romantic novelists, but her father, like all men, did not understand romance as women did. Romance was when you fell in love with someone or something which was denied to you. Romance was not marriage. On their wedding night, when he took off his clothes, Lambert was older than she had imagined him to be, the hair on his chest was grey and when he reared up over her his breathing was harsh and laboured. She knew he wanted a son who would carry on his work, inheriting his secrets, his magic boxes, his mechanical inventions. But the son Emmeline gave him was a dead foetus the midwife took away to throw in a rubbish bin. Then last year, when again she came to term, a girl child, born dead, its tiny face flat and crushed like an abandoned plaster cast. She wept at sight of it and pushed it away. Lambert was in the room and saw her horror. In the next few weeks he spent unprecedented hours in her company, neglecting his work in an effort to ease her depression. And though they were told that a further pregnancy would not endanger her and could well result in a normal birth, he no longer sought to caress or kiss her except in moments of solicitude. She knew that he still desired her: she saw it in his eyes and in his habit of coming into her bedroom, pretending to make conversation so that he could sit, watching her dress and undress. But, in bed he feigned sleep or turned away. At first she was grateful for that, it showed that he was kind, that he wanted to give her time. But when, feeling she must try once again to have a healthy child, she came to bed naked and held him, feeling his penis stiff against her belly, he turned away to masturbate. Why? Was he afraid for her or did he no longer want the son he had so desired? In the nights that followed she would wake to feel his hands stroking her buttocks and breasts but when she turned to him he moved away. And when she asked what was wrong, he shook his head and said, 'Nothing. Nothing. Go to sleep.'

Secretly, she felt relieved. Sex with him had been a duty. After a month he no longer fondled her but slept or feigned sleep, his face to the wall. Again, as in the days before her marriage, she dreamed of sex with strange men. So when he asked her to go with him to Compiègne how could she refuse? She had failed him as a wife.

Next morning after breakfast she went out into the streets of Paris to return the rented jewels. Later that day they took the train for Tours. They arrived at night. The driver of the carriage that met them at the station was a young local man whom they did not know. It was dark, the moon invisible behind heavy rain clouds. They drove in silence over the familiar rutted road, through a small wood, until at last their carriage jolted unevenly down the narrow avenue of oak trees which led to the Manoir des Chênes. Jules, who was sitting in the front beside the driver, climbed out in the darkness and inserted a key in the electric box to the left of the entrance gate. At once, a kerosene torch blazed alight. The carriage horse reared up in fright and as their driver pulled down on the reins, Jules climbed back into his seat. At that moment the life-size marionette gate-keeper trundled out of the gate lodge and, on reaching the iron bars of the gate, lifted the latch. At once the gate rolled open and their driver, now as frightened as his horse, whipped it past the marionette which raised its tin hand in salute.

As was usual when Lambert was expected certain mechanical devices had been set in motion. As their carriage moved through the grounds kerosene torches lit up a grotto in which a bearded sage stiffly bent his painted head as his mechanical hand turned over the pages of a bible. At sight of this their driver started in fear and gripped the reins, bringing the carriage to a near halt. When they reached the main entrance the gardener and a maid came forward to help Jules and the driver unload the luggage. As the last trunk was being lifted out of the carriage, the driver jumped back on to his seat, shook the reins and cracked his whip over the horse's back. The carriage rumbled off towards the gates.

'He didn't wait for his money,' Lambert said. 'I hope I have as much success with the Arabs.'

'What do you mean?'

He took her arm as they entered the hallway. 'Fear,' he said. 'Fear mixed with awe and reverence for the unknown, for something we do not understand. That's at the heart of all magic. That driver, like most country people, is ignorant and superstitious. Yet even he must have seen conjurers, escape artists and card tricksters in fairgrounds. But in Africa, Deniau tells me, the Arabs will never have seen illusions such as I can devise. Believe me, to them I will be the most holy of marabouts.'

In the semi-darkness of the hall, clocks in every room of the manor began to sound the hour of eleven, drowning out his final words. Lambert smiled as though their cacophony of chimes was, for him, a sweet, familiar music.

'Home again, my darling. And it's very late. Tomorrow I must get up at dawn to begin my preparations. I think I had better sleep in my workroom. Good night, my dear. Pleasant dreams.'

He bent and kissed her cheek, holding her by her shoulders. His eyes had that excited look she had seen so many times. He was home again in the only place he really loved: the laboratory of his illusions.

*   *   *

An hour later as the myriad clocks struck midnight Emmeline lay sleepless in her bed. She saw, again, the frightened face of their driver as he whipped up his horse and rushed his carriage towards the mechanical gate, fearing to be trapped in a wizard's house. To the peasants and even the townspeople in nearby Tours her husband was not, as he thought, a person they regarded with fear and reverence. Fear, yes, but it was a fear of witchcraft, of persons in league with the Evil One. Emmeline knew this, as Lambert would never know it, for her mother was a country woman, born in the Bercy, not far from here. Her mother, while pretending to laugh at such superstitions, was, Emmeline knew, no different from her peasant forebears. In the unchanging world Parisians called *La France profonde*, night was host to hobgoblins, witches and will-o'-the-wisps. Even in the bright sunlight of a summer's day you might touch a grassy mound or venture into a field sacred to the fairies, those malevolent others who could cast a spell on you, a spell which brought misfortune. And why should the peasants not believe in such things, passed down from generation to generation? For them the world did not exist outside their townlands. Most did not know how to read or write, few had ever been in a theatre and, even in cities like Tours or Rouen, many among her husband's audiences believed his inventions and illusions were a gift, granted him by that world which lies hidden behind our visible world, a world ruled by mysterious powers stronger than the Church, capable of miracles no saint could match.

And now in the darkness she thought of the weeks to come. What if the Arabs were like the people of the Bercy? What if they saw Henri not as a holy man, but as an agent of the devil?

Part Two

Algeria, 1856

FIVE

'The city is white and on a hill,' Commandant Guizot said. 'All of the Moorish houses are whitewashed and only a few of the newer buildings have windows which face on to the street. As we approach from the sea it looks like a gigantic marble quarry. An extraordinary sight, I assure you.'

'And when do we arrive?' she asked.

The Commandant looked down the dining table to his chief officer, who answered. 'The weather in the Gulf of Lyon is predicted as calm, *Mon Commandant.* I would think tomorrow morning, shortly after dawn.'

Colonel Marmont, head of the marine staff at the port of Marseille who had been detailed specially to accompany them on their voyage to Algiers, turned to Lambert. 'Believe me, it's a sight worth seeing. That is, if you can manage to be on deck at such an early hour.'

But now, thirty-six hours after their sailing from Marseille, as the steamer *Alexander* moved through a dawn mist, Emmeline stood alone on the promenade deck outside the large stateroom which had been provided for their passage. Lambert slept. He was never an early riser. At dawn, on her first sea voyage, on this journey to a new continent, she stared ahead, excited, as, suddenly, the swirls of mist were parted by the vessel's prow and in the distance she saw land and then, behind a long dyke which hid the port, that city on a hill, rising four hundred feet out of the sea. But as the *Alexander* drew closer, its foghorn calling a greeting to the shore, the city seemed to her not like the marble quarry described by the *Alexander*'s captain, but a vast and menacing Moorish fortress, its parapets and terraces sheet-white in the fierce light of an African sun.

Twenty minutes later as the *Alexander* sailed around the dyke and entered the harbour Emmeline went back to their stateroom. Lambert, aroused earlier by the foghorn, sat, fully dressed in frock coat, white linen vest and trousers, carefully arranging a silk cravat around his neck. A steward was pouring morning coffee. Lambert, looking up, saw her in the mirror and said, 'You must wear a more formal dress, my darling. Something light in colour. And a hat. There is to be some sort of official welcome.' He turned to the steward. 'When do we dock?'

'We will tie up at eight-fifteen, sir. You will disembark shortly after nine.'

'So we have plenty of time,' Emmeline said. 'I'll change now, but I want to go back on deck as soon as possible. I can't believe we're here.'

'As you wish, my dear. But *I* do not want to be seen on deck. I should make my appearance at the last moment. From now on, I must play a public role.'

And so, again, she stood alone, looking down over the railing as the gangplank was lowered and from the quay below, a cluster of Negroes (were they slaves, she wondered?) came crowding up the gangway to unload the passengers' luggage. Looking up at the ship were Arabs, a race she had known only from drawings and paintings, now suddenly real, men with short beards and moustaches, their heads shaven except for a long lock of hair on top. They wore ankle-length woollen robes, the garment fastened to their heads by a rope of camel hair which served as a turban. Over this robe many wore long flowing cloaks. They were shod in primitive ox-hide sandals, but Emmeline noticed that a few who seemed of higher rank wore high yellow leather boots. There was also a score of Arab women, most of them young, dressed in wide woollen shirts, tied at the waist with a rope and fastened at the breast with large iron pins. Their hair was plaited in long tresses and on their arms and legs they wore bracelets of silver and iron. Their faces shocked her. Many were tattooed. In their ears were large rings and their nails were dyed red-brown with henna.

The crowd of spectators now began calling up to the ship's Arab passengers who crowded the *Alexander*'s lower decks supervising the Negro porters who carried their trunks and boxes. Followed by the porters, the Arab passengers came ashore to be greeted by bowings, embraces and a round of what seemed to be formal compliments. Breaking into this scene, a troop of French soldiers marched on to the quay, preceded by a young officer in dress uniform, a military band, and a standard-bearer holding aloft the French tricolour. The soldiers, but not their officer, carried long rifles and wore the colourful oriental uniforms of the regiment of Zouave. Now, with military precision, they lined up in a row below the principal gangway. At this point some French passengers who were about to disembark were held back by the *Alexander*'s sailors. Colonel Marmont appeared at Emmeline's side. 'Come, Madame. We are ready for you.' Quickly, he led her to the principal gangway where, impatient, Lambert waited. At a nod from Marmont, Lambert walked alone down the gangway. The military band struck up '*La Marseillaise*'. As Lambert stepped on shore, the young officer, who wore an aide-de-camp's lanyard, snapped his hand up in salute, then, drawing his sword, escorted Lambert along the ranks of the Zouave honour guard.

Colonel Marmont, giving Emmeline his arm, led her down the gangplank and over to a waiting landau. Lambert was already seated in the carriage. The military band struck up a drumroll, the honour guard presented arms and, accompanied by the aide-de-camp who sat opposite them in the landau, they drove slowly past the watching Arab crowds.

As they passed through the gateway to the port they came into a street just wide enough to permit the passage of two carriages. 'This is Rue de la Marine,' the-aide-de-camp informed them. 'It leads to the central market-place. There are only three streets of this width in the whole of Algiers. So our use of carriages is limited.'

He then told them that this was the European quarter and

that most of the houses here were new. Emmeline saw that the new houses had vaulted arcades in the style of the Rue de Rivoli in Paris. Intersecting the Rue de la Marine were dozens of dark alleys less than four feet in width where passersby must turn sideways to avoid someone coming from the opposite direction. These glimpses of a city hidden behind the new European houses, a warren of windowless buildings, their upper storeys projecting over the lower floors in a way which made the alleys dark and ominous even in the noonday sun, filled Emmeline with a sense of foreboding. How could people living in these obscure menacing mazes be impressed by the man who sat beside her, anxiously questioning the aide-de-camp about the safe transport of his magician's paraphernalia through these narrow lanes?

'The theatre that is being put at your disposal, Monsieur, is in the Rue Bat-Azoun, which, as I've mentioned, is one of the three principal thoroughfares of Algiers. It's large and easy of access. As for your exhibitions outside the city, you'll find that camel trains can carry luggage even of the most awkward type.'

'It is not that my luggage is awkward,' Lambert said in an irritated voice. 'But it is delicate. It must be transported with great care.'

Now, as they continued to drive past the Parisian arcades of the Rue de la Marine, Europeans and Arabs walking on the shaded pavements turned to look up at their carriage. Several of the Europeans saluted, the men tipping their hats, the ladies inclining their heads under their parasols. At once, as though he were an official dignitary passing in procession, Lambert waved to the crowd. Emmeline looked at the aide-de-camp. The ghost of a smile appeared on the young man's face. When he saw that she had noticed, he pointed ahead as if to distract her.

'Here we are, Madame. The Governor's mansion. Maréchal Randon isn't in residence at the moment. He has gone to the South with some troops. There is a disturbance in Kabylia.'

'What sort of disturbance?' Lambert asked

'A minor uprising. The Kabyles have not yet been colonized.

But by next year, when our troops arrive from France, they will be.'

Emmeline, half listening, stared ahead as the carriage approached an impressive Moorish building surrounded by a rectangular garden of orange trees. The tricolour flew prominently on its roof. Zouave sentries presented arms as their carriage passed through ornamental iron gates and into a spacious closed courtyard flanked by Moorish arches. Emmeline looked up. Above her, the startlingly blue sky formed a vault over colonnaded halls, the intense sunlight cast a golden hue on veined marble paving, ornate carvings, porcelain walls and, in the centre of the court, flecked the gushing waters of a large fountain with iridescent light. She felt suddenly exhilarated as though she had been transported into the pages of a storybook. This enchanted building did not belong to France, no matter that the French flag flew over it. This sunlight, this courtyard, was Africa; Moorish, magical and strange. Her exhilaration was the intoxication of delight. She no longer saw the alleys of Algiers as dark and ominous. Suddenly, she wished that Africa were her home.

Arab servants came forward to take them to their quarters. An Arab major-domo answered Lambert's enquiries about the arrival of their luggage, saying it would be delivered within the hour.

'I must have a storeroom for certain pieces,' Lambert told him. 'It must be kept locked, and I alone am to have the key.'

'Of course, Monsieur. It will be as you wish.'

The apartments that had been set aside for them were spacious, high-ceilinged and cool, their white marble walls adorned with large plates of painted pottery. The floors were also of white marble, bare except for a few simple mats of plaited palm leaves. In each room there were two beautifully carved, brightly painted chests, and vases filled with rosewater. Amid these simple Arab furnishings, the European bed, dressing table and chairs seemed ugly and out of place. Emmeline went at once to the windows and opened the shutters which gave on to a long balcony with a view of surrounding flat rooftops and, two storeys below, the mansion's garden with its small grove of orange trees. She heard the major-domo whisper obsequiously, 'This is the ambassadorial suite, Your Excellency. I hope it is to your liking. Is there anything you wish for? May I perhaps have some coffee and sweetmeats brought to you now?'

The coffee, which arrived within minutes of the major-domo's departure, was strong and sugared, with a heavy residue of sediment, offered in small china cups, set on a painted tin tray. Beside the cups sat a plate of dates and tiny cakes and a long red earthenware pipe filled with tobacco. As they sat on the balcony, looking down on the courtyard, they could hear in the distance a monotonous unfamiliar music played on a violin, punctuated by the flat beat of a drum.

At 11 a.m. when they had washed and changed, a servant appeared to tell them that they were invited to luncheon with the Governor-General's principal secretary, Monsieur de la Garde. The meal was served in a shuttered dining room cooled by fans, wielded by Negro servants. The food was French and in addition to Monsieur de la Garde there were present three senior diplomatic officers and their wives. The conversation, after some initial welcoming pleasantries, turned quickly to Maréchal Randon's absence.

'I received a message from him this morning,' Monsieur de la Garde told the company. 'As you know this latest disturbance was confined to the region of Souk el Arba. But it seems that three days ago the Maréchal held a meeting with the rebel leaders and, fortunately, a sheikh who spoke for the entire group has declared a temporary truce. It seems this sheikh was told by the marabout, Bou-Aziz, that God has not yet given the command for the peoples of Arabia to rise. And so, our luck holds. Maréchal Randon and Colonel Deniau are on their way back to Algiers. I expect them to arrive the day after tomorrow.'

Emmeline, listening, heard only that Deniau was absent and would be returning soon. She had dressed especially for this luncheon and on entering the dining room had looked anxiously to see if he was present. Now, Madame Duferre, the lady on her left, turned to her and said, 'I believe you and your husband have met Colonel Deniau. You must see his apartments here. They are up in the Arab quarter near the citadel. Quite extraordinary, my dear.'

'Is he . . .?' Suddenly, Emmeline was afraid. 'Is the Colonel married? I never thought to ask.'

'No, no. He is very much a bachelor. One can see why.'

'Oh? Why is that?'

'The head of the *Bureau Arabe* must spend half of his life travelling in the desert. His is the opposite of a domestic existence.'

Monsieur de la Garde turned to Lambert. 'I should explain, Monsieur, that this early return is excellent news for all of us because we have already invited the country's leading sheikhs and marabouts to attend the autumnal ceremonies here, two weeks from now. At that time we hope to show them your special powers. If the disturbance in Kabylia had spread we would have had to cancel the festivities. I hope, Monsieur, that two weeks will give you time to make your preparations?'

'I'll do my best,' Lambert said. 'I believe you have arranged a theatre for me?'

'Indeed, we have. It is in the Rue Bat-Azoun and the façade is particularly handsome. I believe you will be pleased.'

'By the way, your theatre is a former mosque,' one of the officials said. 'There were many, too many, mosques in Algiers when we took over the city. Some, we have converted to other uses.'

'I had forgotten that it was once a mosque,' Monsieur de la Garde commented. 'It might be useful to remember it. The Arabs certainly will. And so, Monsieur Lambert, your performance might well take on the tone of a religious ceremony. A touch of the miraculous, perhaps.'

The luncheon guests laughed at this. Lambert, smiling, raised his glass in toast. 'To miracles,' he said. 'French miracles.'

* * *

That same day, shortly before sunset when long shadows fell on the rooftops of the buildings adjoining their apartments, Emmeline saw Arab women walking on the airy terraces, glancing around as they talked. When they saw her they stared back openly, but when Lambert appeared behind her they turned away, raising muslin handkerchiefs to cover their faces. Then, as though this were a game, they giggled and glanced back slyly at the foreign male.

'It's cooler now,' Lambert said to Emmeline. 'And Lieutenant Lecoffre has invited us to go with him to a café and watch the evening parade. Would you like that?'

In the huge central courtyard of the mansion Lieutenant Lecoffre, the aide-de-camp who had accompanied them that morning, greeted her with a bow, then led them along the Rue de la Marine to an Italian café, where, sheltered under covered archways, they sat on the pavement eating ices and watching the kaleidoscope of passersby.

Emmeline sat entranced, as at a play. Even in Paris she had never seen so many different costumes and complexions.

'But who *are* they?' she asked Lecoffre. 'It's like being in several countries at once.'

The Lieutenant was amused. 'Well, let's see,' he said. 'You can tell from their dress which group they belong to. The Arabs, you'll know from their beards and moustaches. The ones in green turbans have made the holy pilgrimage to Mecca. Those two men in gold-embroidered waistcoats and wide trousers are Moors.'

'And who are those light-skinned ones?' Emmeline asked.

'They are the ones who are giving us so much trouble. They are not true Arabs but Kabyles, Bedouin people from the South.'

He then pointed to a group of Negroes in Arab dress. They seemed different from Negroes Emmeline had seen in France. Their complexion was ashen rather than black. 'Many are slaves, brought here from Southern Africa,' the Lieutenant said. 'And that man sitting behind us is a Turk. And those "Arabs", the ones in black burnouses with dark stockings, are not Arabs but

Jews. In former times they were forced to wear black and they continue to wear black as a mark of pride. Black is despised by Arabs and is the colour they assign to infidels.'

'But we French are infidels,' Emmeline said.

'Yes, but we are the conquering infidels, Madame. Not like the Jews. The Jews are the most despised and maltreated of the races in the Arab world. Yet for myself I find their women beautiful. Look. Those two girls are Jewesses.'

Emmeline stared at two young women who were indeed pretty, wearing long silk robes, silk scarves tied around their hips and embroidered silk shawls loosely tied around their heads. The Lieutenant then pointed to some men who passed, deep in discussion. 'Kuruglis. They control many of the stalls in the bazaars. They are a race apart, a result of the intermarriage of Arab and Turk. You must visit the bazaars, Madame. There are trinkets there that you might like to bring back as souvenirs.'

Mixed in this throng were many Europeans and Emmeline quickly became aware that several of the men looked at her with interest. Lieutenant Lecoffre also noticed and turned to Lambert with a man-to-man smile. 'I must warn you, sir, with a wife as pretty as yours it's wise to be on your guard here. We have too many unmarried men in Algiers. Italians, Portuguese, Germans, Russians and Poles.' He smiled flirtatiously at Emmeline.' And, of course, we French.'

Lambert chose to ignore this comment. 'Tell me,' he said. 'How many of these Arabs, Kabyles, or whatever you call them, are Muslim?'

'All, except, of course, the Jews. Even the Negroes are Muslim. As you'll see, Kabyles, Negroes, Kuruglis, Arabs, Turks, rich and poor, it makes no difference, all kneel together to pray five times a day when the muezzin calls.'

'In the mosques?' Lambert asked. 'Every day?'

'Every day and in any place. They will kneel in the sand in the silence of the desert, or in a filthy lane in a remote village. Anywhere, at any time, when the call to prayer is sounded. Their faith is profound.'

'But don't we try to convert them?' Lambert asked. 'Surely, we have missionaries here?'

'Conversions? You should ask that question of the Archbishop of Algiers. I fear our priests haven't had great success in this part of Africa. The Jesuits are working among the Kabyles and we are told they have made some progress. The Arabs are another story. They consider Jesus as a prophet and therefore as a figure entitled to their respect. But Muhammad is God's great prophet and they revere no other. He has promised that a redeemer will lead them out of bondage and into paradise. They still await this redeemer, whom they call the Mahdi, the chosen one.'

'The Mahdi? Isn't that what they're calling this marabout I'm facing?'

The Lieutenant shook his head. 'He has not yet been accepted as the Mahdi. That will only happen if he calls for a holy war.' He turned to Emmeline. 'I imagine political talk must be boring for you, Madame. Besides, we should be getting back to the residence. We dine at nine o'clock in the cool of the evening. That will give you time to change.'

Change, yes, but the West toilette, designed for the French countryside in November, could not serve her in this African climate and so, coming later into the large dining room adjoining the central hall of the Governor-General's residence, she wore a gown made for her by Madame Cott, her dressmaker in Tours, a dress which, she now realized, revealed her as a provincial Rouennaise, the wife of a man who could never be part of this colonial aristocracy of diplomats and high military officers. For she sensed that this mansion, the official residence of the Governor-General of Algeria, was, like Compiègne, a court, its ruler recently elevated by the Emperor himself to the highest military rank, that of a Maréchal of France.

And yet, easing her discomfort, when she and Lambert entered the dining hall Monsieur de la Garde and his wife were waiting to welcome them and it was de la Garde himself, the senior diplomat present, who offered her his arm and led her to a place of honour at the dining table. The meal was served by Negroes and as soon as the guests were seated, strains of music were heard from the adjoining central courtyard. Emmeline could see the musicians, grouped around the great fountain. They wore Arab dress and were led by a very old man who handled his instrument, a three-stringed violin, with grave dignity, bowing from time to time in their direction.

'The music,' Monsieur de la Garde told her, 'is a concert in honour of your husband. This little orchestra is famous in these parts. That old man who leads it was the favourite musician of the last Dey, the Turkish ruler here in the days of the Ottoman empire. Tomorrow, in the coffee houses, it will be known that tonight he played for your husband, the great sorcerer. These things are not without significance in the Arab world.'

She was grateful for the music. The strains of the violin mingling with the sound of pipes and guitars produced a soft monotonous sound which she found peaceful and lulling, allowing her, as in Compiègne, to appear to listen and therefore be excused from conversation. Lambert, on the other hand, was in his element as the company, interested in this guest from a world they had never known, kept him busy answering questions about his tours to the courts of Russia and England. Tonight he was the centre of attraction and so, at the end of the evening when they returned to their quarters, he stepped out on to the balcony, stretched his arms wide and, staring at the darkened Moorish rooftops all around him, said, 'It's a peculiar thing, but I feel that all of my life has led up to this visit. This, above anything else I have ever done, is what I was put on earth to do.'

She did not answer and after a moment, as though irritated by her silence, he went back into the sitting room and said, 'Tomorrow, I have arranged to go early to the theatre. The Lieutenant tells me that Madame Duferre has offered to take you on a tour of the native markets. That should be interesting for you.'

He took her in his arms and, as so often at home, perfunctorily kissed her good night. 'Sleep well. Till tomorrow, then.'

As usual, when they did not have separate beds, she did not undress and lie down beside him until he had had time to fall asleep, or at least pretend it. Now she walked up and down on the long terrace of the balcony, hearing the night sounds of this strange city: voices calling to each other in an unknown language, the distant beat of a flat-sounding drum. She looked up at the ascending rows of white tomb-like buildings, at the dark veins of narrow alleys winding uphill to the Arab quarter beneath the Citadel, where Deniau had his apartment, that apartment Madame Duferre had characterized as, 'Quite extraordinary. Of course he is rarely there. The head of the *Bureau Arabe* must spend half his life travelling in the desert. His is the opposite of a domestic existence.'

In the desert, riding on camels, sleeping in tents. And here in Algiers he lives up there in the native quarter. Emmeline looked again at those white buildings. Why am I thinking every moment of him, this man I hardly know, this man who may have paid me compliments and given me those meaningful looks simply as part of his scheme to bring my husband here? Why do I think of him now, even more than in Compiègne? Is it because I'm in Africa, where I never thought to be and he is part of the spell of this place, how can I say it, there are no words, from the moment I stood on deck this morning and saw this city on a hill, what was it Henri said just now? 'I feel as if all of my life has led up to this visit.' I can say that too, but I have no mission here, no reason to say or feel it. Yet I do feel it. I do.

SIX

'I'm afraid I will have to disappoint you,' Madame Duferre said. 'Alas, our visit to the bazaars must be for another day. We have just had word that the Maréchal will be returning this afternoon and not tomorrow. Monsieur de la Garde has us all on our toes preparing for a reception this evening for the Maréchal and the officers who accompanied him. We will be hosts to the entire diplomatic corps of Algiers, such as it is, and also to certain Arab dignitaries. Of course, you and your husband will be present.'

But Emmeline heard only that Deniau would be here tonight. At once she thought of herself as she had been in Compiègne and as he would see her now, no longer wearing those elegant gowns, without the services of that old maid who had so wonderfully arranged her hair, no longer sitting by special invitation next to the Emperor at table, but instead returned to the ordinary, the magician's wife who, now that the magician had been won over and put to work, was no longer someone Deniau must woo. And late that afternoon as she sat in the unfamiliar dressing room of their apartments, trying over and over again to arrange her hair in the manner of Compiègne, she felt her eyes wet with tears. How have I let myself get into this state, I didn't want to be a part of that society at Compiègne and I can never be a part of this world of Africa. I am Lambert's wife, that's who I am, the wife of someone sent here to trick these Arabs. What does it matter if I am dowdy and my hair is badly done. No one will notice.

But for the fifth time she let down her hair and tried again.

*   *   *

'We will assemble in the central court at seven,' an aide-de-camp told Lambert. 'Maréchal Randon will arrive at approximately seven-twenty. Those who will be attending this evening are the spiritual and temporal leaders in Algiers and in the regions immediately surrounding the city. The marabouts and sheikhs from other, more distant regions will not be arriving until next week. So, although this is a reception in honour of the Governor-General's triumph in Kabylia, it is also a rehearsal of your presentation to the Muslim élite. Because of that, and because in the Arab world the marabout is a personage more highly regarded than any sheikh or temporal ruler, Colonel Deniau has suggested that you be the first guest of the evening to be presented to Maréchal Randon. Consequently, in Arab eyes, you will be seen as *our* leading marabout, a figure of great power.'

And now, at seven-twenty precisely, Emmeline stood beside her husband facing the colonnaded archways through which she could see the Governor-General and his staff approaching, a group of ten officers in dress uniforms wearing decorations followed by several aides-de-camp, and then by the senior French diplomats led by Monsieur de la Garde. The Governor-General, Maréchal Randon, was, Emmeline saw, a short spare man in his late fifties with the air of an administrator rather than a highly decorated soldier. She felt Henri come to attention beside her, felt his tension as he prepared to step on stage in a role different from any he had played before. But at that moment she saw Deniau, walking a little to the left of the Maréchal but with the air of someone of equal rank to the Governor-General himself. And in that moment he raised his head and looked directly at her. He smiled, gave a slight bow and kept on looking at her as the Maréchal's cortège reached the spot where she and Henri stood. He had not looked at, or acknowledged, her husband and she, for her part, was so transfixed by his gaze that in the moment of being presented to the Governor-General she almost forgot to curtsy. Randon, for his part, bowed in her direction and then, almost theatrically, made a sort of reverence in greeting her husband. Lambert, ever the actor, received this false tribute with a certain solemn dignity, befitting his role of marabout. The Governor-General then passed on down the receiving line, pausing to speak to an old sheikh and to three high-turbaned holy men who had been pointed out earlier as revered marabouts of the Algerine plain. A military band struck up a triumphal march as the Governor's cortège made a leisurely circle of the colonnaded court. At this point Deniau was lost to Emmeline's view behind the plumes of water rising from the central fountain. She stood, impatient, as aides-de-camp brought up various sheikhs to exchange greetings with her husband and, as soon as the presentations ended, hurried across the courtyard, pretending to look for someone, but in reality moving directly to the spot where Deniau stood chatting to an imposing figure who was wearing a richly embroidered waistcoat and a red fez.

Suddenly embarrassed, she hesitated and was about to withdraw when Deniau broke off his conversation, came to her, took her hand and kissed it, saying, 'Madame, good evening. How happy I am to see you here in Africa. May I present Effendi Selim who is the representative of the Dey of Turkey?'

The stout gentleman in the red fez bowed to her, and speaking in a language Emmeline did not understand, said something and laughed, a rich chuckling laugh. Deniau smiled politely and answered in the unknown tongue, upon which the stranger again bowed to her and withdrew, leaving them alone.

'What did he say?' Emmeline asked, watching as the Turkish gentleman made his way slowly towards the refreshments being offered at the central fountain.

'Turks have a vulgar sense of humour,' Deniau said. 'His remark, while a compliment to you, is not fit for a lady's ears. But he is right. You are looking particularly beautiful this evening. How was your sea voyage? I was mortified that

I was not able to greet you at the dock. I wanted to be the first friendly face you saw when you arrived in Africa.'

'I missed you,' she said and blushed. 'I mean . . . I didn't know that you were off fighting a war.'

'No more wars,' he said. 'At least not until we French decide to fight the next one. In the meantime we are counting on your husband to keep the peace. Apropos! Come with me while I pay my respects to the great marabout.'

But as he led her through the robed, exotic throng, passing the knot of dignitaries surrounding the Governor-General, Emmeline turned his phrase over in her mind. 'You are looking particularly beautiful this evening.' Am I? Even in this dress? Even with my hair as it is? Or did he say it because that fat Turk made some vulgar remark? And why did I tell him that I missed him, why was I so gauche? Once again he's my escort as he was when we walked down the great hall in Compiègne and once again I am proud to be seen with him. People bow to him. He's treated as someone of great importance. He is the chief of the *Bureau Arabe*.

Now as they came up to the group of diplomats and Arabs surrounding her husband she did not want to lose Deniau as her escort. She stopped. He turned to her. 'Are you all right?'

'Yes, of course. But tell me something. Madame Duferre says you spend half your life in the desert. Is that true?'

'Did she say that? How odd. But, it's true that in some mysterious way the desert is the place where I feel most at home. It's beautiful in its stillness, its emptiness. Soon, I hope to show you what I mean by that. After the celebrations here next week I'll be travelling with you and your husband in the Sahara, the region they call the South. That is the real Algeria. I hope it will interest you.'

'I know it will,' Emmeline said. 'I have been here for less than two days, but it's love at first sight.'

He took her hand and held it. 'I'm not surprised,' he said and then looked over her shoulder.

'Ah! He has seen us. Your husband.' He released her hand and went towards Lambert.

'Monsieur Lambert, welcome to Africa.'

'Colonel! How went the battle? A great success, we hear.'

'Not a battle, Monsieur, far from it. A minor show of force, that's all. Perhaps the most important part of our expedition was that we had a meeting with the marabout. We hope we've persuaded him to attend your performances next week. But we can't be sure. In any case, as I have just been telling your wife, we plan to take you on tour after the celebrations here. You may meet him then. In the meantime I'd like to invite you and Madame Lambert to lunch tomorrow. I have an apartment in the Kasbah, in the heart of the city's native quarter. You might find it interesting.'

'Thank you, that's most kind,' Lambert said. 'But I am afraid if I am to be properly prepared I will have no time for sightseeing or social life before the celebrations begin. However, I am sure Emmeline would be delighted to see the – what did you call it – the Kasbah.'

'And I will be delighted to show it to her. Madame? Could you be ready at, say, midday? I warn you, the streets are too narrow for carriages. You can, however, travel on muleback. Do you ride?'

'Yes, of course.'

At noon, from their high towers throughout the city, muezzins raised the white flag of faith, calling believers to prayer. Emmeline, who had spent most of the morning preparing herself for this luncheon, now ran out on to her balcony, hoping to catch a glimpse of these Muslim devotions. But as she stood searching the adjoining rooftops the maid assigned to her quarters came to tell her that a messenger from Colonel Deniau was waiting at the main gates of the residence. When she went down through the central courtyard past the Zouave sentries who saluted her as they held open the gates she saw, standing in the street outside, a Negro, so tall he was almost a giant, his ashen grey skin giving him the look of a corpse. He wore an orange burnous and a red fez, and was holding the reins of a small mule which had been fitted with a sidesaddle. On seeing her he bowed and knelt, cupping his hands in a stirrup with which he lifted her lightly on to the saddle. He then took the reins and guided the mule, walking beside her as they moved along the dark narrow street which wound uphill under stone archways and overhanging balconies that completely shut out the hot noonday sun. This street, like a turn in a maze, led to yet another dark narrow lane and then another and as they progressed the ascent became steeper, the mule carefully picking its way, guided by the black giant who, when the animal hesitated, slapped its flanks with the flat of his huge hand, the palm of which was white as a lady's glove. In these narrow lanes when Arab pedestrians came towards them, the presence of the mule forced them to take refuge in a doorway or turn sideways as they eased past. But apart from these passersby the city seemed empty of people. The façades of the buildings were uniformly plain, their infrequent windows small, grated holes which gave no view of the interiors. And yet, as her ear became attuned to the jumble of sounds, Emmeline heard, behind these façades, the murmur of female voices, the cries of children and, once, the disconsolate braying of an ass.

At last, after some twenty minutes of halting ascent, the Negro ducked his head under a low archway and, signing her to do likewise, led the mule through a narrow corridor out on to a small square baked by sunlight. Opposite was a building no different from those they had already passed, its heavy wooden doorway ornamented with iron bolts and a shuttered iron grille. As they approached this door someone within opened to admit them to an interior hall supported by white marble columns. The Negro giant dropped the reins over the mule's head, cupped his hands and knelt. Emmeline again put her foot in this human stirrup and when she had alighted saw coming towards her an elderly Arab, sepulchral in a dun-coloured burnous, his head shaven except for a long topknot of grey hair. He bowed, beckoning her to follow him into a second larger courtyard, also paved with white marble and enclosed by colonnades which admitted the sunlight from above. In the middle of this hall was a small grove of orange trees, a fountain and a lighted iron hearth at which, squatting over smoking earthenware cooking utensils, were two Negresses, one old and stout, one tall, young and slender, her face a handsome oval mask which she now turned briefly in Emmeline's direction. The elderly Arab servant passing by these women approached a staircase ornamented with bright pottery designs, leading to an upper colonnade which encircled the entire hall.

'Welcome, Emmeline. In my Moorish house, may I call you by your Christian name?'

At the head of the stairs, Deniau stood, wearing a long Arab robe of the finest white wool, his ankles bare, his feet in red leather sandals, and at his belt, which was ornate and embroidered in gold, a small curved ceremonial dagger. He smiled and beckoned her to come up. When she reached the head of the staircase he kissed her hand.

'Your house is beautiful,' she said.

'I am glad you like it. In fact, it's a typical Algerian apartment. Come, let me show you.'

He led her into a room covered with luxurious carpets, its only furniture a large vase filled with rosewater and two carved and painted wooden chests, similar to those in the rooms of the Governor-General's residence. But as they went through to a second room and then a third she saw that, unlike the furnishings in the residence, here there were no beds, tables or chairs. And when he led her into the large central room, spread along one wall was a profusion of silken cushions with, in front of them, two long painted trays spread with sweetmeats, fruits, a crystal decanter and glasses. Deniau sat cross-legged on the cushions, inviting her to join him. He poured wine from the decanter, saying, 'Alcohol, of course, is not permitted in a Moorish house. But then, we are not Muslims, thank God.'

He handed her a glass.

'Remember Compiègne? Our *Brüderschaft* toast? Shall we?'

She did not want to do this but did not know what to say

and so, taking her silence for consent, he eased towards her on the cushions, holding his glass aloft then entwining his arm in hers, bringing them close, their faces inches apart as their glasses touched in the toast.

'To our friendship,' he said.

In the ritual of the toast they must drink at the same moment and as she drank a lock of her hair fell forward, spilling against his brow. Their eyes met. He lowered his glass.

'Did I embarrass you? I'm sorry.'

'No, no. It was . . .' She hesitated, trying to think of a polite phrase.

'Gauche?'

'No, not at all.'

'Yes it was. I apologize. Forgive me.'

'No, no,' she said again, desperately embarrassed by now. 'Compiègne, yes. Our picnic. I remember.'

He stood up. 'A wonderful afternoon, wasn't it? I'll never forget it.' He held out his hand, raising her up. 'Now. Let me show you the view from my roof.'

As she put down her glass she had a feeling that she was being watched. She turned and saw in the doorway a handsome, light-skinned Arab boy, his face still as an image in a photograph. He stood, leaning against the lintel, his slight graceful body draped in faded pink silken robes. His eyes stared into the room as though they saw something beyond her. Deniau spoke to him in Arabic. The boy bowed and withdrew.

'That is Si Abeldesselem, one of my servants who will play for us at luncheon. A strange boy, but, as you will see, his music has charm.'

The roof on to which Deniau now led her was sheltered from the midday sun by a stone arcade running around the parapet. He pointed to an irregular mass of white buildings at the very top of the hillside. 'That is the Citadel. It was the residence of the Princes of Algiers. If you look at those loopholes in the walls you'll see where their huge cannons once dominated the city. The Citadel was where the Turkish ruler held court. Over there to the left were the private apartments where he lived with his wives. And then, one morning, almost forty years ago, walking on his rooftop he looked down and saw our fleet approaching these shores. That was the end of Turkish rule.'

'And now, what is it used for?' she asked.

'Barracks, and storehouses. All of its treasures have disappeared, the furnishings looted by our troops. The great cannons were shipped back to France as trophies. I'm told they're on display in the Invalides.'

He walked to the edge of the parapet and stood looking down as though he were alone. After a moment of silence, he turned back to her.

'So here you are, in Algiers. I hope by bringing your husband here I've done the right thing.'

'I don't understand,' she said. 'You want to stop them going to war against France, don't you? If my husband can help you, then of course it's right.'

'It's more complicated than that. Remember, when we were in Compiègne, how the Emperor talked of France's mission to civilize these people and improve their lives. But the truth is, next year we'll complete our conquest of this land. In doing so we'll open new trade routes to the rest of Africa. It is we, not the Arabs, who will benefit. And I ask myself: what will happen to their way of life?'

'There is something about this place, something I would not like to change,' she said.

He smiled and, leaning across the cushions, touched her hand lightly. 'If you had come here today with your husband I would not have worn Arab dress. He wouldn't have understood. But you – you're different. You could fall in love with Africa, as I have. Don't misunderstand me. I love my country. I will fight for France as I have fought for her in the past. And yet Africa has changed me. As I suspect, it will change you.'

'But I am here only for a short visit,' she said. 'In a month or two I will be back at home in Tours.'

'I envy the Arabs,' he said. 'They have a word – *mektoub*. You will hear it on their lips, time and time again. It means 'It is written'. They believe that everything is written beforehand

and the destiny of each of us is the will of God. Perhaps it was written that you should come to Algeria. Perhaps it was written that it will change you.'

He offered her his arm. 'Come, let's go in. Our luncheon will be ready.'

He led her back into the central room and sat beside her on the cushions. Somewhere within the apartment a bell sounded and through the doorway the giant black servant appeared, encumbered with a sort of leather harness on which he balanced an assortment of small jars and pots. The giant deposited these objects on the painted trays in front of Emmeline, then, bowing, withdrew.

'Who is he?' Emmeline whispered. 'I've never seen so tall a man.'

'He's Senegalese,' Deniau told her. 'We call him Kaddour. But I bought him as a slave so I don't know his real name.'

'A slave?'

'Yes, many of the Negroes here were brought from Southern Africa as slaves. He is very loyal. A good soul.'

'But he is your *slave*?'

Deniau nodded and reached for the pots on the tray. 'Today my servants have prepared an Arab meal. I thought it might interest you to see it served in traditional fashion. These are just *amuse-gueules*. The little round cakes are warm, a sort of buttered crêpe. Those are dates from a southern oasis. This is ewe's milk, although I think we will prefer to drink wine. My cooks will bring the main course at any moment.'

She ate one of the cakes and bit into a sweet date but her mind, filled moments ago with the things he had implied and said about her, now echoed dully with one word: *slave*. And as she put down the half-eaten date, the bell sounded again and the two women she had seen in the courtyard below entered, carrying large earthenware pots which they placed in front of Deniau. They then stood, heads bowed, hands joined as in prayer, waiting. Emmeline looked up, first at the older woman and then at the other, tall, young and slender, her eyes now downcast as in submission. Was she, too, his slave?

At a sign from Deniau, the older cook began to serve food from one of the pots. 'This is couscous, a sort of pilaff, the base of any Arab feast. Today my women have made it in two versions, one with mutton and the second a sweet version with sugar and spices.' He gestured to the young girl who, kneeling in front of Emmeline, served the second couscous.

At a further nod from Deniau both women rose and withdrew.

'Slaves?' Emmeline looked at him in fear of his answer. But he laughed and shook his head. 'No, they are my prized cooks, among the best in the city, I'm told.'

'Do they live here?'

'Yes, they are house servants.'

'The young girl is beautiful.'

'She is, isn't she? The older woman is her aunt. Like Kaddour they are devoted to me. I am very lucky.' He handed her a plate. 'The Arab eats with his fingers. They use only the right hand.'

She ate a mouthful of the food but, later, she could not have told what was its taste. For at that moment she heard behind her a thin, high music and turning saw the Arab boy, sitting cross-legged in the rear of the room, playing a small flute, the music monotonous and strange but with a rhythmic cadence. As he played the boy stared at his flute as if he were alone in the room, but when, putting down his instrument, he began to sing in a soprano tone, he looked first at Deniau and then at Emmeline, his look changing from a shocked stare when he sought to lock eyes with his master, to a look of scorn and hatred when he sang to her as audience.

Deniau, eating, listening, lay back on the cushions and from time to time turned to look at Emmeline and smile as though inviting her to share his enjoyment of the singing.

The boy ended his chant, took up his flute, then, graceful as a girl in his faded silken robes, bowed to his master and withdrew.

'Haunting song, don't you think? It's a traditional lament.'

Deniau poured wine from the decanter. She did not pick up the glass.

'What does he do, that boy? Is he a house servant?'

She saw Deniau hesitate. 'Yes. He keeps my accounts, deals with tradesmen and supervises the other servants. I am away a lot. I need a reliable person to look after things.'

'He looked at me as if he hated me.'

'Did he?' Deniau laughed. 'Ignore it. Boys of his sort do not like women.'

Boys of his sort. Henri once had an assistant like that. She knew about them. But for Deniau to have one in his house, there was something – she looked at Deniau now as he lay back on the cushions eating the Arab food delicately with his fingers, she looked at the fine white robe that covered his body, at the curved dagger in his ornate belt, at his bare feet in the red sandals, at his sun-darkened face, this man who made allusions which could lead to an affair but who knew his *Brüderschaft* toast had been a mistake and would not embarrass her further at this luncheon. And as these thoughts rushed around in her head, the women came back into the room and now, as they replenished the dish of couscous, she looked at the younger one, head bowed, submissive as a slave. I am not beautiful. She is. I wish I hadn't come.

The women withdrew. After some minutes, the Senegalese, Kaddour, re-entered the room, carrying small bowls of water and towels. The meal had ended and as she dried her hands on the towel Emmeline saw Deniau watching her as if he knew her thoughts.

'In Algiers after luncheon, the city sleeps,' he said. 'A very civilized custom. I cannot offer you a proper bed here. Cushions, yes. But perhaps you would prefer it if Kaddour took you back to the residence?'

'Yes,' she said. 'Perhaps that would be best.'

SEVEN

It was Deniau and not her husband who showed her the theatre in the Rue Bat-Azoun. She stared up at the elegant façade.

'I could believe I was in Paris.'

'You're right,' he said. 'It's a copy of the Variétés. However, as you'll see, there are differences. Because of the hot climate the stairs, passages and boxes are more spacious than in a theatre in France. Usually, the performances are given by opera or drama companies imported from Marseille or Nice. Last week we cancelled the current performances and we're paying the opera company to stay idle for the period of your husband's rehearsals and performance. The company manager is not at all pleased. But, of course, your husband may have told you all this?'

'I'm afraid I've hardly seen him since he started to rehearse. And he rarely talks about his work.'

'But his secrets, his illusions, you must be one of the very few people to know them?'

'I don't. He believes those are things a magician should not discuss.'

'Not even with his wife?'

'Not even with his wife.'

When they entered the theatre Emmeline saw that Jules was on stage helping Henri and in the background were assembled the cornucopia, the 'inexhaustible' bottle and the glass box which he used for transference of the five-franc pieces. At one end of the stage, sinisterly, was the small copper hinged box which he had used in performances in Spain and Russia. She knew at once that while it would be produced later in the performance to frighten and impress the Arabs, the cornucopia, the bottle and the glass box were opening gambits with which he would puzzle and please them. Now she watched Deniau vault lightly on to the stage and heard him describe to Lambert where the various members of the audience would be seated.

'The Arab leaders, particularly those from the desert regions, have never been seated in a building like this one and it's not their custom to sit in chairs as we do. You must take this into account when you're performing in front of them. There may be a certain amount of fidgeting and inattention.'

'And the Governor-General, where will he sit?' Lambert asked.

'Maréchal Randon with his family and suite will occupy those two boxes to the right of the stage while the Prefect and other civilian authorities will sit exactly facing him. The sheikhs, caids, agas, bash-agas and other leading Arabs will be given a place of honour. They will be seated in the dress circle.'

'And the marabouts?'

'We expect that four will attend and we will seat them in the very front of the parterre, facing the stage so that they will have the closest view of your performance. But I must warn you, at the moment we doubt that Bou-Aziz will journey to Algiers. You will have to perform for him at a later date, probably somewhere in the South.'

'We should not use the word "perform",' Lambert said.

'Of course. You're quite right.'

Deniau then turned to Emmeline.' I brought Madame Lambert with me to show her the theatre. Perhaps you'd let me offer you both a light luncheon at the Aleppo Café?'

She saw Henri look down at her and smile in the guilty way he had when he was about to refuse something. 'Hello, my darling. What do you think of the theatre?'

'It's very handsome,' she said hesitantly.

'By the way, *you* will have an excellent view,' Deniau told her. 'You will be sitting in the Governor-General's box.' He turned to Lambert. 'And our luncheon, Henri?'

'I'm sorry,' Lambert said. 'I must go on working. However, Emmeline might enjoy it.'

Suddenly she decided that Deniau must not be allowed to manipulate her so easily. 'I think, in that case, I'll stay here with Henri. We could have some food sent in.' She looked at Deniau. 'Is that all right, Colonel?'

'Of course, Madame. Although I will miss your company.' He touched his fingers to his kepi, making her a mock salute. 'Well, until Sunday, then.'

'Sunday?'

'Henri hasn't told you? The Governor-General requests that you both accompany him and his party to next Sunday's service in the cathedral. It will be a High Mass in celebration of our recent victory in the South.'

François du Chatel, Archbishop, a gross, towering presence in his white episcopal robes, waited under a parasol held by an acolyte on the steps of the cathedral at the entrance to Rue Divan. At the sound of trumpets which announced that the Governor-General's party had entered the street, a double row of French officers lined up behind the Archbishop came to attention and drew their sabres to form a ceremonial arch. Emmeline, disembarking from her carriage with the official party, stood beside her husband, waiting, as the Governor-General kissed the episcopal ring and was led inside to the surprising accompaniment of an overture from an Auber opera, played by an army band positioned in a side aisle of the church. Fanning themselves in the noonday heat, the congregation made up of diplomatic representatives, the Prefect and his staff, the leading French, German and Syrian merchants, French army officers, nuns and priests from the diocese's convents and seminaries, waited for the Mass to begin. In this former mosque, columns fifty feet high supported the cupola which was lit from above by stained-glass windows. The altar was on the north side, decorated by a painting of the Virgin which had been presented to the cathedral by the Pope. Yet above this painting in prominent relief was a series of ornate, interlaced sentences from the Koran which had not been erased despite the fact that they proclaimed in Arabic that there is only one God and Muhammad is his prophet. Even stranger than this juxtaposition was the Mass itself. As priests and acolytes filed out on to the altar the gay martial music continued. Ranks of soldiers in full regimentals stood before the tabernacle and as the service got under way and the sacramental bell rang to announce the miracle of transubstantiation, the noise of twenty drums thundered under the cupola. At the command of their officer the soldiers presented muskets, at the same time bending the right knee and bowing their heads towards the ground. The thundering drumroll continued until the priest finished his prayer.

Emmeline saw at once that the congregation was inattentive: a few prayed, some listened to the music, while many of the men walked about, staring curiously at the younger women who knelt in pretended devotion, their heads and faces veiled in the Spanish fashion.

When the Mass ended, Archbishop du Chatel rose from his episcopal chair on the right side of the altar and walked down to the gate of the communion rail. At once the entire congregation came to attention in a manner not evident during the religious ceremony. A regimental colour-sergeant marched up the central aisle carrying a flag which, kneeling, he offered to the Archbishop for a blessing. Holy water was sprinkled on the flag, the Archbishop mumbled an inaudible Latin prayer and accepted the colours, raising them aloft for the congregation to see, then handing them to a colonel of Zouave who marched to a side altar and hoisted them to a position of honour beside other, now faded, military flags. Drums thundered; the military band struck up the national anthem as a thousand voices were raised in patriotic chorus.

And now, in this Muslim mosque transformed into a place of Christian worship, Emmeline was transported back to the hurried Sunday Mass in the Emperor's chapel in Compiègne. Here in Algiers, in an outpost of Louis Napoleon's dominions, again, the religious ceremony had been no more than a formality. Today's true devotion was reserved for the flag, symbol of recent victory, displayed not as an act of Christian piety but in a gesture of triumph in the temple of a conquered race. She searched the faces of the official party until she found Deniau who stood among the most senior officers, left hand on his ceremonial sword, his eyes on the newly raised colours, his voice chanting the patriotic verse. Was this the man who, two days ago, lay on silken cushions wearing an Arab robe and telling her that Africa had changed him? Yes, it was. She remembered what he had said: 'I will fight for France as I have fought for her in the past.' He was not here to help the Arabs preserve their way of life. He was here to destroy it. Staring at him now, drawn by his looks, his manner, his charm, knowing that she was half caught up in secret anticipation of an affair, she was, at the same time, filled with the uneasy feeling that by bringing her to Compiègne and now to Algiers he had cast her adrift.

In the next few days, gradually at first, Algiers and its environs began to fill up with thousands of Arab tribesmen, bringing with them horses, camels, sheep, goats, cooking pots, families, children and women camp followers, erecting a warren of tents and huts on the plain of Hussein-Dey just outside the city. This great space in sight of the sea and under the shadow of the hill of Mustapha adjoined the city's hippodrome where in a fête organized and presided over by the Governor-General, Arab and Kabyle leaders had been invited to take part in a demonstration of riding skills, followed by three days of horse racing.

Madame Duferre, who had appointed herself as Emmeline's mentor in social matters, now arranged that she accompany the official party to the hippodrome for the opening day of these festivities. That evening at a dinner party in the Governor-General's residence Emmeline sat silent, pretending to listen to the conversation of her neighbours but in reality lost in a confusion of the sights she had just seen: four hundred Arab horsemen, wheeling and galloping across the hippodrome, uttering strange cries as though on the battlefield, firing muskets, whirling sabres, in a wild and daring display of warrior skills. And this for the benefit of Randon, a Maréchal of France, fresh from his victories in the bloody Crimean campaign, who sat surrounded by his staff, smiling in false approbation of this reckless display of valour, then rising from his seat in the reviewing stand to salute these desert savages whose leaders he would soon bring to subjugation under the rule of France. But, for now, all was festive; a holiday spirit ruled Algiers. That evening Emmeline slipped out of the residence to roam the newly crowded streets and squares, passing stalls filled with the smells of boiling coffee and hot cakes baked in fat, listening to the oriental twang of guitars, the thin monotonous music of reeds, the beat of strange flat drums, making her way through crowds of jugglers, musicians, beggars and pedlars, stepping past the rings of gamblers hunched in circles, intent on play. And then as the sun set above the Citadel, the stalls were struck, the music ended. Vendors and musicians rode out of the city on mules, camels and horses to camp in the vast huddle of tents below the hippodrome, leaving a deep night silence in the city itself.

At the residence, a Zouave guard opened the gates to re-admit her. The cool marble corridors of the great courtyard were quiet as a cemetery at dusk. When she let herself into their private apartments she saw her husband asleep on a daybed in the alcove. He wore a long white nightshirt and, as always before a performance, he had washed his hair and tied it up in a hair net. He lay on his back, arms crossed over his chest as though to protect himself from a blow. She approached and stood looking down at him, filled with a sudden pity for this man who made his livelihood standing on a stage, smiling at strangers, hoping to deceive them. She looked at his hands, white, supple, slender, trained to conceal and reveal, to misdirect and charm, at his mouth skilled in its patter of falsehoods, at his eyes, now closed, eyes trained to see that person in his audience who could be used as an innocent foil. This man, still as a cadaver under his night shroud, his dignity destroyed by the humble hair net which circled his brow, was at once the most famous magician in all of Europe, her husband and, as her father had said, a charlatan. Who tomorrow would try to alter history through a series of magic tricks.

But in that moment of looking down at him, her pity turned to shame for he was also a man who loved her as much as he was capable of love, loved her despite her failure to give him the son he wanted, loved her although he must know she did not love him.

Tears came. She bent and kissed him on the lips. He woke.

'What's wrong, my darling? Why are you crying?'

She shook her head, unable to answer.

'Did you just come home? How were the celebrations? I heard great noise in the streets.'

'Yes,' she said. 'There were great celebrations tonight.' She put out her hand and touched his cheek.' Go back to sleep. Tomorrow is your moment. You must be ready for it.'

'I am. You'll be proud of me.'

French soldiers came to attention at the entrance to the theatre as the first of the Arab military companies arrived in the Rue Bat-Azoun. The marabouts entered last, moments before the Governor-General and his party appeared in the boxes above the stage. During the lull before the curtain rose the Arabs shifted uneasily in their unaccustomed seats, some trying to tuck their legs beneath them as they would in their tents. In 30-degree-centigrade heat the Europeans fanned themselves distractedly with their programmes, the ladies furtively peering into pocket mirrors to see if their mascara had run.

Suddenly, Colonel Deniau appeared before the footlights, bowing first to Maréchal Randon's party and then to the marabouts and sheikhs.

'We bid you welcome.' He spoke in French, pausing between sentences so that the interpreters among the crowd could translate.

'As part of the festivities and celebrations offered by our Governor-General, he has brought here from France a great Christian sorcerer to delight and astonish you but also to show you the truth. The truth is that certain of your marabouts have claimed to be invulnerable to bullets, impervious to bodily pain, to heal the sick and cure the barrenness of women. Because of these claims they would have you believe that they, and they alone, possess supernatural powers and can foretell the future, a future which promises you victory in a holy war. But tonight you will witness powers greater than any you have seen, powers that may give you pause. Let us welcome the great marabout of France. Henri Lambert.'

Deniau stepped down from the stage. The curtain rose. Emmeline, watching from the Governor-General's box, saw at first an empty stage with a table in the rear containing the heavy box, the cornucopia, the top hat, the punch bowl. Then, in the silence of total attention from the audience, Lambert walked out from the wings. He carried his short ivory-tipped baton and wore a light-black silk jacket, a white linen waistcoat, and grey chequed trousers. He held his head high, looking up at the dress circle, then bowing slightly, as a signal that he was about to begin. At this, Jules appeared on stage, wearing the yellow-and-black-striped vest of a French footman. Jules went to the table in the rear, took up the top hat and handed it to Lambert. Lambert tapped it to show it was empty, displaying its insides to the audience. He then passed his baton over it and reaching into it produced, in turn, three heavy cannon balls which he dropped with a thump on to the stage floor. There was a sudden stiffening among his audience. The Arabs no longer shifted in their seats but stared unblinking at the stage.

Again Lambert tapped the hat and this time took from it a

bouquet of flowers. Emmeline, watching the four marabouts in the front rows of the stalls, saw them finger their prayer beads and exchange sidelong glances. There was no applause. Lambert, walking to the footlights, signalled to Jules who came forward and handed him the papier-mâché cornucopia which was about three feet in length and hinged on one side so that Lambert could open it to show that it was empty. He did this, then closed it and, smiling now, turned the cornucopia upside down, spilling from it a rain of ladies' fans, small bouquets of flowers and bonbons which Jules placed on a tray and offered to the ladies in the audience. Now, for the first time, a smattering of applause was heard but Emmeline saw that it came, not from the Arab spectators but from the Europeans.

Jules brought out the punch bowl, a silver cup of the type used in Parisian cafés. Lambert unscrewed the bottom of this cup and passed his baton through the vessel to show that it was empty. He said some words which his audience could not hear and passed his hand three times over the bowl. A dense vapour immediately issued from its opening. Jules then brought forward a dozen small coffee cups which Lambert filled with boiling coffee. Jules placed the cups on a tray and going down among the audience, offered them to spectators in the front row. Interpreters, prompted by Jules, announced that the great sorcerer offered any in the audience a gift of coffee, their favourite beverage. No one accepted, until at last, on Jules's urging, one of the marabouts suspiciously took a cup and sipped from it. Several other spectators then tried the coffee as Lambert kept pouring from the small, seemingly inexhaustible bowl, now handing it down into the audience so that Jules could refill the cups in full sight of the recipients. At last Lambert signalled and the bowl was brought back by Jules to centre stage. Lambert held it up, showing that it was still full. He placed it on the table at the rear of the stage, then took from the table the small solidly built box which was closed with copper hinges. Holding it lightly in one hand he walked to the centre of the stage. And now, for the first time, speaking slowly so that the interpreters could translate, he addressed his audience.

'From what you have seen you may say that I am possessed of unusual powers. And you are right. My powers are supernatural, granted to me by God. I will now give you a new proof of these powers by showing you that I can deprive the most powerful man of his strength and then restore that strength at will. I ask anyone who thinks himself strong enough to try this experiment to come forward now.'

Emmeline looking down from her box saw the four marabouts in the front row lean their heads together. Then one of them pointed to an Arab sitting in the stalls. This man at once got up and mounted the stage. He was of medium height but muscular and well built. He came up to Lambert with a confident air.

'Are you very strong?' Lambert asked him. The Arab smiled and looked down at the marabouts in the front row, then nodded. 'I am.'

'Are you sure that you will remain strong, always?'

The Arab turned to his interpreter and uttered one word which was translated as: 'Always!'

Emmeline saw Lambert pause. Knowing him, she could sense his pleasure at what he was about to do. He faced the Arab in a long silent pause.

'You are wrong,' he said, at last. 'In an instant I will rob you of your strength and you will become as weak as a little child.'

The Arab smiled and again looked back at the marabouts as though sharing in a joke.

'Now,' Lambert said. 'Lift this box.'

The man bent and easily picked up the box, balancing it in one hand and raising it above his head. He turned to Lambert and said contemptuously, 'Is that all?'

Lambert signalled him to put the box down. Facing the Arab, he raised his slender magician's hands making a pass in front of the man's face. He then said, 'From this moment on, you are weaker than a little child. Try to lift the box.'

The Arab confidently reached down, seized the box by its iron handles and gave it a violent tug. But the box did not budge from the floor. Angrily, he bent over it, sweating as he strained to lift it. It did not move. Emmeline heard the audience begin shouting what seemed to be words of encouragement. Again, the Arab bent and strained. He panted and pulled and at last, defeated, let go of the handles and stared up at Lambert in a mixture of fear and anger. But at this moment shouts from the sheikhs in the parterre made him turn and look out at the audience. Emboldened by their cries, in a great show of will, he bent again over the box gripping the handles, his legs straddled for a final effort. Emmeline, who knew what would happen, felt a tremor of fear for this man.

On a secret signal from Lambert, Jules who was now backstage sent an electric current into the handles of the box. The Arab, his hands glued to the box, trembled violently, his chest contracting as he uttered a yell of pain. He fell on his knees, sprawled over the box unable to relinquish his grip.

Lambert watched his agony then stepped forward and waved his baton over the box. The Arab, released from the current, staggered to his feet staring at the infidel sorcerer, then turning away, pulling his burnous around him as if to shield himself from harm, jumped down from the stage, ran through the central aisle and out of the theatre.

In the Governor-General's and Prefect's boxes and among the French officers in the parterre, Emmeline sensed a sudden elation, a moment of triumph mixed with a certain puzzlement, for no one knew how her husband had achieved these effects. But from the marabouts in the front row, to the masses of Arabs in the further reaches of the theatre, there was a grave, uneasy silence.

'*Chitan*,' a marabout called out. The ladies in Emmeline's box turned to the interpreter. 'What is he saying?'

'Satan.'

Now the theatre filled with a hubbub of excited Arab voices. Emmeline saw her husband look down from the stage as though searching for someone in the audience. And then Colonel Deniau came up the centre aisle, pausing at the orchestra pit to face the agitated Arab spectators.

'Some of you know of marabouts who claim to be invulnerable to bullets,' he said. 'But can they prove it? Tonight you see a sorcerer who is truly invulnerable and will prove it beyond any doubt.'

Lambert now came to the centre of the stage, paused, then said, 'I am invulnerable because I possess this talisman which protects me from all harm.' As if by magic, a small glittering glass orb appeared in his outstretched hand. 'With this in my possession, the best marksman in Algeria cannot hurt me.'

He had barely finished speaking when one of the marabouts in the front row of the stalls jumped up, vaulted into the orchestra pit and hoisted himself on stage, in his haste singeing his clothing in the candles of the footlights. He faced Lambert and said, in excellent French, 'I am here to kill you!'

There was a silence. Then Lambert said, 'You wish to kill me? I am a greater sorcerer than you and I tell you, you will not kill me.'

He gestured to Jules who came from the rear of the stage and handed him a cavalry pistol which he offered to the marabout.

'Take this and satisfy yourself that it has not been tampered with.'

The marabout blew several times through the barrel, then through the nipple to make sure there was passage from one to the other, and after a further careful examination of the gun, said, 'The weapon is good and I will kill you.'

'Because you are so anxious to kill me,' Lambert said, 'then put in this double charge of powder and a wad on top.'

The marabout did this, saying, 'It is done.'

'Now here is a lead bullet: mark it with your knife so as to be able to recognize it and put it in the pistol with a second wad.'

'It is done.'

'Now that you are quite sure that your pistol is loaded and that it will fire, tell me: do you feel no remorse about killing me, even though I authorize you to do it?'

The marabout looked at him coldly. 'No. You say you are a sorcerer. Prove it.'

Lambert nodded, then signalled to Jules who came forward

and handed him an apple and a dagger. Lambert stuck the dagger into the apple and held it in his left hand at chest height.

'Now,' he said. 'Aim not at this apple but straight at my heart.'

The marabout at once took aim at Lambert's chest and pulled the trigger. The gun fired. The bullet did not hit Lambert but lodged itself in the centre of the apple which he held in his hand. Lambert brought the apple back to the marabout, saying, 'Take this bullet. Is it the one you marked?'

The marabout pulled the bullet from the apple. He looked, then nodded angrily. Lambert took the pistol from him and handed it to Jules.

'No one can kill me,' he said.

Emmeline saw that even the European spectators were alarmed, and baffled by what they had just seen. The Arabs in the theatre sat stiff as automata, watching as the shaken marabout went back to his seat.

At this point, Maréchal Randon, sitting in front of Emmeline, stood up and applauded, smiling down at Lambert. Following his lead, all of the Europeans in the audience rose and applauded. Lambert bowed gravely in acknowledgement, waited until the applause had ended, then, smiling, holding his hands up in a welcoming gesture, came forward to the footlights and signalled to the interpreters.

'For my next demonstration I would be grateful if one of our Arab friends will come up on stage to assist me. I assure him he will suffer no harm.'

He waited while the interpreters translated, after which there was an uneasy pause. Then, suddenly, a young Arab, tall, insouciant, wearing elegant yellow boots and the embroidered waistcoat of a caid, came down the centre aisle, smiling at his friends in the manner of a boy who has accepted a dare. Lambert stretched out his hand to help him climb on stage. Jules then carried a light wooden table to centre stage and set it down.

'As you can see,' Lambert said, waving his baton under the table legs, 'this table is not attached to anything and contains no concealed drawer or space.' He turned to the young Arab. 'Will you please climb up on it?' The Arab climbed on to the table and stood, looking out at the audience. Jules then brought from the wings a huge cloth cone, some six feet high and open at the top. He and Lambert fitted this cone over the Arab, completely hiding him from view. They then slipped a plank under the cone and each taking an end of the plank lifted it and the cone that sat on it off the table, carrying it towards the footlights where, suddenly, they upended it. The cone was empty. The young Arab had disappeared.

A gasp of astonishment rose in the room. Suddenly, as though someone had called, 'Fire!' people rose in their seats and several, in panic, hurried to the main exit. But the door was locked. Lambert, calm and deliberate, stepped down from the stage and walked through the now crowded main aisle. Those who wished to flee nevertheless moved aside to let the sorcerer pass. Emmeline, from her vantage point, saw the fear in their faces as they stared at her husband. On reaching the main door Lambert stretched out his hand and as if by magic an iron key appeared between his fingers. He unlocked the door, then passing through to the vestibule, returned leading the young Arab by the hand. The Arab seemed dazed, as though drunk. Emmeline smelled the odour of ether as he passed beneath her box. Lambert led the young man back on stage. The Arabs, bewildered but still in a state of extreme agitation, began calling out to their fellow countryman, who, dazed, muttered some answer which the interpreters translated for the European audience as: 'He says he does not know what happened. He feels as if he has smoked *kif.* He forgets.'

Lambert now put his hands on the Arab's shoulders, thanking him for his assistance. But the young man, frightened by his touch, jumped down from the stage and disappeared into the audience. In the ensuing confusion and milling about of the crowd Lambert signalled to the orchestra pit. A drumroll sounded, silencing for a moment the panicked spectators. Lambert turned to the interpreters. Emmeline, watching him, saw his elation, his sense of triumph.

'I am a sorcerer. I am Christian. I am French. God, whom you call Allah, protects me. As He will protect my country from any enemy who dares to strike a blow against France. In the name of your host, Maréchal Randon, I thank you for coming here tonight. We bid you good evening.'

EIGHT

The following day as she went in on the arm of Monsieur de la Garde to a luncheon given by the Governor-General in honour of her husband, Emmeline saw Deniau enter the room carrying copies of a newspaper which he handed out to Monsieur de la Garde and the Prefect. The newspaper was *Le Moniteur Algérien*, the voice of Algiers' French population, and when he opened his copy and began to read it Monsieur de la Garde said to the company, 'Aha! Listen to this! It says here:'

> *Let us add that this year, as always, the races have been the occasion of numerous festivities offered, in part, to honour our Arab chieftains. But neither the banquets held for them by Monsieur le Maréchal, nor the closing ball which brought together the élite of our population, has impressed them as did the astonishing séance given by Henri Lambert whose supernatural gifts they witnessed for the first time. Monsieur le Maréchal is well aware that recently certain marabouts have managed to impress their fellow Arabs by deeds which would seem to hint at unearthly powers and by this means have gained an influence over the native population which they now wish to exploit in a revolt against French rule. By showing them a Christian whose supernatural powers so far exceed any their marabouts can demonstrate, Monsieur le Maréchal and Monsieur Lambert have made an important contribution to re-establishing the atmosphere of peaceful co-habitation essential to our prosperity.*

On hearing this the Prefect came up and shook Lambert's hand, saying, 'Congratulations!' Others crowded around, adding their praise. At that moment Lieutenant Lecoffre entered the room, a sign that the Maréchal was expected.

Monsieur de la Garde holding the newspaper went to greet him. 'Your Excellency, have you seen the newspaper?'

The Maréchal, who this morning wore his dress uniform and the grand cross of the Légion d'Honneur, acknowledged the respectful bows of his staff and the curtsies of the ladies present, then, turning to de la Garde, said, 'No I have not seen it but Lecosse told me what was written. An excellent beginning.'

Maréchal Randon then signalled the servants who at once offered glasses of champagne to the company. 'Let me propose a toast,' he said. 'To Henri Lambert – a great magician and as of today a soldier in the war against France's enemies.'

The toast was drunk. Emmeline saw her husband's elation as, moved by pride and emotion, he told the Maréchal, 'Thank you, Your Excellency. Believe me, it is a great honour to be allowed to serve my country.'

There were murmurs of 'Bravo!' and the company went in to luncheon. As she took her seat on the right of Monsieur de la Garde Emmeline saw Deniau's place card on her left. Moments later as he slipped into his seat beside her he took her hand and kissed it, saying in a low voice, 'I have been dreaming of you.'

She looked at him, worried that Monsieur de la Garde might have heard. But Monsieur de la Garde was engaged in badinage with the Prefect's wife.

'Do you know why I have been dreaming of you?' Deniau said in his confidential tone. 'It is because next week we shall be travelling together. And in the desert, in the real Algeria. It will be enchanting for me. For both of us, I hope?'

At that moment, to her relief, Lieutenant Lecoffre, sitting across the table, leaned forward and said to Deniau, 'Colonel, isn't it true that this performance was your idea? You are also to be congratulated. As you can see, you have a great success on your hands.'

Deniau smiled at her as if in apology for the interruption,

then told Lecoffre, 'Thank you. It's a success, yes, but we have only begun our task.'

'How so, Colonel?'

Emmeline realized that other guests had heard this exchange and now waited for Deniau's answer. And Deniau knew it. Looking down the table and catching the eye of the Maréchal, he said, 'As you know, Your Excellency, in two days' time I will be travelling with Monsieur Lambert to the region where Bou-Aziz is rumoured to be the new Mahdi. Now, Monsieur Lambert must prove himself greater than Bou-Aziz and by doing so weaken his influence among the Arab and Kabyle chieftains. Not an easy task, I'm afraid. Even though I have the greatest faith in my friend Lambert we cannot promise success.'

Randon smiled. 'He has already had great success, Colonel. Yesterday after the performance I spoke with Sheikh Farhat who rules in Constantine. He said, "Our marabouts must now do very great miracles to astonish us."

'"And do you think they will succeed?" I asked him.

'"My hopes are not strong," he told me. "But, if Bou-Aziz is indeed the Mahdi, he must show that he is greater than your sorcerer."'

The Maréchal smiled at the company. 'And so I said to the sheikh, "Allah alone is great. And He will decide."'

The Prefect clapped his hands in approbation. 'An answer in his own coin, Excellency. Wonderful riposte! And He *will* decide. For Lambert – and for France!'

Emmeline looked down the table at her husband. He sat, his head held high, smiling in a sea of smiles.

Next morning, shortly after dawn, Emmeline and Lambert waited with Jules in the courtyard of the Governor-General's mansion for Deniau's arrival in a diligence which would take them on the first leg of their journey to Kabylia. But when the vehicle clattered into the courtyard there was no sign of him.

Instead, the Arab boy who Emmeline had seen in Deniau's apartments jumped down from a seat beside the coachman and in heavily accented French announced that his master had been delayed by 'political duties' and would join them with horses and camels for the second part of their journey in two days' time, when the diligence would arrive at the town of Ain Sefra.

'From Ain Sefra, Monsieur, there is no high road. You will travel on horseback. My master will do his utmost to join you there.'

The boy then bowed to Lambert and opened the carriage door. Lambert turned to Emmeline indicating that she precede him, but the boy barred her path. 'No, Monsieur,' he said to Lambert. 'You must go ahead of the woman. You are the marabout.'

When Lambert climbed into the carriage the boy extended his hand to assist him with the step. But when Emmeline followed her husband the boy did not offer his hand. Instead he stared at her with that now familiar look of hatred and as he closed the carriage door behind her she heard him make a spitting sound with his lips.

When their luggage, including Lambert's theatrical boxes, was loaded and secured on the roof of the carriage Jules took his seat beside the coachman. The Arab boy bowed farewell to Lambert. Zouave guards came to attention, presenting arms as the heavy diligence rumbled out on to the Rue de la Marine. Within minutes they had left the city, the horses moving at a fast trot along a broad highway through outlying villages into a landscape dry as death. Emmeline, sitting beside her husband, who, as usual on a journey, busied himself with reading, stared blankly at the route ahead. She had dressed this morning with special care, rising before dawn to wash and set her hair, choosing a pink silk dress and white lace gloves as though she were going to a luncheon party instead of on a journey, using the stopper of her favourite perfume bottle to anoint her throat, the hollows behind her ears and the backs of her wrists with the delicate scent of *muguet*, for she would be sitting close to Deniau in the confines of the carriage. She did these things somnambulistically, refusing to think of what might happen in the days ahead, but on the arrival of the Arab boy with his news that there would be two days of travelling before Deniau would join them she was filled with a quick anger at the cavalier way he had delayed their meeting, mixed with anxiety in case 'political duties' might keep him from joining her. But because of the disappointment she felt at his absence, she at last permitted herself to imagine that if, in future, he chose to make advances she might not reject them.

This absence, this longing for him, this uncertainty, made the next two days seem endless. Each night the diligence stopped at hotels run by French colonists where, to Lambert's disgust, they were seated at a communal table with French commercial travellers and served indifferent European food. He, like she, worried that these mysterious 'political duties' might prevent Deniau from making rendezvous. But on the morning of the third day when the diligence trundled into the courtyard of the building which housed the *Bureau Arabe* in the town of Ain Sefra, there, bowing gravely as he opened the carriage door, was Kaddour, Deniau's Senegalese slave.

Emmeline's face lit in a smile of pleasure as the giant cupped his hands to help her down. Moments later they were in the presence of Captain Hersant, the *Bureau* chief in Ain Sefra, who informed them that Deniau was already in the town arranging for the hire of camels and would join them at luncheon.

Shortly after noon when the muezzins sounded the call for devotions Emmeline, looking down at the courtyard of their lodgings, saw, behind the field of Arab backs prostrate in prayer below her, the arrival of three camels through the main gates of the building. On the leading camel, sitting cross-legged and at ease, wearing a brown burnous over his military uniform, Deniau, who stayed the little caravan until the prayers had ceased. Then making his camel kneel, he gracefully slipped off its back and strode across the courtyard, looking up at her, waving his riding crop in welcome.

'Henri, he's here!'

'Where?' Lambert came to the window, looking down. But already Emmeline was at her mirror, anxiously rearranging her hair then turning, excited, to hurry downstairs to the main hall. And when Deniau entered the hall she went up to him, saying with obvious delight, 'Oh, we were so worried. I kept wondering – but here you are!'

It was a signal and he knew it. He took her hand, bent low to kiss it, then raising his head, looked into her eyes. 'Yes, here I am.' He smiled, released her hand and said softly, 'Dear Emmeline.'

In the next hour she sat in a state of euphoria, only half aware of the conversation at the luncheon table. But then, she heard Deniau tell Lambert that they should set out as soon as possible and keep up a stiff pace as their tour must end before the coming autumnal rains which made the routes impracticable and often dangerous.

'But when do you expect the rains?' Lambert asked.

'Towards the end of the month. And so, it's my aim to have you back here safe and sound, within a fortnight.'

Emmeline stared at Deniau. *A fortnight. Fourteen days . . . Then it will be over. We will be sent back to France.*

'But I have prepared four performances,' Lambert said. 'You will remember, that's what we arranged.'

'Unfortunately, when we made those arrangements in France I didn't foresee that our Algerian festivities would be delayed by the Kabyle uprising. Now, I'm afraid we must risk everything on one great coup. That's the reason I stayed behind when you left Algiers. I have sent messengers to all of the sheikhs and marabouts before whom you would have performed to invite them to one grand séance in the town of Milianah. We have a military fortress there with a large courtyard which can accommodate a sizeable audience.' He smiled. 'I think, in fact, that it will be the ideal venue. Particularly since there is electricity in the building.'

'Is there? Excellent,' Lambert said.

'I think it's particularly important, as your heavy box is already being talked about even by those who weren't at your

performance in Algiers. The news of that box has spread like –
I was about to say wildfire – but perhaps like an electric current
would be a more suitable metaphor.'

Captain Hersant, who had been told the secret of the heavy
box, smiled knowingly. But Emmeline saw that Lambert was
not pleased.

'The secret of magic is in its mystery,' he told Deniau. 'So
I trust you will not mention electricity to any of our Arab
friends.'

'I apologize,' Deniau said. 'Of course, you're right. The
illusion must be presented to them as a genuine miracle.'

Lambert nodded. 'Good. Now – when will this performance
take place?'

'In four days' time. Maréchal Randon has already received
promises from most of the sheikhs and marabouts that they will
attend. Mind you, it wasn't difficult to secure these promises.
You are already the object of fear and curiosity.'

'And Bou-Aziz?' Captain Hersant asked. 'Will he be present?'

'We have not yet received an answer, but if he stays away, it
may be interpreted to his disadvantage. We, of course, would
at once spread the rumour that he fears Henri's supernatural
powers. In any event we won't wait for him. My plan is that
we will start our return journey at dawn on the morning
after your performance, leaving those who saw it dazzled by
your skills.'

Deniau now turned to Emmeline, his hand on her arm as
if to attract her attention. 'And so, Madame, if it is not too
great a strain for you I would ask that you be ready to begin
our journey at first light tomorrow.'

'How shall we travel? On horseback? Or must I ride a
camel?'

Deniau laughed. 'The camel is not a comfortable mount,
dear Madame. I would not impose that on you. We'll take six
horses from Captain Hersant's stable. We will have two Arab
servants to ride the camels which will transport our baggage
and two on muleback to wait on us. I must warn you, though.
The road will be difficult.'

Next morning as their caravan set out, the sun rose like a threat in the pale dawn sky. The road Deniau had spoken of was a trackless desert landscape with no sign of other travellers. Against the red background of the desert soil neutral shades stood out: their servants' ochre clothing, the rust and beige of the camels' hides, the black and brown coats of the horses; all of these dull colourings seeming to intensify the growing heat. Within two hours the sun became a punishment. She felt her hair grow wet. Rivulets of sweat trickled down between her breasts as she spurred her horse, moving ahead of Deniau, unwilling to let him see her heated face and disarrayed coiffure. Towards midday the desert's rolling dunes changed to a series of steep ravines where her horse slithered and stumbled in a near vertical descent, threatening to tumble her on to the ground. Shortly after noon Deniau halted the caravan, the servants quickly erecting a goatskin lean-to, under which they laid out a frugal meal of dates, ewe's milk and bread. Emmeline retired behind this shelter attempting with soap and a basin of water to make a hasty toilette before sitting down on the carpet where the meal was served. She heard Deniau tell her husband that they would lodge that evening in the house of a sheikh named Ben-Gannah where they would be served a proper meal. 'Tomorrow we will travel on a less demanding road. The worst part of the journey is over.'

Later that afternoon as she sat slack on her weary horse, the desert stretched before her, endless as an ocean, illimitable and dangerous, repelling all intruders. How could she, a few days ago, have dreamed of it as the setting for an illicit romance?

Deniau rode up to ask if she would like to make a stop. She shook her head and said, 'I just want to reach wherever it is we sleep tonight. To be inside, away from the sun. How big is this desert? It frightens me.'

'The Sahara? Three hundred thousand square miles is the figure we have calculated. And yes, it can be frightening. But it is also a spiritual landscape. To enter it you must become, like it, a *tabula rasa*.'

He spurred his horse, moving ahead of her. 'Emmeline,' he called back. 'Believe me, it will change your life.'

She looked to where Lambert rode in tandem with his servant, Jules. 'And my husband,' she asked. 'Will it also change his?'

'I doubt it,' Deniau said. 'He is a great magician. But is there magic in his soul? What do you think?'

She did not answer.

Shortly before sunset she saw, ahead, a cluster of Moorish dwellings, rising like a ghostly castle in the surrounding wilderness. Within minutes, two Arab horsemen came galloping towards them, called out a greeting to Deniau, then, wheeling their mounts, reined up to Lambert and Emmeline and chanted something which Deniau translated.

'They are saying, "Be you welcome, you who have been sent here by God." This is Ben-Gannah, our host for this evening. The young man is his son.'

An hour later, bathed and refreshed with perfumed rose-water, her hair arranged more or less to her satisfaction, Emmeline and the others were ushered into a large reception room where they sat facing their host on a carpeted floor as two servants, their feet bare as a mark of respect, served a meal of mutton and roast fowl which, in Arab fashion, was eaten without utensils. Afterwards, bowls of water with soap and towels were brought to allow them to wash their hands. When this operation was completed the sheikh rose and led Emmeline and Lambert to a small elegantly decorated room furnished only by two divans. He smiled and said something which Deniau translated as: 'This is the room for our most honoured guests. May you sleep in peace under my roof.'

The sheik withdrew. Deniau signalled to servants to bring in their luggage and then, as Lambert gave orders as to where the trunks should be placed, Deniau joined Emmeline on the balcony which looked down on an inner courtyard. He pointed to a balcony on the ground floor at right-angles to theirs. 'That is my room.' He smiled. 'I hope you sleep well.'

He turned and went back into the room. 'Good night, Henri,' he said to Lambert. 'You must be tired.'

'My bones ache,' Lambert said. 'I'll be glad when we reach Milianah.'

She heard Deniau's footsteps on the stone staircase as he went down to the ground floor. She undressed, put on a nightgown and laid her dressing gown on the end of the divan. Lambert was already stretched out on the divan across the room. She lay listening to the night sounds within Ben-Gannah's compound. Sheep and horses quartered inside the walls to protect them from raiders bleated and neighed as though disturbed. Camels uttered their hoarse complaints. After a time these noises diminished. She heard someone beat a flat drum, accompanying the high reedy music of a flute. Then there was silence. She lay, drowsy, remembering Deniau's words. 'That is my room.' An invitation? If she were to go outside now looking down into the moonlit courtyard, would he come from the shadows inviting her to run down the stone staircase and join him? He would be wearing the white robe he wore in his apartment in Algiers. He would lead her past the squatting figure of his giant slave who, guarding the door of his room, would close it behind them, shutting them in. Then in the half-shadows Deniau's arms would encircle her waist. His mouth would find her lips, his hand baring her shoulder as, moving down from her neck, his tongue licked the nipple of her breast. And then as she strained against him he would lift her up and carry her to a divan, laying her down on its cushions, smiling as he let drop his robe. Then, avid and reckless in the drunkenness of passion, she would be his willing partner in what he did to her until at last, sated, she lay by his side on the divan. Smiling, he would retrieve her nightgown and place it on her naked body. When she had put it on, he would rise and walk with her to the door, opening it to reveal the great sloping back of Kaddour who, bowing, would lead her back across the courtyard to the stone staircase which led to this, her room.

She lay, her body soaked in sweat. She looked across the room to where her husband slept, his arms crossed over his chest in his usual posture. She turned her face to the wall.

NINE

Shortly after dawn she heard a sound of knocking on the door, then her husband's voice as he spoke to someone in the corridor. She could not hear what was being said but soon he came to her side, asking if she was awake, telling her they must dress and go downstairs.

'Deniau wants to see me,' he said. 'It seems there is trouble brewing in Kabylia. An officer from the *Bureau Arabe* in Milianah has just arrived here after riding through the night. Captain Hersant says the situation has grown dangerous. They will tell us more at breakfast. Can you be ready soon, my darling?'

Coffee, dates, flat loaves of bread and a jar of honey had been laid out for breakfast in the central courtyard below. The meal was served by Deniau's servants. The sheikh and his son were not present. As Emmeline walked into the courtyard accompanied by her husband, Deniau, Captain Hersant and a junior officer rose to greet them. 'Good morning,' Deniau said. 'May I present Lieutenant Dufour? He has come from Milianah with, I am afraid, disturbing news.'

The young lieutenant smiled and bowed. She looked, not at him but at Deniau who returned her look with one of bland, friendly neutrality as, with a flick of his wrist, he signalled Kaddour to bring a tray on which were tiny cups of Arab coffee. The black slave went first to her. When she took the coffee, he turned to Lambert who, as usual, took a spoon and heavily sugared his cup. As he did this he asked Deniau, 'Disturbing? How? I hope my performance has not been cancelled?'

'On the contrary, Henri,' Deniau said. 'Your performance may be the only way to avoid what looks like serious trouble.

We are told that certain sheikhs who will be attending your soirée have urged Bou-Aziz to call for a holy war to start next month. Lieutenant Dufour who knows them well, as, indeed, he knows Bou-Aziz, tells us that your performance in Algiers greatly alarmed them and they now fear that your feats in Milianah will convince the native populace that you are a greater sorcerer than any of theirs. If you succeed, then Bou-Aziz may not be obeyed if he asks the country to rise against us.'

'And what if I fail?' Lambert said. 'I know I had a great success in Algiers. But I spent days preparing my performance and it was given in a proper theatre. There is a magic to performances in a theatre, a magic which can be greatly diminished when I perform in some desert fortress, surrounded by Arabs who see me as an enemy.'

'My dear Henri, I don't understand your hesitation,' Deniau said. 'A magician of your talents will always make the rest of us believe he has some supernatural power. Even in Paris, before a sophisticated audience, your feats produce uneasiness and bewilderment. That is why we brought you to Africa. Most of the so-called "miracles" of these native marabouts are circus tricks – playing with serpents, eating pounded glass, walking on red-hot coals, etcetera. You've told me yourself that you know the origin of such tricks. But they, or we, do not know the secret of your illusions.'

As he finished speaking Deniau looked briefly in her direction, as though trying to gauge her reaction. It was no longer the complicit, amused look he had exchanged with her in the past but the appraising stare of a participant in discussion. And in that moment she remembered the closed door of last night's reverie. Was it possible that the attraction she assumed they both felt was, for him, part of his plan to make her his ally?

Lambert, his confidence restored by Deniau's remarks, now turned to Dufour. 'Tell me, Lieutenant – this marabout, Bou-Aziz – you know him well. What sort of man is he?'

'Well, first of all he is, perhaps, sixty years of age. His wife is dead and he lives with his daughter Taalith, who is herself a saintly woman and his interpreter because in her youth she learned our language. Bou-Aziz is not war-like, rather, I should say he is a scholar, a peacemaker, who works to prevent acts of violence within the Kabyle community. I have seen him, at the risk of his life, step between two men who were about to kill each other. At sight of him their swords are lowered and peace is made. What is also relevant is his background. Traditionally, the Mahdi will come from the South, from the Sahara, as does Bou-Aziz. And when he proclaims himself the Madhi, he will take the name Muhammad b. 'Abd Allah. All of the would-be Mahdis have used this name. But none has succeeded in ridding the country of us infidels. That's why, even now, with his great prestige, many of the sheikhs doubt that he will be the new saviour of Islam.'

'And, as I told you, every one of them will doubt it when they have seen Henri's performance,' Deniau said.

'And now – ' He turned to Emmeline. 'This lady has not had her breakfast. 'Come with me, Madame. Let us eat and be on our way.'

At that he put his hand on her arm, his fingers increasing then decreasing their pressure on her bare skin in a touch which brought back the ecstasy of last night's reverie. Lambert, Dufour and Captain Hersant followed them to the stone slab on which the food was laid. Jules, Lambert's servant, came forward, offering her a dish of dates. She saw that his hand shook, and that his fair French skin was blistered by the sun. 'How are you, Jules?' she asked. 'Are you not well?'

'I don't know, Madame. I may have a touch of fever.'

'We'll give you tablets for that,' Deniau said. 'Kaddour, fetch my medicine box.'

He turned to her. 'We must take good care of him. He will be needed for the performance.'

The performance. Always, the performance. She watched Deniau open a leather satchel, intent on picking out the tablets from an array of medicines. Again, she had been forgotten. She watched as Kaddour poured water from a pitcher and Jules swallowed the pills. She saw Deniau go over to Lambert, and heard him ask, 'What if your man becomes ill? Will you be able to carry on without him?'

'He is not ill, is he?' Lambert said, alarmed.

'A touch of dysentery, perhaps. Those tablets will help. But, tell me. If you had to, could you manage without him?'

'Absolutely not. I need someone on stage, someone who knows what I am doing and when I will need assistance.'

She saw Deniau lean towards her husband and whisper. Lambert turned and looked back at her. 'No,' he said. 'Let's just hope that your tablets work.'

The road to Milianah was a desert track, monotonous under a burning sun. As the day wore on, Deniau, riding around the fringes of their caravan, kept urging the camel drivers to whip up their beasts, afraid that their party might not arrive before nightfall. And then towards sunset, after a day of Saharan solitude, Emmeline saw coming towards them an extraordinary assemblage of sheep and dromedaries guarded by horsemen armed with long rifles. Other armed men were on foot leading the dromedaries, some of which were loaded with folded tents made of animal skins wrapped around long tent poles, others swaying under the weight of huge brown-and-white-striped sacks which, Hersant told her, contained the furniture and provisions of these nomadic people. But it was the dromedaries loaded with palanquins which caught her attention, for as they came towards her she saw that the palanquins were closed in front with a black cloth which was suddenly drawn aside to reveal women and children, laughing and chattering excitedly as they pointed to her, the children waving as though she were one of them. The women, of all ages but mostly young, were unveiled. Many of the younger women were handsome. They wore white wool tunics, held at the shoulder by a clasp, belted at the waist and opening on one hip. Their turbans of camel hair were carefully arranged to display long black locks which framed their cheeks. At each movement a multitude of bracelets, some iron, some silver, jangled on their necks and arms. Enclosed in their palanquins peering out at her, they reminded her of actors in a puppet show, exaggerated and vivacious and, as their caravan receded into the desert dust amid a hubbub of bleating sheep, the shouts and crackling whips of the men and the yelping of their pack of starveling dogs, it came to her that she knew no more about this country than on the first day of her arrival and that in a few days, following Deniau's plan, she would be forced to leave Africa, never to see again these people who travelled with all their worldly goods in a few bundles, who daily knelt prostrate in prayer before a god whose decisions, terrible or merciful, were met by them with the acceptance of total faith.

And now, as the nomad caravan disappeared over the horizon, Emmeline heard a sudden shout behind her. Turning, she saw Deniau and Lieutenant Dufour wheel their horses around and leap from the saddles. A riderless horse cantered past her, reins loose over its neck. The camel drivers brought their animals to a kneeling position and it was then that Emmeline saw Jules, lying face down in the sand. Deniau and Kaddour lifted him up and placed him on the back of a camel, where he was supported in a sitting position by one of the camel drivers. His head lolled. She rode over to Lambert who was speaking to Deniau.

'What happened? Did his horse bolt?'

'It's probably the dysentery,' Deniau said. 'I'm afraid he is quite ill.'

'This dysentery,' Lambert said. 'What form does it take?'

'Generally, it moves towards a crisis,' Deniau said. 'If it's what I think it is, the crisis comes within three days. Or, if it is less severe, in seven days.'

Lambert turned to her and with a slight movement of his head indicated that she should follow him. As they rode side by side, he said, 'Now what? What am I going to do?'

'What do you mean?'

'The performance is the day after tomorrow. These sheikhs and marabouts are coming from all over Algeria. We can't postpone it.'

'But what Jules does is not so difficult,' she said. 'Someone else could help you.'

'Who?'

'I don't know. Ask Deniau. He'll find someone.'

'He suggested you,' Lambert said. 'He said you would be the perfect person. If it was one of his men it would not have the same effect. Besides, how can I train a stupid soldier in less than two days? Darling, you've seen me perform. I can show you what to do. And as you know, if I succeed we'll save thousands of lives.'

She stared ahead at the camels, their rumps bobbing up and down, their large splayed feet delicately picking their way through the trackless sands. It was Deniau who told him to ask me. Deniau has convinced him that I'm the one he must use. Deniau who uses him, who uses me, with compliments and flattery. Deniau is the magician. We are his marionettes.

She saw her husband whip his horse to make it keep pace with hers. When she ignored his presence, he said quietly, 'Darling, you know I wouldn't ask you if it weren't important.'

Angry, she stared ahead. At last, she said, 'Deniau always has his way, doesn't he? All right. Tell him I'll do it.'

As she knew he would, Lambert chose to ignore her anger. 'Thank you, darling. Thank you! With your help, I know I won't fail.'

Minutes later, the roofs and minarets of a small city came into view and as they came closer Emmeline saw underneath its walls a profusion of tents spread out to form a sprawling nomadic encampment. As they made their way through this crowded staging ground it became evident that these were the separate camps of different sheikhs, each with its tents drawn up in a circle to protect an inner corral of sheep, chickens, camels and horses from robbers and roving packs of dogs. Here and there among the drab goatskin shelters, stately circular tents rose up, topped with pelmets in bright colours, outside which men wearing the richly embroidered waistcoats and high yellow boots of caids sat in conversation, drinking small cups of coffee and passing around a communal pipe. Lieutenant Dufour, riding slightly ahead of Emmeline, reined back to answer her question.

'The most elaborate tents belong to the marabouts. They are always the most impressive. But as you can see, Madame, sheikhs and caids have come from all over Algeria to witness your husband's miracles. So many of them that Milianah cannot possibly hold them.'

'But what about the performance?' Lambert asked. 'Surely we will have to limit the size of the audience?'

'Of course. We have invited only the marabouts, the leading sheikhs and their relatives. To compensate for this we have arranged a series of banquets and receptions for those who have been excluded. But I must tell you that in the last few days the sheikhs have entertained us on a scale we could never match. There have been horse and camel races, displays of hunting skills, feats of daring, even military exercises. Arabs and Kabyles have that in common: they love such shows. Oh, by the way, the *Bureau Arabe* is giving a banquet tonight.'

Dufour looked at Emmeline. 'Men only, I regret to say.'

Emmeline smiled. 'I am delighted to hear it.'

The French fort at Milianah was situated in the heart of the town, a three-storey building looming high above the warren of enclosed Arab dwellings. The walls and buildings of the fort enclosed a large military parade ground. Emmeline, looking down from her third-floor bedroom window, saw, in it, a scene of frantic activity as French soldiers laboured to build tiers of seating which would transform the square into an auditorium. In the centre, carpenters had already erected a stage some ten feet above the ground. On the left side of the stage an impromptu dressing room had been constructed with adjoining wings so that Lambert could appear and retire from sight, as in a normal theatre. Earlier, on their arrival, Lambert had accompanied Jules to the military sick bay and now in the moment before the sudden desert night, she saw him come from the sick bay, cross the square and climb up on to the makeshift stage, inspecting the floorboards, checking on the hidden space beneath the stage where his electrical devices would be placed. He had already told her that tomorrow morning she must be ready to run through at least two rehearsals so that there would be no hitch. The electrical switches which she would manipulate were simple levers but the timing must be accurate.

'However, there's no need for you to worry, my darling. You will be letter perfect when I begin my performance. By the way, Captain Hersant told me he is arranging that supper be sent up to your room tonight. They expect the banquet will continue to a latish hour. I'll try not to disturb you when I come in. I want you to have a good night's sleep.'

Dawn, extinguishing the night's stars, rose red in the sky to reveal like the horizon of a faraway ocean the desert hills surrounding the city of Milianah. Emmeline, already dressed, looked down into the courtyard of the *Bureau Arabe*'s fort where a young French corporal unbolted the door of the infirmary and brought out slop pails which he emptied into a gutter. *Jules.* Jules who, were she at home, would be coming upstairs with their breakfast, now lay behind that infirmary door.

She looked back into the room where her husband slept, then, carrying her shoes so that she would not wake him, slipped out of their apartment and went down the stone staircase, hurrying past the new grandstands and stage assembled for the forthcoming performance. As she walked across the sand-dusted flagstones, the sun, freed of its red beginnings, shone with a clear golden light. From the ramparts above a bugle blared the sound of reveille. And then like an echo in its dying music she heard an older summons: from the towers of the city's mosques, the call to prayer.

When she entered the shadows of the infirmary, the young corporal she had seen earlier came towards her, his forage cap pushed back on his forehead, his uniform concealed by a long white apron, his arms bare, and wet from washing. 'Madame? For Monsieur Guillaumin, yes? He's in here.'

He led her down a corridor past a small ward where six soldier patients lay sleeping and into a long narrow room marked *Isolation Ward.* There were two beds in this room but only one was occupied. Over the backs of each bed was a shelf holding a tin mug and a white spittoon, and above these objects, thumb-tacked to the wall, a printed notice:

> *Milianah Military Hospital*
> *Rules for Health Service*
> *Civilian patients subject*
> *to disciplinary measures*

In the occupied bed Jules turned to face her, his eyes at first glazed as though he could not see. But then, suddenly, he struggled to sit up. 'Madame? Madame? Where is Monsieur? I must speak to him.'

His dark hair, wet with sweat, fell across his brow in black stripes, as though some unseen painter had tried to erase the face of the Jules she knew. She went to his bed, took his hand and held it in hers. In all the years he had worked for her and her husband she had never touched his hand except by accident. And now, when the corporal said the name *Guillaumin* she had not known at first that he meant Jules. Holding his wet and fevered hand, trying to think of words to comfort him, she was filled with shame. I am holding the hand of someone who brings my meals, orders my carriage, helps me in running the house and assists Henri in his work, someone who has lived for years under our roof, and yet, stricken with fever because we brought him here, he remains someone I do not know.

'You mustn't worry, Jules,' she told him. 'Lieutenant Dufour says your illness will pass. In a few days when Monsieur has given his performance and you're feeling well again we will go home.'

'But how can he?' Jules lay back as though the effort to speak had exhausted him. 'Who will work the levers? Who will know what he must be served and when?'

'I'll do it. You mustn't think of that. Rest now and get well.'

He closed his eyes as though to sleep but his hand gripped hers with sudden force. 'Madame! I could die here. If I do, promise me you'll bring my body back to France. Promise me I won't be buried in these sands?'

'You are not going to die.'

'How can you say that, Madame? You don't know. Promise me? Please?'

She looked at his imploring eyes. 'Yes, yes. I promise.'

His hand went slack, releasing hers. The young corporal standing by the door nodded to her to follow him. They went outside.

'This illness,' she said. 'Is it contagious? Why is he in the isolation ward?'

'It could be. But he's there because it's where we put the ones who might die in the night. If the other patients wake in the morning and see a corpse – ' The corporal shrugged.

'So he might die?'

'Yes, of course. We must wait and see.'

'But he – are the tablets working –?'

'You must speak to the doctor, Madame. He's not here at present.'

She went out into the sunlight of the courtyard. Soldiers were beginning to assemble the last tiers of seating. On the stage, army carpenters were erecting the wings to which she and Lambert could retire at certain parts of the performance. Seeing her, the sergeant in charge of this work invited her to join his men for coffee and a slice of the flat Arab bread. 'Monsieur will be here shortly,' the sergeant told her. 'Everything is ready as he requested.'

As she sat drinking coffee from a tin mug Emmeline saw, through the main archway of the fort, a commotion of camels in the streets outside. She watched their drivers make them kneel by tapping them with sticks just below the knees. Other drivers shouted to each other over a sea of camel backs, the camels' heads swaying this way and that, as swollen packs, planks, canteens, and crates bearing Arabic lettering were unloaded and heaped in large bundles on the flagstones.

And then, suddenly, the shouting ceased. The drivers stood silent beside the grey and brown flanks of their animals as a small troop of Arab riders cantered past, clearing the way for two horsemen who now moved slowly up the street. On the leading horse, a tall, thin, white-bearded man, dressed in green silken robes, his head high-turbaned in the manner of a marabout. Behind him a younger rider, wearing a grey burnous. This rider, passing the courtyard where Emmeline sat, turned to look in at her. Despite the burnous and the male pose astride in the saddle, the rider was a woman, small and frail, her face wasted as if from years of fasting.

The sergeant foreman, sitting near Emmeline, rose and ran to peer through the archway. The camel drivers, no longer silent, called out to each other excitedly as the riders and their escort disappeared from sight. The sergeant came back from the archway, nodding his head. 'I was right,' he said, to no one in particular. 'The marabout has come. Our Colonel will be pleased.' He looked at Emmeline. 'And Monsieur Lambert, he will be pleased, very pleased. Eh, Madame?'

'So that's Bou-Aziz,' she said. 'The man in green?'

'Yes, Madame. The woman is his daughter.'

Some minutes later Lambert appeared in the courtyard. He had already been informed of the marabout's arrival. Emmeline saw that this news made him nervous and as he began to instruct her in her duties he was demanding and censorious, making her repeat over and over again each simple task such as handing him the cornucopia, passing out the bouquets and other gifts, helping him move the table to centre stage, sweeping aside the plumes he scattered on the ground. None of these tasks seemed to her to be difficult and she felt a vague irritation when asked to repeat them. But when it came to the levers that controlled the electric charge in the heavy box, she was suddenly unsure. 'The timing is everything,' Lambert told her. 'You will be in the wings, invisible, forgotten. My signals will not be seen by anyone but you. You must react immediately, both by turning on the charge to anchor the box, releasing the charge, and above all, turning this knob at the end of the demonstration to give the subject an electric shock. You must make sure that the shock continues for exactly thirty seconds. Watch the clock on top of the charging apparatus. Don't look at what is happening on stage. Ignore him if he cries out. Just watch the clock. Thirty seconds, no more, no less. That gives the audience just enough time to see his pain.'

'But it's so cruel. I don't know if I can do it.'

'Have you ever seen men killed in a war? Killed by bullets, cannon balls, trampled by horses, buried in mass graves. Or taken captive, beaten, starved? That's what I'm trying to prevent. We're talking of the deaths of French boys, conscripts, sent out here to do their duty. Thirty seconds of an electric shock which leaves no after-effects. Please, Emmeline!'

'I wish you could find someone else?'

'You know I can't. And we promised Deniau, remember?'

'Deniau! Always Deniau!'

'What do you mean?' he said. 'Deniau didn't make me come here, I *wanted* to come. And now that I'm here, now that I have this chance to save thousands of lives, is it going to come to nothing because you refuse to help me? My God, Emmeline! Besides, this performance won't be like any I've done before. For the first time in my life I'm afraid. What if something goes wrong? Everything I do on stage depends on skill, timing, and above all in my ability to hold an audience. This audience! Arabs, savages! I need you, don't you understand, I don't want some stupid soldier bungling everything. You will be wonderful, you will be letter perfect by tomorrow evening, I promise you. All right?'

She nodded. It was always the same. He was the man, he was in charge.

He came to her then and kissed her cheek. 'Thank you, my darling. Forgive me for asking you to do this. But, remember. I ask it for the sake of our country.'

'Our country?' she said. 'And what of this country?'

'This country?' He looked perplexed.

'Nothing.'

Deniau came down into the courtyard, shortly before four, watching as Lambert rehearsed his and Emmeline's performance, for the eighth time. When Lambert had finished Deniau applauded, then vaulted on to the stage and kissed Emmeline's hand, congratulating her. 'Wonderful! No magician in history has had so beautiful a foil. And now I want to ask one last favour of you, dear Madame. As Bou-Aziz has already arrived, we are planning a dinner for him this evening and we very much hope you will attend.'

'I thought your banquets were for men only?'

'The marabout's daughter will be present. She accompanies him to almost every function. I think it's fitting that you should represent us as *our* marabout's wife.'

'So I am to meet Bou-Aziz before the performance?' Lambert said. 'I wonder is that wise?'

'I'm afraid we have little choice,' Deniau said. 'When I invited him to dine with us, he at once said he would be honoured to break bread with Monsieur Lambert. So, of course I assured him that you, too, would be honoured. And we've discovered that this will be the first time that he dines in the French manner. It will be a new experience for everyone.'

The commandant of the Milianah headquarters was a Captain Raoult, who normally would be their host for the evening. But Deniau as chief of the *Bureau Arabe* obviously took precedence and so, that evening, he stood surrounded by his subordinates, welcoming a group of some twenty sheikhs, marabouts and civic leaders as they filed into the dining hall of the fort.

When Emmeline and Lambert arrived Deniau whispered to her husband, 'He's not here yet. Stay by me. You shall be the first to be presented.'

As they awaited the arrival of Bou-Aziz, the sheikhs and marabouts gossiped and looked around in a manner which reminded Emmeline of those days, a few weeks past, when the company had assembled in the *grande salle des fêtes* to await the arrival of Emperor Napoleon and his consort.

Deniau, as host, exuded the same confident watchfulness as the First Chamberlain at Compiègne and when at last, amid a hushed murmur of anticipation, the marabout and his daughter entered the room, Deniau went to them, spoke some Arabic words of welcome, then, turning to Lambert, presented him to Bou-Aziz. The marabout bowed slightly to Lambert then said something which his daughter now translated, speaking an excellent French. 'My father welcomes you and your wife and asks God's blessing on you.'

As the marabout's daughter said this, Bou-Aziz, tall and stooped, turned to Emmeline with a gentle smile as though waiting for her to speak. *What should she answer?* She felt herself blush as she turned to the marabout's daughter and said, 'We are honoured. We thank him.'

The marabout smiled again and turned to a group of sheikhs who came to greet him. Deniau, pleased, moved close to Emmeline, saying softly, 'An excellent beginning, my dear. Thank you.'

And then, to her dismay, Deniau pointed to the dining table. 'You will sit there, in the centre, on his right. His daughter will sit on his left. It will be a surprise for him to sit between two ladies. That is not the Arab custom. But here, as he will see, we are in France.'

With that he approached the marabout's daughter, taking her arm, leading her to a place at the centre of the table, and with a wave of his hand indicating to Emmeline that she should now sit in the place allotted her. When both she and the marabout's daughter were seated, Deniau approached the marabout, and smiling led him to a seat between them. Emmeline saw the marabout hesitate, as though afraid that a mistake had been made. But when he at last sat down, tucking the skirts of his green robe under him, his daughter turned to Deniau with a smile. 'I have told my father that tonight we dine in the French manner. This will be new for him. To sit with ladies!'

'But if he wishes – ' Deniau began.

'No, no, he wishes that everything be done as you would do it in your own country. And he has asked me to tell you that neither he nor any of our countrymen will be offended if you serve wine to those who desire it.'

'That is most gracious,' Deniau said. Emmeline saw him turn to the marabout and say something in Arabic. The marabout answered with a gentle smile then smiled at Lambert who had been seated, also in the centre, facing Bou-Aziz across the table.

And now, temporarily released from the need to make conversation, she could watch the theatre of this evening. The dinner prepared by the commandant's cook was a succession of the most sought-after Arab dishes, but served on a tablecloth with porcelain plates, crystal glassware and silver cutlery. The marabout picked up a fork and, watching his hosts, awkwardly emulated their example. He and the other marabouts and sheikhs drank only water or goat's milk. He spoke little, his few remarks mainly answers to questions put to him in Arabic by Deniau and Hersant. But as the second dish of couscous was served he turned to his daughter, gesticulating in the direction of Lambert. 'My father gives you his apologies and begs you to forgive him. He did not understand when you were presented to him earlier that you are the great French marabout in whose honour he has come to Milianah. He has heard of the miracles you performed in the mosque of Algiers. Allah has blessed you.'

'Tell your father that I thank him for his good wishes,' Lambert said. 'But I performed my miracles in a theatre in the Rue Bat-Azoun, not in a mosque.'

The marabout, smiling, put up his hands as if in self-defence. His daughter told them, 'My father lives here. He has never been in a theatre. He does not know the word. He has been told that you perform your miracles as an act of worship and in a holy place.'

'I wonder who can have told him that?' Lambert said, turning to Deniau as if for assistance. Deniau at once began an explanation in Arabic, speaking urgently to Bou-Aziz, without bothering to translate for Lambert's benefit.

Emmeline saw at once that this angered her husband who, reaching across the table, touched the arm of the marabout's daughter and said loudly, 'Tell your father that I can perform my miracles in any place and at any time. Tomorrow, as he will see, I shall do my work in the open air.'

The marabout bent forward, listening as his daughter translated, then speaking softly, slowly, as if pondering his words.

'My father says that you are right. It does not matter if we worship God in mosques, in the market square, or in the lostness of the desert sands. It is the act of worship that links us to God. Your miracles, I am told, are wonderful to behold. You are blessed in that you can in this manner bear testimony to God's greatness. Tomorrow, through them, He will be praised.'

The marabout then turned to Deniau and spoke in a low voice. Emmeline saw that he seemed weary, his head nodding, as though he were in pain, his left hand agitatedly fingering a string of prayer beads draped around his neck. She looked across him at his plain, patient daughter. 'Is your father ill?'

'No, Madame. But he is asking permission to retire. It will soon be the hour of the fifth prayer, the prayer at darkness. We must leave now.'

Bou-Aziz rose and said something to the other guests. Heads nodded, sheikhs and the other marabouts stood, bowing, murmuring what Emmeline guessed were words of farewell. Bou-Aziz, bowing in turn to Emmeline and Lambert, then went to the door of the dining room accompanied by Deniau. When he left, Emmeline saw the sheikhs gather together in a sudden heated discussion.

After some minutes, Deniau, who seemed to eavesdrop on

their conversation, walked over to Lambert and said, 'They're worried. Tonight, Bou-Aziz did not inspire confidence. I suspect that after tomorrow, if all goes well, *you* will be the great marabout.'

In her dream that night she wore, not the long grey dress which Lambert had decided she should wear on stage, but stood naked, her only covering Jules' black-and-gold-striped valet's vest, open to show her breasts. Facing her in the dream was a wall of Arab faces, male, bearded, inscrutable, watching, as she bent to pick up the plumes which her husband had pulled from the cornucopia and scattered on the floor. And now in the dream she must turn her back on these faces, bending down to expose the nakedness of her buttocks to their view. She woke, sweating in the cold desert night. Her husband lay, seemingly asleep on his couch across the room. She rose and went out on to the balcony overlooking the barrack square and the makeshift stage in its centre. She looked across the square to the infirmary where a solitary light burned in a window. Was that Jules' room?

Suddenly, behind her, Lambert's voice. 'Can't you sleep, my darling?'

She turned. He stood facing her in the moonlight, incongruous in his hair net.

'I had a bad dream,' she said.

'Oh? What was that?'

'I was naked on the stage in front of the Arabs, wearing only a servant's vest.'

'Stage fright,' he said and laughed as though he had made a joke. 'It happens to every performer. But you'll not be naked, far from it. In fact, I've been meaning to tell you. Charles thinks it would be a good idea if you appeared on stage wearing a veil in the Arab fashion. Some of the sheikhs are very conservative. Any woman, even a foreigner, appearing unveiled, offends their eyes. Besides as my assistant you're merely part of the scenery. The audience watches me and only me.'

She stared at him. *Charles.* Charles thinks . . . Again, Deniau, using us like puppets.

'And why wasn't I told this before?'

'Told what, my darling?'

'The veil. Surely he should have asked my opinion?'

'But why? Don't you want to wear a veil? I thought you'd be pleased. I know you hate to make a show in public.'

'That's not the point. I thought *you* were the magician. Is it your performance or is it his?'

'What are you talking about? I don't understand.'

'Nothing. It doesn't matter. How is Jules? Did you visit him tonight?'

'No, but I spoke to his doctor. The fever hasn't broken yet. Let's go inside, shall we? It's cold out here.'

She felt his hand on her shoulder but did not turn round.

'I'll come in a moment. I need the air.'

She heard him pad across the floor in his loose felt slippers. Outside the walls of the fort, a pariah dog howled provoking a brief barking chorus of response. Into her mind came an image of the Emperor, his long waxed moustaches, his satyr's pointed beard, his hand, languid, holding a half-smoked cigar. '*In the spring I will complete our conquest of the entire country.*'

TEN

Noon. In the city's mosques, in the enclosed courtyards of private dwellings, in dark alleys, in narrow lanes, and, outside the walls of Milianah throughout the great encampment of tents and huts, men covered their heads, removed their shoes, unrolled carpets and rugs, prostrating themselves in prayer. In the barracks square of the French fort, the Kabyle workers who had erected the stands, ignoring Lambert, Emmeline and Deniau who stood under the shaded arches of the square, knelt in unison, heads turned towards Mecca, murmuring their prayers as though each were alone with God. Emmeline, as always moved by this devotion, turned to Deniau and asked, 'I have been wondering. What is it they are saying?'

'The prayer? It's from the Koran,' Deniau said, seeming pleased to display his knowledge. 'It says, "Praise be to God, the Lord of the worlds, the merciful, the compassionate, the ruler of the Judgement Day. Thee we serve and Thee we ask for aid. Guide us in the right path, the path of those who are gracious: not of those with whom Thou art angry, not of those who err." I suppose you could call it their version of the Lord's Prayer. Not very different, is it?'

'I think it is,' Emmeline said. Both men looked at her, as if surprised that she would have an opinion.

'Oh?' Deniau said. 'In what way?'

'They don't ask for favours, for daily bread, for forgiveness of trespasses, deliverance from temptation and evil. All they ask is God's help to guide them in the right path. Isn't that what all of us should ask?'

'Dear Madame!' Deniau said, smiling in amusement. 'You

constantly amaze me. And now . . .' He opened his briefcase, taking from it a white cotton headdress and a veil of white lace which he handed to her. 'Here is your Muslim disguise. I tried to find a pretty veil. Now Henri, we will start to seat the various sheikhs and goumier companies shortly after one. Bou-Aziz and his attendants will be the last to arrive. When he is seated I will begin my introduction. You will appear only after I finish. I would like you to walk past the ranks of sheikhs and marabouts ignoring them, and go up on to the stage turning to face the entire audience. Bow and then begin. I think that will be very effective.'

Lambert slid his ivory-tipped baton out of his sleeve with the ease of a master conjurer and touched it to his forehead in a mock salute. 'At your orders, *Mon Commandant.*'

'And I, what shall I do?' Emmeline asked.

'I'm afraid I want you to take up your position hidden in the wings, shortly before one. I know it will be an hour's wait there, alone, behind the stage. I apologize. But it is one way of ensuring that Henri's entrance has the maximum effect.'

'Before we start,' Lambert said, 'I must warn you, Charles, that my performance today will not be as elaborate as that evening in Algiers. We will not perform the trick of having an Arab disappear as Emmeline would not be strong enough to help me carry the table on which he stands. I shall also omit the punch bowl which dispenses supplies of coffee. I have decided that today's performance must hinge on my two most convincing illusions, the heavy box and my invulnerability to bullets. These Kabyles are unsophisticated men of the desert. I suspect that they are not, like an Algiers audience, willing to be entertained. Fear is the weapon I must use on them.'

At one o'clock in the arid midday heat, Emmeline, wearing the long grey dress Lambert had chosen for her and carrying the headdress and veil given her by Deniau, came down from the apartments and, unnoticed by the workmen who were putting the last benches in place at the rear of the square, entered the makeshift room in the wings to the left of the stage. There in a corner were the electric levers she must pull, the cornucopia she must hand to her husband, the feather plumes he would scatter on the floor for her to pick up, the bonbons and favours which she must offer to the audience. She sat at a small mirror, first covering her hair with the headdress, then fitting the veil over her face so that only her eyes and forehead were visible. When she had done this a masked Arab woman stared at her through the mirror as though by this simple act of disguise Emmeline Lambert was no more. Minutes later, from the streets outside, she heard the clatter of horses' hooves, the shouted cries of camel drivers, the distant firecracker sound of rifles. Turning to look through the slats of the dressing room she saw the first of the Arab companies arriving in the square of the fort. An unseen French military band struck up a martial air as below her vantage point a colourful mass of Arab men, wearing white, red or blue burnouses, many carrying old-fashioned rifles, some with swords and daggers, came strolling through the aisles where French soldiers and a handful of interpreters waited to show them to their seats. There were no women in this audience. She looked again at the veiled female in the mirror. She looked at the levers, those black handles which she must pull to inflict pain. Today, Henri depends on me. He will not forgive me if I fail.

Time passed. The music changed, the military band switching to operetta airs. Suddenly the music faltered, trailing off as a hubbub of voices rose from the packed benches below. Emmeline, rising from her seat, peered through the peep hole at the side of the wings. Slowly, bowing this way and that, in humble acknowledgement of the greetings and salutations offered him from every side, Bou-Aziz came down the centre aisle on the arm of his daughter. Ahead, Deniau, wearing decorations and sword, stood below the stage, waiting to show the marabout to his place in the front row. As soon as Bou-Aziz had taken his seat, Deniau signalled to the conductor of the military orchestra. A roll of drums and a fanfare of trumpets were followed by the strains of '*La Marseillaise*'. Deniau raised his arm over his head for attention. 'Today, to the sands of the Sahara, to the fiefdom of the Kabyles, comes the greatest marabout in all of France. I give you Henri Lambert.'

Emmeline did not see her husband come down the aisle because on his instructions she must now move into the wings. When she reached the place where he had told her to stand she saw that he was already on stage. He bowed to the audience, a signal that she should appear. She stepped out into the sunlight and walked to the table at the rear of the stage taking up the top hat that sat there. Coming downstage she handed it to Lambert, then retreated, continuing to face the audience as Jules did when assisting his master. Now, Lambert, his back to her, wearing not his usual frock coat, cravat and linen waistcoat but dressed as though for a boating excursion on the Seine, in an open-necked white shirt and trousers, passed his ivory-tipped baton over the hat and reaching into it produced, in turn, three heavy cannon balls which he dropped with a thump on to the stage floor. As in Algiers this opening gambit at once fixed the attention of his audience. They watched in awed silence as again he reached into the hat and this time pulled out two doves which he let fly up into the arid desert sky. This was, she knew, the signal for her to bring him the papier-mâché cornucopia which he accepted without deigning to notice her presence. He opened its side hinge to demonstrate to the audience that it was empty. He closed it, then turned it upside down, spilling out a dozen bonbons, and other small favours which she must crouch to pick up and offer to the audience. But when, trembling, nervous, uncertain, she advanced to the front of the stage and handed the favours to interpreters who at once offered them to those in the front rows, Emmeline saw only one face. The marabout, leaning forward, his turban a crown framing his high forehead, his thick grey beard streaked yellow by the desert sun. His eyes, clouded yet intense, closed on Emmeline, locking her in his gaze. Transfixed, she stood, statue-still, as an interpreter took from her hands the last few favours to be distributed among the audience. In that moment she saw, not the marabout she had met last evening, but a face, mysterious and strange as the bruised visage of the crucified Christ imprinted on the shroud of Turin.

Now, in gentle dismissal, the marabout bowed his head, releasing her from the spell of his eyes. She turned back to Lambert who, displaying to his audience the empty cornucopia, passed his baton over it then drew from it with agile conjurer's fingers first, one feather plume, then many, scattering them at her feet on the stage floor. And now as she began to scoop them up and place them in a basket, Lambert, stepping down from the stage, went among the front rows of the audience, plucking from the ear of one sheikh an egg, from the nose of another a five-franc coin. He picked up an empty slipper which one of the sheikhs had cast off and holding it aloft suddenly showed that it was filled with five-franc coins which he tossed out among the spectators. This manoeuvre seemed to delight the audience who cried out, '*Douros!*' which the interpreters translated as a request for more five-franc pieces. Lambert, carefully avoiding the place where Bou-Aziz and his daughter were seated, then walked, smiling, along the aisle, producing again and again '*Douros*' from the noses and ears of the astonished audience. This manoeuvre eventually brought him back to the steps from which he had stepped down. There, he held up his baton to still the cries and applause.

At last, when there was silence, he re-mounted the stage, turning to face the audience. He glanced briefly at Emmeline, reminding her that this was the moment when she should retire. She, her arms full of the feather plumes, still confused and moved by her encounter with the marabout, was slow to respond to Lambert's covert signal. As she went past him, he whispered angrily, 'Be ready!' then walked to the rear and took from a table the small, solidly built wooden box adorned with iron handles. Holding it lightly in one hand he came back to the centre of the stage.

And now Emmeline heard him begin to give the speech he had given in Algiers, boasting that: 'Through the powers granted me by the Almighty I will show you that I can deprive the strongest man of his strength and restore that strength at my will. I ask anyone who thinks himself strong enough to try this experiment to come forward now.'

On hearing this, she abruptly dropped the bundle of feathers and went shakily towards the black levers. A young Kabyle chieftain, his fair hair worn long, a small Greek cross tattooed between his eyes, mounted the stage.

Lambert bowed in welcome and asked, 'Are you very strong?'

Smiling, the chieftain nodded.

'You are wrong. In an instant I will rob you of your strength. You will become as weak as a woman.'

In Algiers, Emmeline remembered, her husband had said 'as weak as a little child', and the audience had reacted with amusement. But here, when his remark was translated, the word 'woman' seemed filled with insult. In the packed benches which filled the square there was a sudden hostile silence. But the Kabyle chieftain did not seem offended. He smiled, shrugged his shoulders and gestured towards Lambert as if asking him to continue.

'Now,' Lambert said. 'Lift this box.'

The young man bent and easily picked up the box, balancing it in one hand as Lambert had done earlier. He looked at the magician and again shrugged his shoulders.

'Put it down, please,' Lambert said.

The young man put down the box at Lambert's feet. Lambert raised his hands making a pass in front of the young man's face. He paused, then looked out at the audience. 'From this moment on, he will be weak as a woman.'

He turned to the young chieftain. 'Now. Try to lift the box.'

As he spoke, Lambert looked past the chieftain, staring into the wings in a pre-arranged signal. Emmeline, jerky as an automaton, at once pulled back the first of the black levers. The young man reached down, took hold of the box by its iron handles and gave it a savage tug. But the box, held by the magnetic force of the lever, did not move.

The young chieftain straightened up, panting, half turning

in Emmeline's direction. Although she knew he could not see her she felt herself stiffen and draw back from his gaze. Beads of sweat on his forehead moistened the tiny cross tattooed between his eyes, eyes which now, in bewilderment, stared into the darkness in which she hid.

From the benches in the square, half a dozen men rose to their feet. The young chieftain nodded and waved to them as if to say he understood. Bending down he tried again, shifting his feet as he straddled the box, straining and straining until, at last, defeated, he let go of the handles.

Lambert stood, tapping his ivory-tipped baton against his trouser leg, like an animal trainer about to signal a new trick.

'Now. One last try?' he said.

The interpreter repeated his words in Arabic, whereupon four or five Kabyle leaders rose again from their seats, urging the young chieftain not to give up. Emmeline, distracted by their cries, looked out at the audience, something that Lambert had forbidden her to do. In the front row, Bou-Aziz sat quietly with his daughter, his gaze fixed not on the chieftain but on Lambert himself. Emmeline, nervous, looked out at her husband, just in time to see him give her his second covert command.

The young man bent once again and took hold of the trunk's iron handles. Trembling, closing her eyes as though it were she who would suffer the pain, Emmeline pulled down the second black lever. Above it was the clock with which she would measure the thirty seconds of agony. The young chieftain, his hands suddenly glued to the box, trembled violently but, despite the shock of electricity which surged through his body, he did not cry out. Her eyes blurred with tears. Convulsively, she reached for the lever to shut off the current but remembering her husband's strict injunction at the last moment she waited, looking out at the stage. Lambert, whose timing was impeccable, moved forward at the precise moment that the clock's second hand registered a thirty-second advance. She pulled the lever. Lambert waved his baton over the box. The young chieftain, released from the current, his face still contorted in pain, stood swaying unsteadily, staring at the sorcerer.

Emmeline had been told by Lambert that if the victim was still in shock from the electricity it was her duty to come on stage and help him back to his seat. Now, with a tiny gesture, Lambert summoned her to re-appear. But when she stepped out into the cruel sunlight and went towards the Kabyle, putting her hand on his arm, he turned, as if struck, and shook her off. In the silence which had come down like a cloud on the audience, the young Kabyle went to the edge of the stage and, ignoring the steps, jumped down on to the sand, falling as he landed, almost at the feet of Bou-Aziz. The marabout rose, lifted him up and putting his hands on the young chieftain's face, said something which no one except the young man heard. The young chieftain then took the marabout's hand and kissed it. Together they went to the marabout's bench where Bou-Aziz's daughter moved aside to make room for them to sit together.

While this took place Lambert stood, looking straight ahead at the tricolour which flew on the ramparts of the fort. Emmeline, as instructed, moved back into the wings to wait for his next command. In the shadows, standing beside the levers, she pulled aside the covering of the peep hole and, filled with shame, looked down at the place where Bou-Aziz sat, his face grave and still, eyes clouded, withdrawn as in a state of trance. Beside him, the young Kabyle chieftain seemed recovered and at peace, while behind them, sheikhs and marabouts turned to each other, whispering uneasily, fingering their beads and staring from time to time at the enigmatic, quietly alarming figure on stage.

Lambert, master of his audience, knew the precise moment when he must resume. In a pre-arranged signal, he held up his ivory-tipped baton as if to examine it. At this, on cue, Colonel Deniau rose from his seat and came to the steps below the stage, turning to face the audience. He spoke in Arabic.

'What is spiritual power? The Koran tells us it is a gift that Allah grants to holy men and women in gratitude for their devotion. It is the gift of miracles, the gift of lifting the curse from a woman who was barren, of delivering from his enemies a prisoner who was in chains, of cooling the bullet wounds of the injured and, the greatest gift of all, the gift that makes men in battle invulnerable to the bullets of an enemy. This last gift, you have been told, will be granted to the Mahdi, the chosen one of God, who will lead your armies to victory over us. But what marabout has this gift? What marabout has proved it before your very eyes?

'I say no one. No Mahdi has risen among you. But here on this day, our marabout will show that he, guided by God, has been granted this power.'

Emmeline, standing in the shadows, heard this, her cue. She picked up the morocco-leather case containing the two cavalry pistols which her husband used in his performance, and came out at the rear of the stage.

Lambert, who had been standing at the centre of the stage, now walked towards the audience. He paused, his eyes searching among the massed faces in a way which held their attention. Then, speaking quietly, he said, 'As I have demonstrated in Algiers I am invulnerable because I possess a talisman which protects me from all harm. No marksman can injure or kill me.' He now looked down directly at Bou-Aziz. 'Bou-Aziz, I ask your help to prove my claim.'

Emmeline saw the marabout look up at her husband and again felt the strange attraction of his gaze. He spoke in Arabic to his daughter, who said, 'My father does not kill.'

At that, a tall heavily built Kabyle sheikh wearing an ochre burnous stood and walked towards the steps leading to the stage. He spoke in a slow guttural French. 'You wish to be killed? I will help you.'

Lambert signalled him to mount the stage. When he did, Lambert turned back to Emmeline, gesturing to her to come forward. Obedient, she opened the pistol case as he had taught her to do and showed the two cavalry pistols to the audience. She then went up to Lambert who took one of the pistols from the case and offered it to the Kabyle sheikh.

But the sheikh shook his head and putting his hands into his burnous pulled from a sash two pistols of a similar type. 'Now, my marabout,' he said. 'Choose one of *my* pistols and we will load it and I will fire at you. You have nothing to fear. You said in Algiers that you possess a talisman which can ward off all blows. Let us see this talisman and witness its power.'

Emmeline, holding the unwanted pistols, waited, confused, watching Lambert who looked directly at the sheikh, then, nodding as in agreement, handed his own pistol back to her. She saw Deniau, sitting in the front row of the audience, rise in his seat, alarmed. And now she knew that the pistols she held had been in some way tampered with and that if her husband failed in this ultimate test of power on which the success of the journey depended, his mission would be aborted and his pride destroyed. She saw Deniau come forward as if to mount the stage and halt the proceedings. But Lambert signalled him to wait.

He turned to the sheikh and reaching into the air produced, as if by magic, the small, many-faceted glass orb, which glittered in the sun.

'This is the talisman you speak of,' he said. 'With it, I am invulnerable. But I have decided not to use it today, when I stand before the marabout Bou-Aziz, who many of you believe is the Mahdi, the chosen one of God. Today I wish to show you that my power is greater than that of any talisman. Take the talisman.'

The Kabyle sheikh reached to take the glass orb offered him. But at once it disappeared from Lambert's hand.

Lambert smiled. 'Look in the fold of your sash,' he said.

The sheikh slid his fingers into his orange silk sash and, astonished, took from it the small glass ball.

'Guard it well,' Lambert said. 'I must explain that to do without the talisman I must now retire and spend six hours in prayer. Tomorrow morning, if you will permit me, I will return to this place and prove to you that I am invulnerable, even without my talisman. It will be proven when you fire your pistol directly at my heart in the presence of these sheikhs and marabouts.'

He turned to the audience and addressed himself to Bou-Aziz's daughter. 'Tomorrow, at dawn, I shall be ready. Will you ask your father to do me the honour of attending?'

Touching her father's arm, Bou-Aziz's daughter spoke to him

in a low voice. At that, Bou-Aziz rose, gathering the folds of his green robe around him. He turned to his daughter who took his arm. In an electric pause, watched anxiously by the Arab and Kabyle leaders, he nodded his head in agreement, then, frail and slow, made his way towards the archway which led out into the streets of Milianah. At once, in a hubbub of talk and movement, the audience began to disperse, glancing back at Lambert who laid down his baton and walked out of sight into the wings. Emmeline followed, still holding the pistol case. She saw that Lambert's face was wet with sweat and that he held his fists at his sides, tightly clenched as though to prevent himself from trembling.

Footsteps sounded on the stage behind her. Deniau greeted her with a nod, then said to Lambert 'What are we going to do now? Couldn't you have persuaded him to use your pistols? No one can see they have been tampered with. Why didn't you try?'

'A magician must honour his promise,' Lambert said. 'Even if it means that tomorrow I will be killed.'

Emmeline saw that Deniau was not concerned for her husband. His voice, his face, showed anger and frustration. 'And if you are killed, everything we've planned will be lost. Tomorrow you must use your own pistols. I will make an announcement. I will say that you have been insulted and that anyone in the audience is free to examine your guns and satisfy himself that they are not false.'

Sweating, tense, Lambert sat on the solitary chair beside the electric levers which controlled the heavy box. He put his head down as though he felt faint, then said, 'I can't go back on my promise. I said I am invulnerable. If I am invulnerable, how can I refuse to use the sheikh's pistol? Charles, I have spent my life before an audience. The audience is like an animal. If you fail to dominate it, it will turn on you. Today by dispensing with my "talisman" I made them feel my power. Now I must prove it. I have a slim chance of doing that, the glimmer of an idea which I must work on before morning.'

'What is this idea?' Deniau asked.

Lambert did not answer. He sat, his head bowed as if deep in thought.

Deniau turned to Emmeline. 'Do *you* know what it is?'

'She knows nothing,' Lambert said. 'Come, Emmeline. We will go back to our rooms now. Bring the pistol case with you.'

'But this idea,' Deniau said. 'If you won't tell me what it is, tell me, at least, how I can help you?'

Lambert forced a smile. 'I must not be disturbed at my "prayers". Make sure of that, will you? Send supper up to our rooms. And remember, if I fail the government of France must provide for my wife. I entrust her to your care, Charles. She will need your help.'

She folded the Arab veil and put it on the mirrored table. Lambert stood, impatient, by the flimsy door of the dressing room which he closed and locked as they went through the wings and out on to the stage. Deniau, who had preceded them, waited at the foot of the steps and now as she followed her husband across the square, going towards the archway which led up to their rooms, Deniau took her arm, delaying her. Lambert did not seem to notice. He walked quickly, not looking back, disappearing into the shadows of the colonnade.

At that, Deniau put his face close to hers and whispered, 'You mustn't let him do this. What if he's killed? It's pride and foolishness. You must make him use his own pistols. Do you realize that by this time tomorrow you could be a widow? Besides, it's not just his reputation that's at stake, it's more than that. Please, help me?'

'Help *you*?'

'I mean . . .' He paused and smiled guiltily. 'I mean, help *him*. Look, you'll be with him now, you must find out what it is he plans to do. I'll come to your rooms later. Perhaps you can slip out for a moment and we can talk?'

'Emmeline? Emmeline?'

She looked up. Lambert stood on the balcony overlooking the courtyard. 'Come along! I need that pistol case!'

'I'm coming.' Ignoring Deniau she hurried under the archway and up the stone steps leading to the second floor of the fort. Her husband was already standing by a table in the sitting room and when she entered he held out his hand for the pistol case and sat down, opening it and removing an object which she did not recognize.

'Fetch me one of those candles,' he said. 'And matches. And pray that this will work.'

'What are you going to do?'

He put the object on the table, then looked up at her. She saw that his face was pale and drawn. 'Something I haven't done before. Dangerous. When I prepare an illusion I rehearse every move over and over again to make sure it's perfect on stage. But tomorrow there will be no rehearsal. I will be working with a savage who wants to kill me and with this.'

He looked again at the object on the table. 'This is an ordinary bullet mould.'

He stood, went to his writing case and took out a card, bending up its four edges to make it into a trough. He then melted down a piece of candle wax and placed it in the trough. He made a sort of lamp black by running the blade of a knife over the candle and mixing the result in with the melted wax which he then poured into the bullet mould. 'This is the difficult part,' he said in a half-whisper as he turned the mould over to allow the portion of the wax which had not yet set run out, leaving a hollow ball in the mould. He did not succeed.

'How many candles do we have?'

She went into the bedroom, counting. 'Seven – no – eight.'

'Good. Bring them here. I will need to practise. I must have a perfect hollow wax ball which looks exactly like a bullet.'

'So there will be a trick,' she said. 'A false bullet?'

He did not answer. He bent over the table, as she had seen him do hundreds of times in his atelier, shut off from her, engrossed, patient, perfecting his art.

'You said there's a danger. You could be killed.'

Again, he did not answer. She sat on the divan, watching him. He could be killed. And for what? Why has it come to this?

'Henri, did you hear me?'

He was now fashioning his third wax bullet. 'It's still not right,' he said, as if to himself. 'But it's better. And with luck and application it will be better still. It must seem like a lead bullet when I hold it up. I must practise – practise. It must be done very naturally, a simple holding up of the bullet so that both the sheikh and the audience can see it. That will be the moment of risk. These desert people have keen eyesight. It must be perfect.'

'What are you talking about? Henri, you've made your fortune. You're famous. You said you wanted to settle down, to live a normal life at home in Tours.' She hesitated, then said, 'I know you want a child. We could try again.'

'Nonsense. That has nothing to do with it.' She looked at him, stunned. *I know you want a child. We could try again.* After all these years, at last I managed to say it, to blurt it out. I never thought I could. When I think of the times I lay awake at night feeling guilty, knowing that it was up to me to urge him to try again. But now when I say it, he doesn't even notice. Doesn't he care about us? What *does* he care about? His career, his fame, his inventions, his 'posterity'.

'Well, what about your inventions? You tell everyone that your mechanical marionettes are the finest ever made. Are you going to ignore all that to play a trick on some African sheikh? Tomorrow morning, you could be killed and for what? To please the Emperor? To help him conquer another part of Africa? Don't you see? Deniau has tricked you into this. But, to be fair to him, even Deniau is telling you to use your own pistols and not risk your life.'

Carefully, he poured the melted wax back into the cardboard trough. It was as though she were not in the room.

'Henri, you say you love me. I know I haven't been everything you wanted, but *do* you? Tell me the truth.'

Now he was decanting the melted wax into the bullet. He

nodded his head, as if remembering something. 'That's it. I can draw blood from my thumb. An English magician showed me how, some years ago when I performed in London. The second bullet filled with blood will have to be more solid than the first one.'

'Henri!'

He looked at her. 'Darling, this has nothing to do with the things you're talking about, the ordinary things, love, marriage, children. I was put on earth for more than that. Perhaps to be here in Africa and tomorrow at dawn to confront this challenge. Because I am Lambert, because I have been given these gifts, I can't refuse it. If I do, shame will dog me for the rest of my life.'

'Shame? Listen to me. Deniau says you'll save lives if you prevent Bou-Aziz from starting a holy war. But next year when our armies arrive in Algeria there'll be war just the same, a war in which thousands of French soldiers will be killed and thousands and thousands of Arabs and Kabyles will die. And for what?'

'It will be a war that France will win,' he said. 'And perhaps in some small way it will be won because of the risk I take tomorrow morning. I may be killed. So be it. It's no more than any French soldier would do for his country.'

He held up the hollow wax bullet and pierced its end with the tip of his knife. Squinting at the tiny orifice, he nodded his head as though agreeing to an invisible suggestion. 'If he fails to kill me, I will use this. It will frighten them. Now, please! Go out, go to the other room, but go away. I must be alone.'

She went out on to the balcony, pushing aside the bead curtain of their quarters, hearing it rustle as it closed behind her. The late afternoon light struck down across the courtyard of the fort, intersecting it, leaving the stage in shadow. She stood swaying slightly, as though her mind had ceased to command her body. Then, aimless, she walked down the stone steps, crossed the square and went out into the narrow streets of Milianah, mingling in the crowd, standing in doorways to allow small trains of camels and mules to pass, then, amid covert glaces from the Arab and Kabyle passersby, wandering among the stalls of an impoverished bazaar, unseeing, lost in painful reverie, not knowing where she was going, or why, her mind returning again and again to those words: *I was put on earth for more than that. More than the ordinary things, love, marriage, children.*

Again hearing his irritated voice as he said it, the voice of someone explaining an obvious fact of life to a stupid girl.

And, I who lay awake night after night in Tours, guilty because I didn't want another miscarriage, or even a healthy child, his child. Tonight I found out the truth. To him, marriage and having a child is something 'ordinary', not to be compared with the triumph of earning a place in history as the magician who brought glory to the Emperor and to France.

Yet why should I judge him? I married him, knowing I didn't love him, I dreamed of making a cuckold of him with Deniau, who's nothing if not his twin in that ambition to rise above 'ordinary things'. Anyway, what do I know about those 'ordinary things'? I never had them.

She walked on, lost among the aisles of the bazaar, ignoring the importuning smiles of stall keepers, their outstretched hands inviting her to inspect their wares. Ahead, a file of loaded camels moved in strange undulations. The cries of their drivers, the smack of whips against the camel hides, the odours of coffee and spices, the small boys running alongside her holding up clusters of dates for sale, the sputtering, sporadic crackling of rifle fire in the distance, all of these sounds, sights, smells, suddenly, inexplicably, filled her with panic. She hurried on, crossing a square, entering the narrow streets of the inner town, a labyrinth of hidden courtyards, closed gates, and blind façades. In these surroundings, so unlike any city, any landscape she had known at home it was as though the Emmeline she had been slipped out from her body, leaving it null. She leaned against an archway, lost.

The African sun fell below the horizon. Night came down like a blind. Slowly, one by one, lights flickered on in the narrow windows of the surrounding dwellings. In desperation, she looked this way and that until at last she saw, high above the roofs of the city, the tower of the French fort. She went towards it, running as to a beacon. As she ran, she wept.

ELEVEN

The Zouave on guard duty at the entrance to the fort went into the guardhouse and told his sergeant, 'The lady has returned.'

'Has she gone to her quarters?'

'No sir. She went into the infirmary.'

At once the sergeant put on his belt and ran out, hurrying up the flight of steps which led to Colonel Deniau's quarters. He found the Colonel, asleep on a divan, wearing a white robe, a volume of poetry lying open on the floor beside him. The smell in the room told the sergeant that *kif* had been smoked. But at once, on hearing the sergeant's news, the Colonel rose, threw off his robe and putting on his dress tunic hurried down to the courtyard. Lights were on in the infirmary. The door was open. An orderly saluted and showed him into the dark night shadows of the isolation ward. The Colonel saw that there were two beds in the room, one occupied, one empty. In the occupied bed he saw Lambert's servant, his face wet with sweat, his eyes wild and terrified in a way which reminded the Colonel of a frightened horse. Sitting on a camp stool by his bedside was Madame Lambert. She had been weeping and was holding the sick man's hand and trying to speak to him. The young corporal in charge of the sick bay stood at the head of the bed, wiping the patient's soaking face with a towel. At sight of the Colonel he came to attention and saluted.

When she saw the corporal salute, Emmeline realized that someone had entered the room. She turned. Deniau at once went to her and put his hand on her shoulder. 'You're back. I was worried for you.'

But she turned away from him, bending over the sick man, saying, 'Jules? Jules? It's Madame. Can you hear me?'

Deniau looked at the corporal. 'Where is the doctor?'

'He was here earlier, sir. He left because Lieutenant Dessault's wife is in labour. Besides . . .' The corporal shook his head.

Again, Deniau touched Emmeline's shoulder. 'I'm afraid he can't hear you.'

But she ignored him, clasping the sick man's hand, saying again, 'Jules, Jules, it's me. Can you hear me?'

An orderly appeared at the door and said to the corporal, 'The priest is here.'

The corporal, again wiping the sick man's brow, said quietly, 'Madame? Madame? The priest is here. Monsieur Guillaumin asked for him earlier today. He will give Monsieur Guillaumin the last rites.'

Emmeline looked up, distraught. A bearded Jesuit monk wearing a robe and sandals stood behind her, carrying a small box containing the viaticum and holy oils. He nodded to her and to the Colonel then, putting down his box, draped a stole around his neck. 'He may wish to confess,' the Jesuit said. 'Will you please leave us?'

She nodded but bent again over the sick man, saying, 'Jules? Jules? I will be back. Can you hear me? I will be back.'

Deniau, waiting, walked with her into the corridor. 'Can I get you something? A drink, something to eat? You haven't had supper.'

She shook her head. 'No. Nothing. But can you find the doctor?'

'The wife of one of our officers is in labour. There is a fear that she might miscarry. So the doctor is with her. But I will speak to him soon. In the meantime, tell me about your husband?'

She looked at him as though she did not understand.

'I mean, how is he getting on with his preparations? I knocked on his door a while ago but there was no answer. And when his supper tray was sent up, he sent it back, untouched.'

'He is trying to make bullets,' she said. 'He says if what he's doing goes wrong he could be killed.'

'False bullets?' Deniau said. 'You must be worried for him. As we all are. But, as you know, he's very resourceful. I wish, though, that we could persuade him to use his own pistols. If anything goes wrong tomorrow, it could be a disaster.'

'A disaster,' she said. 'For you?'

'I'm sorry. I didn't mean . . . I mean, for him, of course.'

'Go away! Leave me alone!'

Deniau, ignoring her anger, said gently, 'I am truly sorry. You misunderstood me. Your husband's life is precious. Let's see what he proposes and if we still think it too dangerous we won't allow him to proceed.'

But she looked past him as though he were not there, then walked back towards the isolation ward. The corporal was waiting outside the closed door.

'Has the priest finished?'

'No, Madame. But he is giving the last rites now. It will not be long.'

Deniau, watching, saw her bow her head. Her body trembled as though she wept.

He turned and went out of the building.

Several minutes later, the Jesuit came from the isolation ward, holding the viaticum box carefully in both hands as though he were about to go up on to an altar. When he saw Emmeline waiting he paused and said, 'Madame Lambert?'

'Yes, Father.'

'He is asking for you.'

She nodded and went in, following the corporal who carried an oil lamp which he placed on the shelf above the sick bed. A harsh yellow light lit the sweat-soaked face of the patient who, now conscious, twisted around under the sheet, and staring up at her, held out his hand, palm upwards like a beggar. For a moment she did not recognize the Jules she knew in this figure with its pinched face, the skin colour eerily bluish, the voice so weak that she could barely hear it. 'Madame, Madame? Do you remember your promise?'

'Yes, of course.'

Seating herself on the camp stool, she took his hand in hers.

The room was filled with the stench of excrement. His breathing was rapid as though he could not get air into his lungs.

Now, in an almost inaudible voice, he asked, 'Where is Monsieur? He didn't come to see me. Is he sick too?'

She closed her eyes in shame. 'No, no. I will bring him to you very soon.'

'He won't come. He's forgotten me, that's all. I know Monsieur, I know him better than you do. He's working. He won't come. Maybe you . . .' Weeping, he did not finish the sentence.

'What is it, Jules? Tell me.'

'Maybe you will speak to him. It's for my wife and my boy. When I am dead, what will happen to them? I have worked for Monsieur for twenty years. Twenty years, Madame. From the beginning, in Paris before he became famous and then in his theatre in the Rue Monge. And when he wanted to live in Tours, as you well know, I brought my wife and my boy from Paris to live in the stables across the yard from your house. I was loyal to him, I was always loyal. Long before you came into his life, I was there. Every day, helping him. And on stage, in all of his travels, Russia, Spain, all those countries. And now, because I followed him to this hellish place, it is the end for me. I will die here tonight. I will die alone. And what will happen to my family, Madame? They will not have a sou. Please, Madame. You are kind. You are not like Monsieur.'

'You are not going to die, Jules. And you mustn't worry. Monsieur Lambert *is* kind, he's a good employer. I promise you. You mustn't worry. Soon, you will be home. Try to rest now. I will stay with you all night. I promise.'

The corporal approached, and beckoned her to come with him to the far end of the room. There, watching the sick man writhe on his bed, he whispered, 'I have seen this many times, Madame. *Hélas!* He is close to death now.'

'Please,' she said. 'Can you send someone to my husband's rooms? Tell him Jules is dying. Tell him he must come at once.'

'I am sorry, Madame. Earlier, I went myself, because I thought

Monsieur Lambert should know. But I wasn't able to speak to him. He was asleep and had left instructions that he was not to be wakened. I asked Colonel Deniau what I should do. He told me on no account must Monsieur Lambert be disturbed. Perhaps if Madame goes herself?'

She looked back at the bed. Jules was staring at her, his breathing frighteningly rapid, his mouth opening as though he were trying to vomit.

'No. It doesn't matter. I will stay with him. That will be best. My father is a doctor and I used to help in his clinic.'

'I will be in the main ward with my other patients,' the corporal said. 'Call, if you need me.'

Shortly after two o'clock, the sick man who had writhed and twisted about in an oblivion which seemed to lift him into a world in which he was not aware of her presence suddenly lay still. She leaned over him, afraid. But he opened his eyes, saw her and dragging himself up in the narrow bed, asked, 'What day is it?'

'Monday. Are you feeling better, Jules?'

'Madame? Madame? Did I tell you about my wife and my boy?'

'Yes, Jules, you did. Now lie back. Try to rest.'

He lay back in the bed. Should she call the corporal? She rose from her seat. Jules, eyes closed, whispered, 'Don't leave, Madame. Don't leave!'

She leaned over the bed and lifted him to her, cradling his head on her breast as though he were a child. The sweet sickening smell of excrement came up in a wave and she saw that he had again fouled himself under the sheet. She could feel his fetid breath on her neck as he snuggled his sweating head under her chin. But she held him tight, held him until, minutes later, his body contracted in a rigid spasm and with a groan he pulled away from her and vomited. As she brought a basin and attempted to wipe his face, gradually his body slackened, his mouth fell open. With eerie certainty, she was in the presence of death.

After a time she rose, turned down the lamp and drew a sheet over the dead man's face. On the shelf above his bed she saw, again, the incongruous printed notice:

Milianah Military Hospital
Rules for Health Service
Civilian patients subject
to disciplinary measures

She went out into the corridor. The orderly corporal saw her and came from the main ward.

'Madame? How is he? Can I help?'

She shook her head.

'I am so sorry, Madame. He was your servant. You'll miss him, I know. These deaths are a terrible thing. I have seen so many go like that. Sometimes I think this country is accursed.'

'No' she said. 'It's we who are accursed.'

The beaded curtain shielding the doorway to their quarters rustled like rain as she entered the darkened rooms. As she blindly felt her way towards the dressing table she stepped on a sheet of paper, anchored by one of her slippers. Picking it up, she went to the lamp and lit it, turning down the wick so as not to wake him. In his strange, almost medieval, handwriting, she read:

My Darling,
I have left instructions that on no account am I to be wakened before 7 a.m. I have taken a sleeping draught because it is essential that I be well rested. Otherwise my concern about what will happen to me tomorrow morning might weaken and distract me from the task ahead. I do not know where you have been and trust that you will return safely. But when you do, please let me sleep. I am

*hopeful but not yet confident that tomorrow I will succeed in this
ultimate test.*
Sleep well,
H.

She went to the door of the sitting room and looked in, but in
the darkness she could not see him. She went to the bed where
she slept alone, turned off the lamp and stripping herself of
her clothes, lay down, covering her naked body with a woollen
blanket. She thought of the corpse. Where would it be buried?
Not in France as poor Jules had wished but here in Milianah,
in a French cemetery, far from home. Into her mind came a
face she remembered imperfectly, the face of Jules' wife, a
Breton woman, who spoke no French, but the Gallic language
of her region, a woman she could not converse with, a woman
who, although she worked as their laundress, Emmeline barely
knew. Jules' child, a small dirty boy, sometimes rode a donkey
around the manor pathways, beating it with a switch, shouting
in mysterious joy. Mother and child were living out their lives
tonight, not knowing that an hour ago those lives had changed
for ever.

At seven, as though an alarm had gone off, Lambert woke and
came into her room. He went to her dressing table and peering
in the mirror, removed his hair net and carefully combed
his hair.

'Jules is dead,' she said.

He did not turn round. He folded the hair net into a square.
She could not see his face.

'He died in the night. He asked us to take care of his wife
and son.'

'His wife and son? Yes . . . we must do what we can.
Poor Jules.'

'He asked for you.'

Now, at last, he turned and looked at her. 'What did you say?'

'I said he asked for you.'

'No. I meant what did you tell him? Did you tell him I have a crisis on my hands? He would understand.'

'Understand?' she said. 'He was dying.'

'Yes. Of course, you're right. Poor Jules. I hope it's not an omen.'

She sat up on the divan and watched him as in the other room he began to dress in the clothes he had worn during yesterday's performance.

'By the way,' he said. 'I won't need you on stage this morning. We will be using the sheikh's pistols. He will hand them to me. Perhaps you had better stay here. If something goes wrong, I don't want you to see it.'

'Have you spoken to Deniau?'

'Not yet. Why?'

'He told me last night that if what you propose to do seems to him too dangerous he won't allow you to proceed. He believes you should use your own pistols and not risk a disaster.'

He stood staring out of the window, flexing his fingers as she had often seen him do before he performed a card trick. 'I am not under Deniau's orders. He mustn't try to dissuade me.'

'And if you don't succeed?' she said. 'You'll have made two widows in twenty-four hours.'

He turned from the window and stared at her. 'Two widows? What are you talking about?'

'You have already made one,' she said. 'Madame Jules Guillaumin.'

'My darling,' he said, but his tone was one of irritation. 'You will not be a widow, don't talk nonsense. Listen? They are arriving.' He went past her, pushing aside the beaded curtain and stepping out on to the balcony. She followed him outside. Below in the square the crowd of sheikhs, marabouts and caids who had attended yesterday's performance were outnumbered sixfold by a multitude of Kabyles, men, women and children, crowding and pushing their way through the gates to witness the death of the infidel sorcerer. And now she saw Deniau and Captain Hersant come up the stone steps, Deniau saluting ironically as he approached her.

'Will you take breakfast?' Captain Hersant asked. 'There is time. Bou-Aziz has not yet arrived.'

Lambert looked at her. She shook her head.

Deniau, staring at the milling mass of people in the square, said, 'I'm sorry about this. We tried to keep the populace away but it was no use. The story of what happened yesterday and what might happen this morning has spread far beyond Milianah. This will be an historic occasion. And now, Henri, tell me, what is it you propose to do?'

'You will see,' Lambert said.

'But I must know in advance. If you fail it will be a tragedy. But also it will be the end of everything we have worked for until now. So I have a right to know. What risk are you taking?'

'I cannot tell you that,' Lambert said. 'But, believe me, I know what I am doing. In the meantime I have two requests.'

'Please?' Captain Hersant said. 'How can we help you?'

'Order champagne for lunch. We must celebrate when this is over. Can your doctor stand by, just in case?'

'The doctor and stretcher bearers are waiting below,' Deniau said.

'Good. And now if you gentlemen will leave me, I would like to be alone with my wife.'

Captain Hersant, looking out over the square, said, 'Ah! That must be Bou-Aziz.'

At the fort's entrance three horsemen dismounted and made their way through the packed masses in the square. As they proceeded, the crowd pressed back to make a path for them, many bowing and reverently touching the green silken robe of the marabout who as always leaned heavily on his daughter's arm. Preceding them was Sheikh Ben-Amara brandishing above his head the pistols he had displayed on the day before. At sight of his weapons, the crowd shouted out a hoarse welcome.

'What are they saying?' Lambert asked.

Captain Hersant looked at Deniau as if for permission to translate.

'They're telling him to kill the Roumi sorcerer,' Deniau said. 'Sheikh Ben-Amara is the chief rabble-rouser hereabouts.'

The sheikh, still brandishing his pistols, looked up at their balcony. Pointing a pistol barrel in Lambert's direction he cried out in French, 'Roumi, your time has come.' He turned and made obeisance in the direction of Bou-Aziz. 'Behold, the Master of the Hour has arrived. The kingdom of the just is at hand. The time is right!'

But as the sheikh spoke, Bou-Aziz shook his head, as though weary of this boasting. Quietly acknowledging the greetings of the crowd who pressed around him, he made his way to the bench where he had sat the day before. A place was cleared at once for him and his daughter.

Deniau looked at Lambert. 'We will wait for you below. Good luck.'

'Thank you,' Lambert said. He took Emmeline's arm. 'Gentlemen. Give us five minutes.'

Pushing aside the curtain he led her back to the inner room. 'Darling, I'm sorry to put you through this. But I must tell you that it may not be possible for me to substitute the false bullet. I've never done it this way. I may fumble it or be unable to fit it in his barrel. Or he can simply shoot me in cold blood before I have time to prepare. I tell you this, not because I want to alarm you, but if things go wrong . . . What am I saying? They *won't* go wrong. Give me a kiss. I must go.'

'Henri. I'll ask you one last time. Use your own pistols.'

'Darling, I can't back out now. I'd be disgraced.'

'If you had a son, if you had a child, alive this morning, would you still do this?'

Ignoring her words, he came to her and kissed her on the cheek. 'Wish me luck. They're waiting.'

The beaded curtain rustled as he went outside. A moment later she heard the crowd utter a great moaning sound as he was sighted on the balcony. She felt herself tremble. He's not properly prepared. He's going to die. Where's Deniau? He must stop him.

She ran through the rooms, pushed aside the curtain and went out on to the sunlit balcony. Below her, flanked by Deniau and Hersant, she saw her husband walk slowly towards the stage, moving impassively through the milling mass of Kabyles and Arabs who, at sight of him, fell silent and drew back.

And now, nodding to Bou-Aziz who sat in the front row of spectators, Lambert mounted the bare stage and stood, looking out at the thousands of faces below.

'I am ready,' he said.

An interpreter repeated his words. Emmeline, high on the balcony, heard it as a knell. She saw the crowd make way for Sheikh Ben-Amara, who, bearded and moustachioed, wearing a white burnous, yellow high boots and gold-embroidered waistcoat, advanced, smiling, and again holding up his heavy cavalry pistols. Disdaining to use the steps, with one leap he bounded on to the stage and turning to face Lambert cried out in heavily accented French, 'Now, sorcerer. Do you wish to inspect my pistols?'

Lambert nodded and took the weapons in his hands. Looking down at the marabouts seated below, he said, 'I need a volunteer to inspect these vents and see that they are clear.'

One of the marabouts at once rose and came up on the stage. Gravely, like a performer in a play, he inspected the vents, holding the pistols up against the light.

'Clear?' said Lambert.

'Clear,' said the marabout.

'Continue,' Lambert said.

The sheikh took from his pouch a charge of powder and drove the wad home, first in one pistol and then in the other.

'You have your own bullets?' Lambert asked.

The sheikh, smiling, offered a leather case filled with bullets. Lambert chose one, held it up for the crowd to see, and loaded it into the pistol. He took up the second pistol, again choosing and loading one of the sheikh's bullets. He held the pistols aloft then put them on a table beside the sheikh. When he had done this, he looked up as if searching the sky. Emmeline, watching from the balcony, saw that his eyes searched for her. She raised her hand and waved. He saw her and raised his right hand in salute. Had he succeeded? Or had he failed and was this his farewell? His face, impassive, told her nothing but in that instant panic filled her. He had failed and this was his goodbye.

Like a duellist marking out his position he moved exactly fifteen paces across the stage, then stopped and turned round. In a silence so profound that in the streets outside the faint cries of morning commerce were heard by all, he looked directly at the sheikh.

'I am ready.'

Sheikh Ben-Amara took from the table the first pistol and, holding it steady, aimed directly at Lambert's chest. His bearded face, grave until then, split in a ferocious grin. 'The kingdom of the just is at hand,' he cried out. 'Roumi, your time has come.'

He fired. The pistol exploded with shattering power. Lambert did not fall. He stood, swaying slightly, then pointed to his mouth. He was holding the bullet between his teeth.

Emmeline, dizzy with relief, heard below in the square a vast collective intake of breath.

Lambert removed the bullet from his mouth, held it up to the crowd, then walked quickly towards the sheikh, handing it to him for his inspection.

Ben-Amara, agitated, looked at it, dropped it on the table, then reached for the second pistol. Lambert forestalled him, quickly taking up the weapon and holding it aloft.

'You have not been able to injure me,' he said. 'No one can. But now you will see that my aim is more dangerous than yours. Look at that wall.'

He turned to the whitewashed wall which formed the rear of the stage. He pointed the pistol and pulled the trigger. In the noise of the explosion, suddenly, a patch of red appeared on the whitewashed surface, besmirching the wall. A red liquid trickled down from the edge of the patch. Sheikh Ben-Amara stood, his head bowed as though he and not the wall had suffered this injury. He raised his eyes to face the sorcerer, awe and fear in his face. At last he turned and looked out at the crowd.

Emmeline, on her balcony, went forward, her hands gripping the stone parapet. In that moment, so great was the silence in the square, she could hear the faint scuffling sound of her shoes on the ground. Motionless, as though frozen in the frame of a painting, the multitude of faces stared in terror at the red patch on the wall.

In that moment of fear and panic, Bou-Aziz rose from his seat in the front row. Carefully, with the tread of an old man, he ascended the stage, went to the wall and, dipping his finger in the red liquid, raised it to his mouth and tasted.

'Blood?' Lambert asked.

Bou-Aziz nodded. He then turned to face the staring, frightened eyes of a thousand witnesses. When he spoke, his voice was grave and quiet. The crowd seemed to gasp, their eyes shifting from him to Lambert. When he had finished speaking many in the crowd cried out:

'Muhammad b. 'Abd Allah!'

'Muhammad b. 'Abd Allah!'

Bou-Aziz raised his hands as if to still the shouting. He then gestured to his daughter, who ascended the stage and spoke in French to Lambert and the assembled foreigners as Emmeline, high on her balcony, strained to listen.

'My father says that in our time we have not seen, nor will we see a sorcerer such as you. Heaven has sent you like thunder and lightning to warn us of the power granted by God to those infidels who conquered us in the past. My father knows that many of our people, Arab and Kabyle, believe that he, Bou-Aziz, is the Master of the Hour, the chosen one of God. Because of this belief he has been asked to declare that the time is now. If the time is now, the jihad must commence. If the time is now and the prophecies are to be fulfilled, my father must be the true Mahdi, come at last, blessed by a baraka greater than any possessed by an infidel.

'But he says that yesterday and today we have seen with our own eyes you, an infidel, perform miracles unknown to man. We have seen that you, without benefit of a talisman, have been shielded by God from what, for other men, would be certain death.

'My father says: As always we know that God alone is great. Everything comes from Him. Everything, including the miracles you have performed today. Because of that, my father wishes to withdraw for a short time to a place of khalwa, a place of retreat. He will remain alone in prayer and meditation, asking God if, indeed, the time is now, or if, by sending us an infidel sorcerer possessed of such spiritual strengths, God is telling us that you are the strongest.

'Lastly, my father asks that, for the period of his khalwa, the sheikhs, the caids, the agas here assembled, remain in Milianah and pray for an answer to this question: Will the reign of the impious now come to an end and the reign of the true believers begin? Has the time come for my father to take the true name of the Mahdi, Muhammad b. 'Abd Allah, the chosen one, who will drive the infidels from our land?'

When Bou-Aziz's daughter had finished speaking she took her father's arm and helped him down from the stage. Together, they walked towards the gate where their horses waited. Sheikh Ben-Amara, taking up his pistols, followed. Emmeline heard over and over again the chant of 'Muhammad b. 'Abd Allah' from the crowd, who, despite their reverence for the marabout, kept glancing, even as they chanted, at the slight silent figure on stage.

Lambert, with his unerring actor's instinct, had not moved during the entire translation and now waited until Bou-Aziz had left the square before coming down from the stage and, walking with a slow solemn step, moving into the thick of the crowd, staring ahead as if they were invisible. As in Algiers, the sheikhs, marabouts and caids drew back as if unwilling to come within arm's length of the sorcerer and again Emmeline heard the murmurings uttered in the theatre in the Rue Bat-Azoun.

'*Chitan! Chitan!*'

But now the word was spoken in terror. Her husband, Henri Lambert, an ordinary man, was for these people more than a saint. He was *chitan*, the devil incarnate.

Then, as Deniau and Captain Hersant came forward to shake Lambert's hand and congratulate him, Emmeline ran down the steps leading to the square, hurrying towards him, remembering that moments ago he had risked death to win this victory. When she ran across the square, crowds of Kabyles drew back to let her pass, staring in astonishment as she embraced the sorcerer, weeping, stroking his cheek.

'It's over, my darling,' he said. 'Take my arm. We must make our exit.'

And so, confused and frightened by the hostile eyes of the Kabyles, she walked with her husband, Deniau and Hersant through the doorway which led into the main hall of the fort. When they went in a Zouave sergeant closed and barred the heavy wooden doors. Then, and only then, Lambert smiled and clapped his hands in triumph. 'Well, gentlemen. Did we or did we not?'

'You did!' Deniau said. 'Congratulations, my dear fellow. But *how* did you do it? Amazing! You must tell us.'

'No, no,' Lambert said, chuckling to himself in delight. 'A miracle cannot be explained. As the marabout said, "Everything comes from God."'

Now, officers and the few wives who had accompanied them to this distant outpost crowded around Lambert, offering their praise. Army orderlies appeared bearing trays of champagne. Emmeline, forgotten in the rush of congratulations, stood slightly outside the circle, watching as Lambert smiled at his admirers. This man who, moments ago, walked like Satan among innocent Africans is what my father always said he was, a charlatan. She thought of Bou-Aziz, of his grave, dignified speech, of his resolve to pray for God's guidance. And in that moment in the courtyard of a French fort surrounded by illimitable desert she remembered the Emperor's study in Compiègne, the Emperor with his waxed moustaches and his lecher's smile, puffing on his long cigar. 'I have great plans for

Algeria. In the spring, I will bring our armies to Africa, subdue the Kabylia region and complete our conquest of the entire country.' But this conquest that the Emperor desired would not 'civilize' these people as he promised but instead bring more forts, more soldiers, more roads, more French colonists to profit from Algeria's trade and crops. And more mahdis, more jihads, more repression.

A luncheon gong sounded. Lambert, breaking away from his admirers, came to her, taking her arm and leading her into the dining hall of the fort where a festive celebration was about to begin. A major-domo seated them, her husband on her right and Colonel Deniau on her left. As in Compiègne, where the Emperor and Empress had occupied the centre seats at the long table, so, this morning in far-off Milianah, she and Lambert were given the place of honour.

As the first course was brought in, Deniau turned to them and said, 'Of course you realize that things have changed. We have been deprived of our triumphant exit.'

'I was going to ask you about that,' Lambert said.

'He's not the paramount marabout for nothing. What else could he do? He has to buy time, to save face, to plan some action he hopes will devalue this morning's miracles. I don't think he's going to succeed, but we mustn't help him by disappearing from the field of combat.'

'But this period of "meditation" could take weeks, Lambert said. You told us we have to get back to Algiers before the rains. Before the end of the month.'

'I'm sorry, Henri. I'm sorry, Emmeline. We can't leave now. But I hope this "meditation" won't last more than a few days. He can't prolong it. These sheikhs and marabouts are important people in their own communities. They don't want to wait around in Milianah.'

'But what if the rains come? What if we miss the steamer?'

'We'll deal with that problem when we come to it. In the meantime it's important that you be seen in the streets of the city. That you and your powers remain fresh in their minds. We'll arrange a further reception for the sheikhs at which you, of course, will be present. You are Bou-Aziz's nemesis. Already, I'm sure there's doubt among many of the sheikhs that he is the promised Mahdi. He'll have to dispel that doubt by some great feat. And what can he do? His "miracles" aren't so much miracles as faith-healing and this unproven legend that he is the chosen one of the prophet. Those things can't compete with what the sheikhs saw here in the past two days. I'm very hopeful. Very!'

'Hopeful?' Emmeline said. 'What is it you hope for? That Henri's performance has discredited Bou-Aziz and that his following will desert him? Or that he will renounce the idea of a holy war?'

'In truth,' Deniau said, smiling, 'I don't really want him to lose his following. I hope that he'll put off a decision by some ruse such as an interior jihad. It's been used in the past by would-be Mahdis to give them time to rally support.'

'An interior jihad?' Lambert said. 'What does that mean?'

'Instead of calling for a holy war, he'll tell them that they need to turn inwards towards prayer and work to strengthen their faith. That would fit *our* plans perfectly. We know that General MacMahon is already assembling the forces he'll need to land here in the spring. Once our armies disembark in Algiers, that will be the end of it.'

When he said this Deniau tapped his knife on the edge of his glass, calling for attention. He then rose and proposed a toast to: 'A patriotic Frenchman who this morning risked his life and displayed his genius in the cause of France's mission to civilize these lands and make them an important link in our chain of empire. I give you Monsieur Henri Lambert.'

Chairs were pushed back as the company rose for the toast. Emmeline saw her husband smile and bow his head in mock humility. Of course he's happy to stay here for a few more days. He knows no 'miracle' Bou-Aziz can perform will equal what *he* did today. There'll be receptions and dinners in his honour. But when this is over, what's going to happen? He'll no longer be content with his paid performances in theatres. Today is the high point in his life.

Deniau turning to her as the first course was served put his fingers gently on her arm in an effort to re-establish that air of covert complicity which excluded her husband. 'And you, dear Emmeline, how do you feel about staying on longer? I must confess I dread the day when I'll stand on the quay at Algiers and wave farewell to the *Alexander* as it steams towards Marseille.'

He smiled, tilting his head sideways, almost coquettishly, waiting her answer.

'When are they going to bury Jules?'

'Jules? Oh! Henri's man. Is he . . .? Of course. When did it happen?'

'Early this morning.'

'Then it's possible that they may have buried him already. With cholera, they like to get the bodies out of sight. The men fear it, and of course they're right. In Algeria cholera has killed more of our soldiers than all of the battles of the past forty years.'

'Cholera? No one told me it was cholera.'

Deniau shrugged. 'We didn't want to alarm you.'

'But you knew he was going to die?'

'It wasn't certain, it never is. If they don't die after three days it runs its normal course and by the seventh day they begin to recover. One never knows. Besides, I wanted to spare you.'

'Spare me?'

'And spare your husband. Knowing his assistant was about to die might have made it difficult for him to perform. I may seem heartless but believe me there would have been no point in telling either one of you.'

She put her napkin on the table and, turning from him, said to her husband, 'He tells me that Jules may already be buried. I'm going to find out. If there's to be a funeral, of course we must attend it.'

'Wait,' Lambert said. 'Let Charles find out. We're the guests of honour today. Please?'

But she stood up and left the room. Outside in the inner

courtyard of the fort the heavy wooden doors leading to the main square were barred. Zouave sentries came to attention as she approached. A sergeant saluted.

'Madame is going out?'

'Yes.'

'There is a crowd outside in the square,' the sergeant said. 'We tried to remove them after the performance but they refuse to leave. They say they're waiting for your husband. Are you sure you want to go out, Madame?'

'Yes. I must go to the infirmary.'

'I will go with you. You may need an escort.'

The heavy doors opened. When she stepped outside accompanied by the sergeant, a frieze of faces greeted her, a great throng of men and women dressed in the worn and ragged garments of the Kabyle peasantry. At first they turned away from her, disappointed that the newcomer was a woman and not the sorcerer, but then, as she made her way through the mass of people filling the square, she was recognized as the sorcerer's wife and at once was surrounded by people calling out questions she did not understand.

'What do they want? Do you know?' she asked the sergeant.

The sergeant turned to listen to the cries. 'Some of them are asking if the Roumi sorcerer can heal the sick. And some are saying he is the devil. Pay no attention, Madame. The Kabyles hate us, they have always hated strangers. But these are not dangerous. Come.'

They had reached the door of the infirmary.

'Shall I wait for you, Madame?'

'Thank you. No.'

When she entered the infirmary she was at once confronted by the sight of seven soldier patients wearing long nightshirts queued up at a desk in the corridor where an army doctor, wearing a white coat over his tunic, was giving injections.

The doctor, who recognized her from yesterday's luncheon, at once abandoned his patients, coming towards her with a smile: 'Good afternoon, Madame. I hear this morning was an enormous success. I had hoped to be there for the celebration, but as you see, I have work to do. May I ask what brings you here?'

'My husband's assistant, you remember he had cholera. He died earlier today. I wanted to know about his funeral.'

At the word cholera, the doctor gave her a warning look, then, taking her arm, led her down the corridor, away from his waiting patients. 'Sergeant?'

A swarthy medical orderly who had been assisting in the giving of injections came hurrying towards them. 'Sir?'

The doctor, momentarily abandoning Emmeline, went off to whisper something in the orderly's ear. The orderly turned to Emmeline: 'The body is no longer here, Madame. Father Benedict came for it about an hour ago. Monsieur Guillaumin will be buried in the Jesuit cemetery, just a few streets away.'

'But when? Why did no one tell us?'

'The Colonel signed the authorization early this morning. He did not leave instructions that you or Monsieur Lambert were to be informed. The priest came for the body about an hour ago.'

'I am sorry about this,' the doctor said. 'Of course you should have been told. But perhaps Colonel Deniau didn't wish to upset your husband before this morning's event?'

'Where is the cemetery? You said a few streets away?'

'Yes, Madame. It is attached to the Jesuit church.'

'Would you like to go there?' the doctor asked. 'I can send someone to show you where it is.'

The building that housed the Jesuit mission and the cemetery differed only from its neighbours by the fact that a stone cross had been erected on its roof and by an ornamental plaque affixed to the archway of its front entrance:

Mission de Milianah
Compagnie de Jésus

The Zouave soldier who had accompanied Emmeline pushed open the gate, revealing a large courtyard, with at its centre a statue of the crucified Christ. 'The church is that building over there,' the soldier said. 'The cemetery is at the rear. Father Benedict is probably there now. We brought the corpse here about an hour ago but they have to dig a grave. This way, Madame.'

He led her through the small church, out into an area surrounded by a high blank wall. Small paths criss-crossed a little field of rough headstones. At the far end of this place a horse and cart waited, its driver, a Zouave soldier, dozing on his seat. Two Kabyle grave diggers laboured in a muddy trench. Watching them was the Jesuit priest she had seen last night. At first she did not realize it was the priest, for he wore a burnous over his cassock and had covered his head with a fez. He was reading his missal and when he saw her he closed it and came over. 'I am Father Benedict,' he said. 'Forgive me. I didn't introduce myself last night. Will you stay? It will not be long. The grave is ready.'

As he spoke she saw the Kabyles come up out of the trench and toss their spades aside. They went to the cart, removing the tailboard to let them slide out Jules' body which had been sewn into a rough sack. They stepped over the heap of freshly dug earth and rolled the body down into the trench of the grave. At that, Father Benedict nodded to her and together they walked towards the open pit. The Kabyle grave diggers picked up their spades. The driver of the funeral cart now joined the soldier who had accompanied Emmeline, both men removing their caps, to stand respectfully behind the priest who opened his missal and in a droning voice began to read in Latin which Emmeline did not understand. In the distance she heard a cry, the mid-afternoon chant of a muezzin calling to the faithful from the minaret of a central mosque. At once the Kabyle grave diggers, as though alone in this place, knelt on the edge of the grave, heads touching the ground, prostrate in prayer.

Emmeline, turning slightly, saw the two French soldiers, cap in hand, waiting patiently for the Latin to end so that they could return to their barracks. They did not pray. She looked again at the prostrate Kabyles on her right. Prayer, said by millions of these people, kneeling, heads bowed, prayer five times each day for each day of their lives, prayer not of petition but of acceptance.

Everything comes from God.

While we stand uneasily by this grave, listening to words we do not understand, we who have not known a faith as strong as theirs, we who cannot accept death, who fear hell and only half believe in heaven. What is God to us? What is the meaning of this priest's words as he reaches down and throws a handful of dirt over the corpse in the grave?

The grave diggers, their devotions ended, stood up and lifting their shovels set to work filling in the pit. As they did, the soldiers put on their caps and with a nod to the Jesuit went towards their cart. The soldier who had brought Emmeline here turned, as though remembering.

'Madame? Would you like to come back with us?'

She shook her head.

TWELVE

'There will be an escort,' Deniau said. 'It will consist of a troop of Arabs, armed, on horseback. The Sheikh tells me the first part of the escort will arrive at the fort, shortly after sunrise. Can you both be ready by eight o'clock?'

Lambert looked at her. 'Whatever you wish, my darling. Will that be all right or would you prefer to stay here?'

'I will be ready,' she said.

Earlier, when she returned from the graveyard, he had asked about Jules. She said she did not want to talk about it and so they went into dinner in hostile silence. Now, joined by Deniau and Hersant for a discussion of the plans for tomorrow, Lambert was anxious to conceal their rift.

'I think you will enjoy it,' Deniau said. 'Bou-Allem is the leading Aga in this region and the fact that he has invited us to a special feast is quite significant.'

'In what way?' Lambert asked.

'Our spies inform us that in a recent meeting of the sheikhs and marabouts in Algiers he tried to discount the claims of Bou-Aziz. We are told he warned them that even though the French presence in Algeria is a calamity, endorsing a false prophet, even one who seeks to eliminate the infidels, is equally disastrous. And so, your triumph yesterday played into his hands. By inviting you to a feast tomorrow he is signalling to the other sheikhs that he doesn't believe that Bou-Aziz is the Mahdi.'

At eight o'clock the following morning Emmeline and Lambert saw, circling below in the courtyard, four horsemen: Deniau,

Hersant and two young lieutenants of a Zouave regiment. Two additional horses were held by grooms, waiting their arrival. Once mounted their procession trotted out into the streets of Milianah. There, ten Arab riders, wearing red burnouses and armed with rifles, moved in as escort.

'Bou-Allem's men,' Hersant said. 'And this is only the beginning.'

When they reached the gates of the town, a further twenty armed Arabs dressed in red burnouses joined the cortège. Two hundred yards further on a third escort surrounded them and as they reached the open plain yet another twenty riders joined them. At once, the entire Arab escort, now numbering seventy horsemen, started off at a gallop, leaving them behind. About six hundred yards further on they reined their horses to a sudden stop, dividing and forming four troops. The Arabs of the first troop wheeled around and galloped full tilt towards Deniau's party, holding high their rifles and shouting war-like cries. Faster and faster they came on, until it seemed they would crash into the Europeans. At the last moment, suddenly, in unison, they fired their rifles over their heads, reined their horses to a plunging stop, the animals rising on their hind legs as they wheeled around and raced back. The moment they regained the main body of red-mantled Arabs, a second troop rushed towards the Europeans, repeating the dangerous manoeuvre at the same breakneck speed. Troop after troop came on, until the entire seventy-man escort had discharged their guns. Then, suddenly silent, they drew up as in a parade ground and fell in, in orderly ranks behind their guests.

Deniau, reining in beside Emmeline, said with a pleased smile, 'That, dear Emmeline, is what the Arabs call a fantasia. A surprise, a special welcome. Magnificent, no? And you were marvellous. I watched you. You didn't, even for a moment, flinch.'

Ahead on the plain, shimmering like a mirage in the noon sun, Emmeline saw an encampment of tents grouped around a large, high-domed, gaily pelmeted central structure. Camels, horses, sheep and goats were enclosed in a sort of paddock, guarded by armed horsemen. Deniau, now riding between Emmeline and Lambert, told them that the Aga would be waiting to receive hem. 'Even when he is travelling, as he is now, he moves with a large entourage of warriors, wives and servants. As you can see, this is no ordinary encampment.'

Several hundred yards away, a rider came out from the huddle of tents, moving at a slow trot towards the Europeans and their escort. As the rider came close, the escort troop raised its rifles and fired in the air as a signal of greeting. Emmeline now saw that the rider was dressed in the high turban and embroidered waistcoat of a sheikh. He was a man of middle years, light-skinned, bearded, with cold appraising eyes. Reaching their party, he reined in his horse, nodding first to Deniau. He then bowed respectfully to Lambert and said something in Arabic which Deniau translated as: 'Be you welcome, you who have been sent by God.'

Following the Aga's prancing stallion, they entered the city of tents. Their escort riders reined in and waited as Deniau's party rode through the confusion and noise of the encampment. Men, women and children ran out, clustering in a circle at the entrance to the Aga's ceremonial tent as the visitors were ushered inside.

Inside the tent they were invited to seat themselves on a large carpet. Coffee was served and Emmeline remained in the rear of the group, largely ignored by the Aga and his sons as they offered pipes of tobacco to the male guests. After a half-hour of smoking and coffee drinking the Aga clapped his hands. Servants pulled wide the flaps of the tent and Emmeline saw, approaching, a procession led by two men carrying what seemed to be furled banners. But when they entered the tent she realized that the long poles they held aloft contained, not banners, but sheep roasted whole. The sheep bearers were followed by fifteen men, each of whom carried a dish which was to be a part of the feast. Roast fowls, different sorts of couscous, sweet cakes, dates and other dishes which she could not identify were placed before them as a head cook unspitted the sheep, arranging them in a great heaping dish which he and his assistants laid before the Aga and his guests.

In the midst of these festivities Emmeline thought of the sight she had just witnessed, the riders of the fantasia, their rifles held high, their pride in their horsemanship, their triumphant warrior stance. Into her mind came a memory of the *grands boulevards* of Paris, those immense straight thoroughfares where, some months before, thousands of soldiers marched past the Emperor in a celebration of his Crimean victories. On that day, she had seen the might of France's army: gun carriages, cannons, regiments, foot soldiers, cavalry; flags and standards held high to commemorate wars fought and won against other great powers. In the spring that military might will send these Arab horsemen crashing to the ground like toy soldiers swept off a game board. In the spring, this Aga now courting Deniau and my husband will become the victim of a magician's tricks. And what if my husband had not come here, what if these people's belief had not been shaken by Henri's 'miracles'? What if Bou-Aziz could ignore them, call for a holy war and, with it, drive us from this, their land?

Deniau, leaning towards her, offered a strip of the roast mutton from the heap of meat. 'It's delicious,' he said. 'You must try it. I told you this would be a feast.'

'I am sorry,' she said. 'I have no appetite.'

'You are not ill?'

'No.'

'Are you sure? We travelled with your husband's servant. I believe we ate the same food and drank the same water. I don't want to alarm you but we are still at risk.'

'I am not ill,' she said. She leaned forward, dipping her fingers into the heap of meat, and, as she had seen the others do, tore off a strip and began to eat it. 'You see? You don't need to be alarmed.'

'Good. It's delicious meat, don't you think?'

As he said this, smiling, he turned from her to speak in Arabic with a young caid sitting on his left. It was, she knew, a subtle dismissal. Now that he had succeeded in his mission of bringing her husband to Africa and putting him through his performing tricks, this devious, handsome diplomat need no longer woo the magician's wife. In a few weeks when we sail on the *Alexander*, he will remain here, planning, scheming, listening to his spies. A year from now he may not remember my Christian name.

As the luncheon proceeded, again she was largely ignored. And in her aloneness, shut out of the talk, she remembered Deniau's warning. *Cholera.* It was, of course, something she had thought about, something frightening, but which in the guilt and grief of Jules' dying, she had dismissed. Now, the memory of his wasted dehydrated body, his pinched face, the cheeks a bluish tint, his rapid breathing, his inaudible voice, the stench of excrement, the tearing retching noise as a drool of vomit spilled over the sheets, these sights, these sounds came back to her under this richly canopied tent, filled with voices, laughter and bowing servants offering a surfeit of food. It was as though Jules, no longer buried under a heap of dirt in the Jesuit cemetery, had come through the opened tent flaps to walk among the celebrating sheikhs and Frenchmen, the spectre at this feast whose deathly hand might at any moment touch her, Lambert, Deniau or Hersant. *We are all at risk.*

'Did you hear that?' Lambert said, leaning over to her.

She started in surprise as though she had been asleep. 'No. What?'

Lambert turned to Hersant. 'Would you mind telling my wife what you just told me. Interesting. Very.'

Hersant, who sat on her right, said in a confidential tone, 'The Colonel says that just before our luncheon the Aga told him that yesterday evening in Milianah the assembled sheikhs held a conclave and agreed that, despite your husband's performance, if Bou-Aziz decides to proclaim himself the Mahdi, all of them, in fact all of Algeria, will rise with him. But the Aga, who is one of the very few leaders who doubts that Bou-Aziz is the Mahdi, told the Colonel that, from now on, each day he hesitates to declare himself he will lose an important part of his support.

For that reason we must keep the pressure on. Tomorrow, we will invite the sheikhs to a feast at which your husband, the guest of honour' – he turned to Lambert – 'will astonish them with – what will you do?'

'Sleight of hand, making things appear and disappear, conjuring, of course, but done in a spirit of friendship.'

Hersant laughed. 'Friendship? Any trick you perform from now on will merely enhance your reputation as a familiar of the devil. Which is what we want. But I must say, yesterday, watching you on stage, I thought if you'd worn a burnous and were bearded like an Arab, you, not Bou-Aziz, would be their Mahdi.'

Suddenly, unthinkingly, Emmeline said, 'Nonsense! That old man is holy. You know it the moment you are in his presence.'

'Holy?' Captain Hersant seemed amused. 'My dear Madame, these marabouts are charlatans, every one of them, self-proclaimed saints in a religion which, frankly, is childish nonsense. Really, you mustn't romanticize them. You wouldn't if you knew them as I do.'

But at that moment, the Aga rose, clapped his hands and spoke to his guests. It was, Deniau said later, a speech of welcome, but also a signal that the luncheon must end. It was the hour of mid-afternoon prayer.

Half an hour later, after a round of farewells, an escort of ten riders, clad in the red burnous of the Aga's goumiers, led them past the staring crowd of tent dwellers out on to the road to Milianah, passing distant hills of a brownish mauve colour, pitted with myriad crevices. Soon they were riding past plantations of date palms and gardens intersected by walls of dried mud. Ahead on the mountain slope Emmeline saw a village with high-walled houses, their roofs marked with a design of clay bricks, their flat terraces looking over courtyards and gardens full of fruit trees. As they passed by the road leading up to these habitations, Deniau reined in his horse and pointed to a blue-domed building a little way from the village. Behind this building the mountains stretched, range upon range, menacing in their barrenness, melting at last into the fading blue of the sky.

'That's his zawiya.'

'His what?' Lambert said. 'Who are we talking about?'

'Bou-Aziz. That's where he lives, and teaches his pupils. Zawiyas are a sort of marabout seminary and in my opinion they're more dangerous than any army the Arabs can put in the field.'

'What will he decide, I wonder?' Hersant said, smiling. 'Is he thinking of changing his name?'

'To Muhammad b. 'Abd Allah!' Deniau sang out mockingly, shouting towards the distant blue-domed building.

Hersant, laughing, echoed the cry. 'Muhammad b. 'Abd Allah!'

The Aga's Arab escorts, listening to this, stared at each other in wild surmise.

That evening, at dinner, she said to Lambert, 'This lunch for you tomorrow, they won't need me. I am *de trop* at these affairs. I think, if you don't mind, I'd like to go riding instead.'

'Would that be safe?' He turned to Deniau. 'What do you think?'

'Perfectly safe,' Hersant said, smiling at her. 'Who would dare to lay hands on the devil's wife?'

The sergeant in charge of the livery stable remembered her from yesterday and at once saddled for her the roan mare she had ridden on her journey to Bou-Allem's feast. She had risen shortly after sunrise, dressing while Lambert slept, and in a state of agitation, afraid that he would waken and question her, left hurriedly without writing a note. As she rode out of the stables, she heard the muezzin's call from the minaret of a nearby mosque and moments later she passed a group of men, heads bowed, kneeling in the dirt of the narrow street. She spurred her horse, trotting in and out of the maze of market stalls which led to the main gate of Milianah. Once through the gate she forced the roan mare into a canter. The road ahead was empty but minutes later she heard behind her the clanking of bells and, turning, saw three Tuareg riders, their faces half masked in the fashion of their tribe, advancing on her, whipping their giant racing camels as they came up on her and passed her, the iron harness bells worn by the great beasts clanking at every step, their riders high on Tuareg saddles adorned with woollen tassels, the long camel necks swaying as, with undulating strides, they vanished in a cloud of dust.

Again she was alone in the silence of this vast plain, the sun above her hot as a stove, its heat seeming to singe her garments. And then, ahead she saw the bleak range of mountains, the cliffs of pitted rock rising against the sky, a landscape so barren that for some minutes she rode on uncertainly, believing that she had taken a different track from the day before and had lost the direction of the village and the zawiya. But soon she sighted the wall of the cemetery which lay beside the road and coming closer saw inside the wall a field of strangely shaped stones marking hundreds of anonymous graves. Above the cemetery a narrow track divided in two, a few hundred yards from the village. She took the left fork and rode up to the gate of the blue-domed zawiya. Entering a courtyard she saw a small group of young men, seated in a circle, reciting a monotonous chant which seemed to be a prayer.

Emmeline slipped off her horse's back and stood, tense and uneasy, until, from a darkened archway, an old man, barefoot, wearing a ragged robe, emerged and signalled her to follow him. She was led through an inner courtyard and into a small shaded room where, seated on the ground on a sack of folded wool, she saw the marabout's daughter who at once rose and took her hands, saying in her precise conventional French, 'Welcome, Madame. I am Taalith. My father has trained me to help him in his work. You wish to see him?'

'If I may?'

Still holding Emmeline's hands the marabout's daughter drew her down to sit beside her on the folded sack. Emmeline was, as before, moved by the sight of her body, frail as a child's under the burnous and veils, her face wasted, her voice hoarse yet gentle and welcoming.

'Today, my father is meditating. If you will be so kind, tell me what it is you wish to say to him.'

For a long moment Emmeline did not speak. Like a soldier who has crossed a no-man's-land and stands on the rim of enemy lines, hands raised in surrender, she felt a sudden ending of the tension, the anger, the shame which had led her to come here. The marabout's daughter seemed, like her father, to possess baraka, that mysterious gift which Deniau said was a holiness, an expression of divine grace, a gift which made those in her presence feel at peace. These people are not my enemies. If I speak now it's not to betray my country or Henri, but to tell the truth, to right a wrong.

'It is about my husband,' she said. 'He does not possess supernatural powers. Everything he showed you here and in Algiers is a commercial illusion, a magician's trick. I can explain these things to your father. And I can tell him why these things were done and what is the true purpose of our visit.'

The marabout's daughter leaned towards Emmeline and took hold of her hands. 'It was good of you to come. I will tell him what you have told me. If you please, wait here.' The marabout's daughter rose and went out of the room.

Moments later an Arab servant entered carrying a tray with coffee and a glass of water. He smiled at her, said something in Arabic, then withdrew. Outside, she heard the endless chant of the young men in the courtyard. Behind those voices was a world of silence as though their praise of God rose into the heavens in total submission to divine will. Never in France, in cathedral, convent or cloister, had she felt the intensity of belief everywhere present in the towns, villages, farms and deserts of this land. It was a force at once inspiring and terrible, a faith with no resemblance to the Christian belief in Mass and sacraments, hellfire and damnation, sin and redemption, penance and forgiveness.

Everything comes from God.

Now, waiting to see if the marabout would come, the sense of peace she had felt in being here was replaced by despair. As of this moment she no longer belonged in the world of

Tours, Paris and Compiègne. And yet she must return to it. There was no other choice. For this world of total fervour, of blind resignation, was one she neither could, nor would, wish to enter.

After some time she heard voices in an inner room. Three men wearing the high turbans of marabouts came from that direction, entered the chamber where she was seated, stared at her in silence, then went out into the courtyard where they broke into urgent whispered speech. And then she heard a dragging footstep. Bou-Aziz, leaning as always on the arm of his daughter, came into the room, greeting her with a gentle smile and some words in Arabic which his daughter did not translate. The marabout then sat on the bare floor. His daughter sat beside Emmeline on the folded rug. The marabout spoke again, his eyes on Emmeline, waiting as his daughter translated.

'My father thanks you for your visit. I have told him what you said and now he asks if you will tell him why you have come here.'

'Because I am uneasy at what has happened,' Emmeline said. 'If I keep silent about the truth of these events, I will be guilty for the rest of my life.'

The marabout nodded and made a whispered response. 'My father thanks you for that answer. Now, please tell him what you wish to tell.'

On the journey here from Milianah she had rehearsed what she might say but now, the planned words forgotten, she began by telling the secret of the heavy box and the substitution of the false bullets. 'My husband is a professional entertainer. He is celebrated throughout Europe for his illusions and his inventions. But his feats are the result of scientific skills and endless practice. They are not miracles. In Europe, magicians are not thought to be possessed of supernatural powers but to be skilful deceivers. My husband is the greatest of these and that is why the Emperor sent him here.'

'And why was he sent?' the marabout asked.

She hesitated. And then she said it out, telling of Deniau's belief that greater 'miracles' performed by her husband would discredit Bou-Aziz and any claim he might make to be the Mahdi and so buy time until the spring, when Louis Napoleon's armies would sail from France to complete the conquest of Algeria.

As she spoke, she must pause while Taalith translated. During these pauses she felt herself tremble, her throat dry, her heart beating against the wall of her body. But then when it was time to go on, these weaknesses abated and she spoke, impassioned as never before in her life. When she had finished, again she felt weak and febrile, drained of emotion, as though her confession had not been voluntary but forced from her by some other will.

The marabout leaned towards his daughter and spoke for some time in a half-whisper. Taalith nodded, then said, 'My father asks if your husband knows that you are here?'

'No. No one knows.'

'My father says in that case what you have told him today will remain in this room. It will not be necessary for him to betray your confidence to anyone. He and he alone must decide his course of action. But what you have told him will help him discover God's will in this matter.'

When Taalith finished speaking the marabout rose and came towards Emmeline, taking her hands in his, smiling and bowing his head in farewell. He turned and left the room.

Taalith then said, 'Are you hungry? Do you wish to eat? Would you like to rest for a few hours before returning to Milianah?'

She shook her head. 'No. I must go back.'

Taalith rose from the folded sack and stretching out her hands drew Emmeline to her, briefly clasping her in an embrace. Emmeline felt under the burnous a body fragile as that of a small bird, soft, yet bony, a body now racked by a hoarse and ominous cough. Taking her hand, Taalith led her through the rooms which gave on to the courtyard. Outside, the circle of praying students finished their chant and at once began again. Emmeline's horse, reins slack on its neck, stood in the shade of an archway, its tail switching to beat off a cluster of flies. Again Taalith pressed Emmeline in an embrace and stood, small and frail as a child, waving farewell as Emmeline rode out.

Under the implacable sun, on the empty, dusty desert road, Emmeline, confused, feeling, despite Taalith's embrace, alone and rejected, rode slackly, allowing her horse to slow to a walk. Almost two hours later, when she at last reached Milianah, the Zouave sergeant at the sentry post told her that the luncheon for the sheikhs was almost over. 'Monsieur Lambert should be back very shortly.'

She went up to her rooms, ordered a tub of bath water and lay soaking in its coolness. What had the marabout meant when he said that no one would know what she had told him? This morning, on her way to the zawiya she had resolved that if she told the truth to Bou-Aziz she would not hide what she had done from Henri. For she knew that while she was acting out of a sense of shame and anger, she was not doing this solely to right an injustice, but also in some way settling scores: with Henri for his callousness in the matter of Jules' death and with Deniau for the arrogance of treating her like his puppet. But now it seemed possible that this morning's action, at once the bravest and the most shocking thing she had done in her life, might not bring the anger and retribution she had been prepared to accept. Now, if she hid the truth from Henri, whatever decision the marabout would make might never be blamed on her. But was the marabout to be trusted? It was true that in his presence she had felt that mysterious sense of sainthood, but what did she really know of these people and their beliefs? Their faith was not more spiritual than Christianity, but it was stronger, frightening in its intensity, with a certitude Christianity no longer possessed.

*　　*　　*

'How was your excursion?' he asked, as he came into the room. 'Did you ride out into the desert?'

'How was your luncheon?'

'Strange, very strange.' He removed his linen jacket and sat down on the room's solitary sofa stretching out his arms and staring up at the ceiling. 'You know,' he said, 'I learned something today. In Europe when I perform an illusion my audiences are in awe of what I've done. But they don't think of it as evil because in some way they sense that they're being tricked. And so they don't hate or fear me as those Arabs did at luncheon. It's a very unpleasant, almost frightening feeling. Believe me, I'll be glad when all this is over.'

She watched as he got up, stripping off his shirt and, with his back to her, washed his face and neck in a basin. She could see the bald spot which he combed over carefully before each performance. With his bent slightly stooped shoulders and narrow chest, he seemed a humble figure, a servant, not a *seigneur*. The fame he had courted, the dream he held of his importance, now seemed a pathetic delusion for, if what she had done today inspired Bou-Aziz to launch the jihad, he would be deprived of his greatest triumph, one in which his feats would have become legend and he a part of history.

Now, having finished washing, he put on a robe and went out on to the balcony. She sat, sick with anxiety, her mind stumbling among a set of explanations, none of which could possibly deflect the anger and outrage she expected. For she could not use the lie of silence. She must tell him the truth.

Slowly, like an ill person, she rose and went out on to the balcony. At that moment a soldier ran up the stone steps leading from the courtyard below and handed Lambert a folded sheet of paper, saluting as he did. 'Sir, shall I wait for a reply?'

She saw Lambert unfold the note and read it. 'Thank you. No reply.'

The soldier, again saluting, ran back down the steps, his boots loud on the stone. Lambert stood staring at the note as though reading it over and over again. Then, seeing her standing nearby, he held up the sheet of paper and said, 'It's from Charles Deniau. Bou-Aziz has called a meeting of the sheikhs in the courtyard of the grand mosque tomorrow morning. He has asked that we be present, Charles, myself and, I don't know why, he also wants you to attend.' He looked again at the sheet of paper. 'Charles believes that tomorrow we'll have our answer one way or another. But, it's odd. Why would the marabout ask for you?'

She stood, silent, looking at him. 'It is too warm to stay outside,' she said. 'Come. I have something to tell you.'

When they entered the inner chamber he went to the buffet and poured himself a glass of water. 'Well? What is it?' He seemed preoccupied, half listening. But when she began to speak he stood transfixed, his back to her, his hands still holding the glass of water and the pitcher.

'This morning I went to see the marabout in his sanctuary in the hills. I spoke to him and to his daughter. I told him why you have been sent here. I told him the truth about the heavy box and the false bullets. I told him about the offensive next spring. He listened to me, then said that he would not betray my confidence, that no one would know what I had told him. But even if that's true, I can't hide what I have done from you. I won't even tell you that I'm sorry. I know that this is probably the end of our marriage. But I had no choice. I don't believe that we should be the conquerors of these people or that we should try to make Frenchmen of them, or use their country for our gain. I did not want to be a part of it.'

She watched as he put down the glass and pitcher then turned to face her. The anger she had expected was absent from his face. Instead, he seemed to be puzzling over something, as though trying to discover a trick behind what she had told him. At last he said, 'So he knows. Interesting. It annoyed me to have to play the role of one of those saintly fools, a simple vessel used by a divine power. Now he must realize that I have perfected skills which ignorant marabouts like him could never master. Good! But how do I deal with this? I must think about the next move.'

With that, he went back out on to the balcony, leaving without a look in her direction. She saw him pace up and down, his head bent, sometimes nodding to himself, sometimes shaking his head in disapproval. He stopped walking and stood, his hands gripping the rail of the balcony as he stared down at the open-air stage below. At last he came back inside.

'He said he wouldn't betray your confidence and that no one would know what you told him. Tell me. Do you believe him or do you feel he was lying?'

'I believe him,' she said.

'Very well. *Why* would he tell you that? I think I know the answer. Because the hundreds of people who watched me perform my "miracles" believe what they saw and it would be difficult for him to prove that I tricked them. The secret of the heavy box and the false bullets are *my* secrets. He'd have to demonstrate how they work and he cannot do that. That's why he will keep quiet about what you said. And I think we should also keep quiet. You mustn't tell Deniau about this.'

'Why not?'

'Because there is nothing he can do to change the situation. Besides, why should I let the world know that you went behind my back in an effort to destroy me? If, tomorrow, Bou-Aziz declares a holy war, my actions here will be forgotten. If, on the other hand, he steps down, then tomorrow is the day of my triumph, a triumph which will last for the rest of my life. Bou-Aziz now knows that my "miracles" are the victory of science over superstition. I hope that knowledge will work in my favour.'

He came towards her holding up his hands in his odd manner, as though to show he had nothing to conceal. And now she saw at last that he was moved and upset, that he was asking for something, something he had difficulty in putting into words. 'Emmeline,' he said. 'One more question. And may I have an answer, even if it goes against me?'

'What do you mean?'

'A moment ago you said that this is probably the end of our marriage. Is that what you want?'

'No.' She said it without thinking, thinking only that he had misunderstood her.

He came closer and put his hands on her shoulders. His face was strained as though he were afraid. 'I am grateful for that,' he said. 'I mustn't lose you. I know I've made mistakes in the past. I saw what happened to you in Compiègne where you were fêted and admired. It was wrong of me to shut you up in Tours. We must travel more. I'll take an apartment in Paris where you can see friends and amuse yourself. You must know, you are everything to me.'

'Everything?'

'Yes. I have only you and my work.' When he said this he bent and kissed her cheek. 'Captain Roualt and his wife have invited us to attend a small supper party in their quarters. Deniau will not be present as he is dining with some sheikh. It might be pleasant. What do you think?'

'I think there is something *you* should know,' she said. 'I am not sorry for what I did today. You must remember that.'

'Of course. My darling, you don't need to feel sorry. I don't understand your point of view but I respect it. Besides, I love you and because I do I'd forgive you anything. Anything!'

'I didn't ask for your forgiveness,' she said. 'What time is the supper party?'

THIRTEEN

Deniau, riding ahead, made a path for them through the crowd of Kabyles who filled the streets outside the courtyard of the grand mosque. French Zouave grooms took charge of their horses as they dismounted at the main entrance.

'You must go first,' Deniau told Lambert. 'We will act as your entourage. Walk towards the orange trees in the centre of the court. Under these trees is the basin where the faithful wash their hands, feet and faces before entering the mosque itself. That courtyard is where Bou-Aziz will deliver his verdict. I don't know how you will be received. They may try to kiss the hem of your clothing as a mark of reverence. On the other hand they may spit at you. More likely, they'll draw back, as they did yesterday. You are the infidel sorcerer. They fear you. Ignore them. Stare straight ahead.'

Emmeline walking between Captain Hersant and an army interpreter heard the uneasy clamour of the crowd milling around in the yard like a great herd of animals in a pen. Ahead of her, walking alone, Lambert moved past a frieze of white marble columns and was suddenly recognized. A murmur passed through the crowd, signalling that the Roumi sorcerer had arrived. She walked, imitating Henri, staring straight ahead, aware of the burning scrutiny of these dark bearded faces. In front of her she saw the orange trees. Waiting at the fountain beneath them were the Aga Bou-Allem, their host of two days ago, and Sheikh Ben-Amara, who had fired the pistol in an attempt to kill her husband. The Aga bowed in welcome. Ben-Amara nodded coldly to Deniau, ignoring Lambert.

'The Mahdi is here,' he told Deniau in Arabic. 'He is at prayer in the mosque and will join us soon.'

'The Mahdi?' Deniau said. He looked at Lambert and translated. 'Is that our answer, I wonder?' He turned to the Aga. 'So Bou-Aziz has decided to proclaim himself the Mahdi? Does that mean the jihad? If so, why were we asked to come here? To be spat upon?'

'Colonel, I have not been informed of the marabout's decisions,' Bou-Allem said. 'Sheikh Ben-Amara may know them better than I. In any case we do not have long to wait. Listen.'

As he spoke, Emmeline heard a chanting start up behind her. She turned to her interpreter. 'Madame, they are saying Muhammad b. 'Abd Allah comes. The Master of the Hour is here.'

She looked at Lambert, and saw him stare ahead as he had been told to do, but, no longer able to sustain his role, his body slack with disappointment. Everything he had planned and executed with such skill was wasted: worse, it had caused Jules' death. The visit to Compiègne, the Emperor's commission, the hopes he had entertained for medals and praise, all of that was over. There would be an insurrection in which Arabs, Kabyles and French soldiers would die, but now it might be a war the Arabs would win.

Standing by her husband's side, Emmeline saw the crowds again part to make way, but in reverence, men touching the hem of the marabout's robe, fingering their prayer beads as in supplication, chanting over and over again: 'Muhammad b. 'Abd Allah,' the Mahdi's name. Bou-Aziz, nodding in acknowledgement, made his way slowly towards the fountain, as always on the arm of his daughter. As they came up to Lambert's group the marabout greeted the Aga and Sheikh Ben-Amara, then Deniau, Hersant and, at last with a low bow, Lambert.

Sheikh Ben-Amara, his face creased in a triumphant smile, turned towards the waiting throng, raising his arms to catch their attention.

'Silence for Muhammad b. 'Abd Allah.'

Bou-Aziz moving away from his daughter now stood alone, his back to the fountain, facing the crowd. As he began to speak the interpreter huddled close to Emmeline and Lambert, translating in hurried whispers.

'My brothers, I have meditated and asked God's orders. I have accepted the new name that God has given me, the name of Muhammad b. 'Abd Allah, the name of the Mahdi. But I do not claim to be the redeemer who will lead Islam to the triumph of the true religion and the end of that humiliation which our subservience to unbelievers has brought upon us. My claim today is that I am God's messenger and the message God gives me is that our triumph will come only when we face the truth. The truth is that we have strayed from the right path. Reform and regeneration of our faith is now the duty of us all. This is a time for prayer, for a spiritual, not a war-like, jihad. To conquer our enemies, we must first increase our obedience to God and to the Prophet. If we do, one day our faith will be so strong that the Christian world will be powerless against it and the infidels will pass for ever from this land.'

As these words were spoken, Emmeline heard a murmuring of disbelief and anger from Ben-Amara and the other sheikhs. But the vast crowd was silent and attentive. The marabout continued.

'Brothers, I am the messenger of God. In these last days he has given me access to the invisible world. Because of that I know that the unbelievers will be driven from this land, that the way of Islam will triumph and that the passage of the French through our country is temporal: it will not last. In the end it is in the mosques and zawiyas that we will find our victory. Everything comes from God.'

Bou-Aziz then turned to Lambert. 'For now, you are the strongest. You have shown us miracles beyond any we have ever seen. Our eyes were never before dazzled by such prodigies. But are they miracles as we know them?'

At this, Bou-Aziz paused and looked past Lambert at Emmeline, his eyes fixed on her as if seeking some bond.

And then he said, 'No matter. For they come from God. Everything comes from God. And so he has thrown you down among us like a bolt of lightning to prove that for now, none but He, the Almighty, can oppose your will.'

As he finished speaking, Bou-Aziz held up his hands as if to signal that he had finished speaking. Taalith at once came forward and said to Lambert, 'My father thanks you for your visit and wishes you a safe journey to your home.' Then, small and frail, she went to Emmeline stretching up like a child to put her arms around Emmeline's neck, her soft face touching Emmeline's cheek as she whispered, 'My father knows he has made the right choice. He thanks you for helping him decide.'

At this point Deniau joined them, his face not concealing his delight. 'Come. We must leave now.'

As they walked away from the fountain, a muezzin was heard high above in the minaret, chanting the call to devotions. Among the vast throng in the square, all eyes followed the marabout and his daughter, as, moving among the marble columns, they entered the mosque.

Suddenly Emmeline felt herself pushed aside by Hersant in a quick convulsive movement. She saw the crowd ahead of her draw back to reveal at fifty paces a young man, in the high turban of a caid brandishing a pistol which he now pointed at her. The gun exploded.

Lambert, walking a few feet ahead of her, stopped and stood staring at the assailant. In a terrible silence, the young caid stared back, then dropping his pistol, turned and flung himself into the crowd. Lambert did not look to see if she had been injured, but having paused momentarily, continued to walk towards the gates. And in that moment, from the awestruck stares of the surrounding crowds, she realized that the assassin had fired not at her but at her husband and that he had not missed. She ran forward, coming up beside him. He stared straight ahead and said, 'Don't touch me. We are leaving. Keep walking.'

The bullet had entered his body just below his right shoulder. A stain of blood spread like a dark rose on his white linen jacket.

But he did not falter in his walk, nor show the slightest weakness or pain. Deniau, coming up beside her, gave her a warning look. 'Emmeline, do as he says.'

All around them, staring frightened faces, as the sorcerer, seemingly unharmed, reached the gates of the courtyard where the French grooms waited with their horses. She saw Lambert brace himself and for a moment tremble in pain as he put his foot in the stirrup and mounted, using his left hand to grip the pommel. Quickly, Deniau and Hersant followed suit, the grooms helping Emmeline into her saddle. Then, with Lambert's horse in the lead, they rode out into the dusty, crowded streets, the horses, impeded by the narrow lanes and staring pedestrians, moving at a slow walk, Lambert, gripping the reins in his left hand, his right arm slack by his side.

Emmeline, in panic, kicked at her horse's sides and moved up beside him. 'Henri, Henri?'

She saw his face contort in anger or in pain. 'Pretend!' he said. 'Pretend!'

The French fort was three streets away from the mosque. Spurring his horse Deniau rode past her, saying, 'It's all right, it's all right. I'll get the doctor. We'll be there in a moment.'

And then, turning his head, he called back to Lambert, 'Hold on, Henri. Hold on! You were wonderful!'

The Zouave sentries rolled open the gates as Deniau cantered up. 'Close them again, the moment we are inside,' he shouted.

Captain Hersant, riding beside Lambert, dismounted in the yard and reaching up took Lambert in his arms, lifting him from the saddle. 'Good man, good man! We're home. You'll be all right.'

But at that moment Lambert fainted. Deniau, already at the infirmary door, shouted orders and at once two soldiers came running across the courtyard with a stretcher. Emmeline saw the blood seeping in a dark clot across the chest of her husband's soaking jacket. She ran beside the stretcher, leaning over him, calling his name. But when the stretcher bearers entered the infirmary Deniau came over and took her arm. 'The doctor is here and is ready to operate. It will be all right, it will be all right. Sit now, sit.'

He seated her on a bench in the corridor beside the intensive-care room where Jules had died. Across the hall she could see two doctors in white robes and masks going into a room marked SURGERY: Deniau and Hersant hurried out into the courtyard as though on their way to an important meeting. A white-aproned orderly passed her and went into the surgery, carrying what seemed to be a tray of instruments. She sat, numb, her mind shuffling and jumbling broken images as in a dream: Henri walking through the courtyard of the mosque without flinching, Henri, fainting, falling into Hersant's arms, the dark rose stain on his linen jacket, Henri, hunched over a desk, pricking his thumb to draw blood for the false bullet he used in his performance, the young assassin firing, his eyes dilated in insane concentration, the Jesuit cemetery with its freshly dug grave into which the rough sack containing Jules' body rolled, the electric gates of the Manoir des Chênes in Tours opening to admit a carriage in which she sat, dressed in widow's weeds.

And now, the coldness she had shown him last night came back like a wound. I turned against him and if he dies I'll never be able to tell him that last night I was angry and arrogant and that, with all his faults, he is my husband, who has cared for me and in his way loved me, and without him I will be alone.

The smell of ether wafted from the surgery as an orderly opened the door and came past her, carrying a tin basin in which she saw blood-soaked instruments. Ether: he is unconscious, his mind in limbo, no longer the servant of his will. What was it he said before he fainted?

'Pretend! Pretend!'

But could he still pretend?

*   *   *

The surgeon, bearded, burly, with a squint in his right eye, came towards her, smiling, wiping his hands on a towel. 'Madame Lambert?'

She stood up. He offered his hand and she shook it.

'Well, your husband was lucky. We have extracted the bullet. It entered just below his shoulder. There may be some nerve damage. Can't say just yet. Have you seen Colonel Deniau?'

'No.'

'I must find him and give him my report. Your husband is still under the ether. Ah! Here he is.'

She looked back at the room marked *SURGERY* thinking that the surgeon referred to Henri. Instead, he nodded to her in farewell and went down the corridor to meet Deniau who had just arrived. They talked, and after a few minutes Deniau joined her. 'Very good news, eh?'

'Yes.'

'Even better, the doctor tells me we will be able to leave tomorrow.'

'Leave?'

'Back to Algiers. And put all this behind you. It's been a very difficult time for you, I know.'

'But how can we leave tomorrow?' she asked. 'Henri is ill.'

'Our doctor tells me Henri is fit to travel. And the first stop in our journey, is, if you remember, just a few hours away. We'll stay again at Ben-Gannah's camp. The important thing is to get him out of here as quickly as possible.'

'I don't agree,' she said. 'I'm sure he's in no condition to start on a journey.'

'Dr Laporte doesn't agree with you. And he knows a lot about bullet wounds. I trust his judgement completely.'

'Henri is still unconscious,' she said. 'How can you tell if he's fit. Besides, I think it should be my decision, not yours.'

'In the end it will be Henri's,' Deniau said. 'He has been incredibly brave. We must capitalize on that bravery. If he rides out of here tomorrow morning the sheikhs and marabouts, the whole of Algeria in fact, will know that once again he has proved he is invincible. What happened today will add to his legend.

My dear, don't you realize we've won? Henri has succeeded in everything he set out to do. Because of him there will be no jihad. Because of him, your friend Bou-Aziz has been discredited. We mustn't let anything spoil this triumph.'

'Bou-Aziz discredited?' she said. 'I don't think so.'

'Ah!' Deniau looked at her. 'Well, of course, you know him better than I do.'

'What do you mean?'

'You spoke to him the day before yesterday in his zawiya. What did you talk about? I'm curious. Did you urge him not to declare a holy war?'

She did not answer.

'This land is filled with spies,' he said. 'We have them too. We call it military intelligence. Let me make a suggestion. If you help us now, I mean, help us get Henri away safely, then in return I promise you I won't mention to him that you visited the zawiya.'

'He knows. Now go away. Please?'

At that moment, the door of the operating room opened and her husband was wheeled out on a trolley. He was unconscious, his body covered by a white sheet. She got up at once and leaving Deniau walked beside the trolley, looking down at the pale unconscious face. The trolley was wheeled into the small intensive-care room where Jules had died. As the orderlies pushed it into place against the wall, she saw Deniau signalling to her from the doorway.

'Please, Emmeline. I won't disturb you. Look – I'm sorry for what I just said. Forgive me. Let's stay friends. I'm not your enemy.'

She did not look at him. 'But you are.'

She sat down by the bedside. When she looked again, he had gone.

She lost as she knew she would. When, two hours later, Lambert woke, he was drowsy, weak and nauseated by the ether. But his first question was: 'Did they see me? I fainted, didn't I? But I was inside the yard at the time?'

She reassured him. She told him about the operation and its success. And then, when she mentioned what she termed as 'Deniau's mad idea to leave tomorrow', she no sooner said the words than he sat up on the trolley with a strange half-gasp of triumph.

'Well, that means I've done it, doesn't it? Despite what happened, the Arabs still believe I'm invincible. Of course, Charles is right. The thing to do now is ride out in triumph as we always planned to do. Get away from here, the sooner the better.'

Shortly before dark, Deniau and Hersant came to see him. When they entered the sickroom she moved away from the bedside, but stood in the rear, listening to what was said.

After congratulations and praise, Deniau told him: 'Henri, we're planning to leave tomorrow. Did Emmeline tell you? I know she's against it but – '

'No, no, she told me and I agree completely with your idea.'

'I'm glad. It would be a pity to spoil things. Besides, the doctor thinks you'll manage quite nicely as long as you don't use your right arm. Well, of course, you can't use it just now, can you? But you will ride with a cloak over your shoulders. They won't see the bandages.'

'And we're planning to ride out at dawn,' Hersant said. 'There won't be many people around at that hour.'

'But the sheikhs will be told you've gone,' Deniau said. 'And of course our friend the former Muhammad b. 'Abd Allah.'

They all three laughed. Deniau glanced back at her, then said, 'I feel rather sorry for him. All this talk of a spiritual retreat won't sit well with the Kabyle leaders but as he's still the country's leading marabout, they'll have to accept it. And of course there's a tradition behind what he said today, a hope of defeating us through prayer. That's what he'll now try to sell to the Kabyles. And he'll succeed, at least, for a time.'

'At least until summer,' Hersant said and again they laughed.

THE MAGICIAN'S WIFE

'I'll send Dufour on ahead to give Maréchal Randon the good news,' Deniau said. 'Algiers will pass on the word to Louis Napoleon himself. We must see to it that Henri's bravery is rewarded. Alas, the Emperor can't give you his new *medaille militaire*, because that's reserved for soldiers. But the Légion d'Honneur? Yes.'

'The highest level of the Legion is what?' Hersant asked. 'Grand Cross?'

Lambert sank back on his pillows. He seemed exhausted, but exhilarated as though he were drunk. 'On any level,' he said, 'I'll feel honoured. *Vive La France!*'

They rode out through deserted streets, past shuttered market stalls, through the main gates, spurring their horses into a canter, the sun now floating like a kite in the sky as they passed up the road bordered by the temporary encampments of the visiting sheikhs. Children and barking dogs ran out to see them go: women watched from the openings of goatskin tents, while their menfolk sitting in a circle under awnings drank their morning coffee, glancing up with studied incuriosity as the Roumi troop, Lambert, Emmeline, Hersant, Deniau with his servant Kaddour and three camel drivers, switching the flanks of their heavily burdened beasts, left Milianah behind, their caravan growing smaller and smaller on the horizon.

In mid-afternoon they reached the Moorish dwellings of Ben-Gannah who rode out with his son to greet them as before. Lambert dismounted stiffly, still concealing his injury. Refusing his host's offer of coffee, he went at once with Emmeline to their room. There, she helped him remove his sweat-stained jacket and unlaced his boots so that he could lie on the divan. His arm was in a sling and when he lay on his back in the bed, he tried to raise it. It fell back on his stomach. He turned his head to look at her and she saw his alarm.

'My shoulder,' he said to her. 'It's not so much pain as

212

something else. My arm feels dead. When they changed the bandage last night, that surgeon said something about nerve damage. Do you remember?'

'I remember that he didn't seem worried. He said you were very lucky.'

'But he *did* say something. He said they didn't know yet.'

'Look,' she said. 'It's less than forty-eight hours since you were shot at. Of course, your arm doesn't feel normal. Now, try to rest. The trip tomorrow will be more difficult than it was today. Remember the steep ravines on our way here? That's my worry. How will you manage?'

'We won't be on stage then,' he said. 'I can let my guard down. Deniau's servant will lead my horse.'

But on the following day when, in the ravines, their horses stumbled and slithered in deep descent, the giant Kaddour took Lambert down from his horse and carried him through the most dangerous of the passes. And then, towards sunset as they at last approached Algiers, Deniau rearranged Lambert's cloak and tunic, while Emmeline bathed his face and neck as he positioned himself for the ride into the city where Arab eyes would survey his passage. And, as always when he felt himself to be in the public gaze, Lambert displayed the discipline in deception that was the cornerstone of his skills.

But the following evening when he was fêted and applauded at a reception given by Monsieur de la Garde, attended by all of the senior officials and their wives, Emmeline saw that something had happened to him. He, who had always been avid for approbation, now seemed restless and inattentive, anxious for the evening to end. At first she put it down to fatigue and his wound but that night as she helped him undress, he looked at her and said, 'This is the end for me.'

'What do you mean?'

'I am a cripple now.'

'Nonsense!'

'No. The doctor who came to dress my wound this afternoon is Colonel Pouzin. He's the senior medical officer in Algiers and Maréchal Randon's personal physician. So his is the best possible opinion. I described my symptoms and he made some tests. There is severe nerve damage. I may be able to raise my arm to waist-level, or I may not. In any event, my career is over. I am crippled for life.'

She looked at him, desperately searching for words of denial and comfort. But instead saw him as he once was when he entered a room, holding up his slender, graceful hands as if to show that nothing was concealed. Or standing on a stage, diverting the attention of his audience by quick skilful movements, his right hand holding his talismanic ivory-tipped baton to draw attention away from that other hand which would make the covert movement necessary to produce an illusion. That right hand, that right arm, now a dead weight at his side.

'But your inventions,' she said. 'You told me you no longer needed to perform, you said you wanted to devote more time to your mechanical inventions, to your marionettes.'

He took hold of his useless right arm, holding it carefully as he eased himself down on the bed. 'Inventions? Who would remember me if I were merely a clockmaker? Who, when they watch a mechanical marionette perform its tasks on stage, asks who *made* it? No, they watch me, the magician, the man who can make people disappear, the man who can bring flowers and fruit endlessly from a cornucopia, the man who – why do I tell you, you've seen how people admire me, even fear me, you saw what happened here in Africa where I have managed to prevent a war! I am Henri Lambert, known throughout Europe as the greatest magician alive. And now because some drugged savage fires a pistol, my life is over.'

'Your life is not over,' she said. 'You're famous, you have money, you can work on your inventions. And you have me. You said I mean everything to you.'

'You do.' He looked at her and shook his head.

'What is it?' she said.

'Do I have you? Or is that another of my illusions?'

'Henri, listen – Henri?'

But he turned his face to the wall.

*　　*　　*

Two weeks later, the steamer *Alexander* sailed from the port of Algiers on its normal passage to Marseille. On the promenade deck Lambert stood with Emmeline, his left arm around her waist as they looked down at the dock where Monsieur and Madame de la Garde and Colonel Deniau smiled up at them. As the steamer's siren hooted and the mooring ropes were slipped, those on shore waved in farewell. Instinctively, Lambert tried to raise his right arm in salute. But it fell back against his side. Emmeline looked down at Deniau and the others. She did not wave.

The following year, in the summer of 1857, French armies under the command of Maréchal Randon and General MacMahon subdued the tribes of Kabylia, thus completing the conquest of Algeria by France.

In the summer of 1962, Algeria officially declared its independence, ending the French presence in that country.

Brian Moore was born in Belfast in 1921 and was educated there at St Malachy's College. He served wih the British Ministry of War Transport during the latter part of the Second World War in North Africa, Italy and France. After the war he worked for the United Nations in Europe before emigrating to Canada in 1948, where he became a journalist and adopted Canadian citizenship. He spent some time in New York before moving to California, where he now lives and works. Five of his novels have been made into films: *The Lonely Passion of Judith Hearne*, *The Luck of Ginger Coffey*, *Catholics*, *Cold Heaven* and, most recently, *Black Robe*.

Brian Moore won the Authors' Club First Novel Award for *The Lonely Passion of Judith Hearne*, the W. H. Smith Literary Award for *Catholics*, the James Tait Black Memorial Prize for *The Great Victorian Collection*, and the Sunday Express Book of the Year Prize for *The Colour of Blood*. He has been shortlisted for the Booker Prize three times with *The Doctor's Wife*, *The Colour of Blood* and *Lies of Silence*.